THE CRIMSON CHALICE

When a party of marauding Saxons destroy her father's villa, young Roman girl Gratia, 'Tia' escapes. She comes upon the body of the heir to the chieftanship of a British tribe in the west. Baradoc, a prisoner of Phoenician traders, was sold as a slave and is also escaping the Saxons. However, after being attacked he was left for dead by his cousin, the next heir. Tia nurses him back to health, and they continue together to the safety of her uncle's villa in Aquae Sulis . . . Their son, Arturo, inherits his father's desire for uniting Britain against the Saxons.

Books by Victor Canning
Published by The House of Ulverscroft:

BIRDS OF A FEATHER
THE BOY ON PLATFORM ONE

The Arthurian Trilogy:
THE CRIMSON CHALICE
THE CIRCLE OF THE GODS
THE IMMORTAL WOUND

A2 994 350 4

VICTOR CANNING

THE CRIMSON CHALICE

Book One

Complete and Unabridged

ULVERSCROFT
Leicester

First published in Great Britain in 1976

This Large Print Edition
published 2012

British Library CIP Data

Canning, Victor.
   The crimson chalice.
   1. Historical fiction.
   2. Large type books.
   I. Title
   823.9'12–dc23

   ISBN 978–1–4448–1207–7

Published by
F. A. Thorpe (Publishing)
Anstey, Leicestershire

Set by Words & Graphics Ltd.
Anstey, Leicestershire
Printed and bound in Great Britain by
T. J. International Ltd., Padstow, Cornwall

This book is printed on acid-free paper

For my wife, Diana, with love

Contents

Forest Meeting

As the sun tipped the eastern reaches of the forest and fired the pewter sea to silver at the far end of the valley, the May morning was full of song. Through the belling of tits, the monotonous sawing of the chiff-chaffs and the melodious pealing of thrushes and blackbirds, Lerg, the big grey wolfhound, caught the clatter of a distantly falling stone on the valleyside path. Except for a slight lift of his muzzle from his couched forepaws, he made no move; but his grey-flecked green eyes watched the turn of the path where it entered the wide glade. To his right Aesc, the water dog with the long drooping red-furred ears, had heard the stone fall some few moments after she had caught the human scent coming up on the morning breeze from the sea. On the left of Lerg, Cuna, small, short-legged and wire-haired, neither heard, nor saw, nor smelled anything. Not long out of puppy-hood, he was curled into a ball and, empty-bellied now for twenty-four hours, dreamt of vole and rat and hare and the dark tunnels of fox earths and badger sets.

Above them the body hung. The hide

thongs about the ankles still bit tight, but those about the wrists, which held the body suspended from the stout horizontal branch of an oak, had stretched so that the balls of the tied feet just touched the ground. But it had been twelve hours since there had been any power in legs and feet to take advantage of earth's touch to ease the dragging weight of the body on shoulder muscles. Bluebottles, and a small cloud of midges and early gnats, clustered over the crisp-curled head of hair and the brown, sweat-dried face. An hour before sunset a pair of red kites had spiralled down, forked tails splayed, to roost on the upper branches of the oak. Bran, the raven, had given an angry *carp, carp* and had flown at them, chasing them away inland over the rolling green sea of forest.

Bran sat now on the oak top and watched the newcomer moving up the path towards the glade. Twice during the night a lone wolf, ancient and pack-exiled, had come to the glade's edge and Lerg had driven him away. Now, five miles away to the east, the wolf fed on a calf among the slaughtered cattle in a stockyard close to the fire-black ruins of a homestead, and had for company cohorts of crows, kites, buzzards and eagles. In the dust of the forecourt an old woman sat holding her long grey hair over her face to keep the day away, keening and moaning softly to herself, numbed and half-crazed by the memory of the horror which had filled the last two days.

★ ★ ★

The newcomer turned the swing of the path and came to the edge of the glade. It was a girl grown close to young womanhood. The hood of her short brown woollen mantle was pushed back on to her shoulders, leaving her fair hair free. Around her waist, over a white, dust-streaked linen tunic, she wore an embroidered belt with a bronze clasp in the shape of two dolphins. On her feet were leather sandals held by a cross-gartering of red-dyed doe-skin thongs which ran up her bare legs and were tied beneath her knees. Over her right shoulder she carried a bulky sack made by the knotting of four corners of a bed cover of green and yellow striped silk.

Standing at the edge of the glade she saw the three dogs, saw the rapid mouse-movement of a tree-creeper work up the rough trunk of the oak, saw the raven at the top of the tree, and breathed with a slow, anguished tightening of her face as she saw the body. For a moment she closed her blue eyes against memory. A low rumble from

Lerg startled and frightened her. To turn away she knew, for she was no stranger to animals, might bring the dogs after her. To go forward, too, she reasoned, could start the trio of guarding beasts into a violent, rushing attack. She stood where she was and waited, her eyes on the dogs and the bowed head of the body that hung from the tree, ringed with a moving halo of flies and gnats.

Lerg growled low again and Cuna, awake now, slowly sat up but knew better than to move past Lerg. Lerg was the leader. Aesc and Cuna waited.

The girl waited, too, her body trembling under the swift assault of her fears. The strengthening sun burned against the skin of her right cheek. Across it ran a dark smudge of black ash, and above her right eye, dark against the fair skin, was a bruise as large as a crab-apple. She waited and watched and saw the quick flirt of a red squirrel into the top of a young ash tree, saw the bending of the slim branches whip back into place, the silver grey bark flashing in the sun. Lerg growled again and then slowly rose to his feet. The other dogs made no move. Long-legged, lean-bodied, the grey coat shaggy as lichen, he stood as high as a month-old calf and she knew his kind, for they were highly prized now far beyond Britain for their speed and courage in the killing of wolf and deer. And the other dog, too, she knew, with its red coat and long ears — a kind that loved water as much as the otters and wild fowl they hunted. Then, remembering that her father had often said, 'There is no dog which cannot read the cast of any mortal. Feel fear and they scent it and give no trust. Harbour villainy and they will return it. Offer friendship and they will accept it — but at their own gait', she forced herself to stand where she was and watch the slow movement of the hound towards her. He came, not directly, but on an arc which took him away to her right where she lost sight of him. Without words, the cry locked silently in her mind, she pleaded with the hound . . . *your master suffers . . . there is suffering with me, too . . . leave me free to help him . . .* She stared ahead at the hanging body. Its top half was covered with an undershirt, its front open, stirring slightly in the morning breeze. The lower part of the body was sheathed in tight-fitting leather breeks reaching just below the knees. On the feet were heavy, metal-studded, thick-soled sandals fastened by thongs at the ankles.

The hound paced back into her view and circled to her left, but this time halted within her sight. He raised his head, looked back at the oak tree and the other dogs, then swung his head slowly round and eyed her. Her instinct was to make some move, some show of friendliness, but she held still. Fear ran steadily in her, but it was a fear now which she fought to control. Slowly swamping her own misery and recent griefs there rose in her a warm compassion for the being who hung from the tree, who might still live and need her help. The hound lowered his head and moved towards her, stiff-legged, hackles part risen. He stopped close to her and reaching out his muzzle sniffed at her left hand which hung against her side. She felt the warm breath on her fingers and caught the strong, rank dog smell in her nostrils. Suddenly the hound licked her hand, gave a low, easy growl and turned from her. Lerg walked back to the other dogs and sat on his haunches, his eyes on the girl.

Then, as though possessed by some strange power never known to her before, the girl felt her trembling ease, the quick beating of her heart die down and without hesitation she walked forward. The dogs' heads turned as she came up to them, passed them and went to the body. There was no fear in her now. She eased her bundle to the earth and unknotted the covering. Reaching inside she fumbled around for a while and brought out a small sharp-edged dagger. She put the haft in her mouth, then crouched and jumped for the overhanging branch. She got two hand holds, then swung her legs up and worked herself to a prone position on top of the branch. She eased herself along and began to saw at the thongs of the left wrist. As she cut the last one the body lurched sideways, spun slowly on the stretched thongs of the right hand and the bound feet dragged across the earth.

The dogs watched but made no sound.

She wormed herself further along the branch and with a few quick slashes cut the thongs of the remaining hand. The body fell in a heap to the ground. As it hit the earth there was the sound of a long-drawn moan. On the oak top Bran called sharply *carp, carp* and launched himself into the air in a clumsy spiral.

The girl dropped to the ground. The body lay face downwards. She cut the ankle thongs and rolled the body over on to its back. For the first time she saw the face clearly. It was the face of a youth of about eighteen, a lean, strong, tanned face, streaked with sweat and dirt, a young tawny-red beard growth fuzzing the square chin. Across the right side of his face was a jagged cut over which the blood had dried in a hard crust.

Oblivious now of the dogs which had

accepted her, she went back to her bundle and brought out a small bronze cooking cauldron. She ran across the glade and along the path by which she had arrived. A little way down it a small spring sprang from the hillside feeding a shallow cress-covered pool. She filled the cauldron and went back to the youth, and pulling a small earthenware beaker from her bundle, squatted on the ground and lifted the youth's head and shoulders up on to her knees. With a firm hand on his chin she forced his mouth open and poured water between his cracked lips. He moaned a little and choked, the water spilling over his face and neck. She tried again and this time eased only a little water into his mouth, her hand shaking, chiding herself, 'Gently, Tia, gently'.

Slowly she fed him water and when she judged he had had enough, she lowered his head to the ground, cushioning it on a woollen blanket from her bundle. She tore a long strip from the edge of her linen tunic and bathed his face, keeping the water away from the hard crust on his wound as much as she could since it was a better protection than any she could devise. His wrists were raw and bloody with the thong-marks so she tore the linen face cloth into two strips and bound them around the wounds.

The sun was climbing higher in the sky. In a little while she knew the glade would be in full, hard sunlight. She would have to find shade for the youth and — since the times were what they were — some kind of concealment. There was little charity abroad these days. There were men about who would murder for a worn pair of leather breeches and a pair of old legionary sandals.

She hurried away to the edge of the glade. As she went Lerg moved to the youth and lay down at his side, but the water dog, Aesc, followed her and, after a moment's hesitation, so did Cuna.

Not far from the edge of the glade she found a stunted yew with a tangle of wild clematis in fresh leaf trailing over its lower branches to form a narrow bower. She went back to the youth, took off her cloak belt and, looping it under his arms, began to drag him into the forest. Within the hour she had him in the bower, resting on a couch of old bracken growth and fresh branches, his head and shoulders propped up on her travelling bundle. She refilled the cauldron, fed more water to him, drank herself and ate part of a wheat cake she carried. She undid his wrist bandages, laid dock leaves around the wounds and replaced the bandages. Then she covered him with her mantle and sat by him, looking down at him. In all the time she had been with him he had never opened his eyes, but now and again he had given a long groan. He was young, strong and hardened, and tight-muscled and there were no wounds on him except for his wrists and the cut cheek. She sat patiently watching him, knowing that time and the water she had given him would do their work. A spear's length away from her Lerg lay couched under a bush. Of the other two dogs there was no sign. Unknown to Tia, Bran sat high up in a nearby ash tree on a roost which gave him a view through the forest's canopy of the dark fringe of the yew bower and Lerg's shadowy couched form. Before roosting Bran had robbed a magpie's nest of its two blue-quilled fledglings and had eaten well. Somewhere Cuna and Aesc were hunting. Only Lerg lay still and close to his master and would not eat until he knew that it was safe to leave him.

And Tia, elbows resting on her knees, chin cupped in her hands, remembered the night which had passed and the days before it, and knew that there could be nothing in the future which could replace all that had been lost . . . her brother and his wife dead, the villa and the homestead huts plundered and burned, cattle slaughtered, and most of their own workpeople turned against her and the family. Only the devotion of her maid's husband, Tullio, had saved her from the savagery of the estate steward who had laid a drunken claim to her from which she had been saved by the dagger thrust of Tullio's old service *pugio*. She began to sob. In a few short hours the peace and ease of her life had been shattered, her loved ones killed and the security of her sheltered, rich life destroyed. She covered her face with her hands and her body shook with quick spasms which she could not control.

Lerg gave a low whine and Tia straightened up, the spasms passing. As she did so the youth stirred and opened his eyes. He stared without moving at the dark roof of the yew branches overhead, and she saw that his eyes were a dark, shining brown reminding her of the colour of the closed sea anemones that studded the low water rocks of the beach that marked the estate's southern boundary. She reached to her side and dunked part of the hard wheat cake in the water of the cauldron. Cradling his head on her arm she tried to feed him, but he closed his eyes and turned his head away. She filled the beaker and offered him water. With his eyes still closed he drank, and this time he swallowed the water avidly. When she lowered his head and shoulders back on to the bundle he sighed.

She sensed the slow ease taking his body as its strained muscles relaxed. He slept and his breathing, which at first was heavy and troubled, took on a regular, slow rhythm.

The sun climbed higher. Aesc and Cuna returned and settled a few paces away. Cuna slept, curled into a ball, but Aesc lay couched, her eyes wide open watching the youth. Somewhere, Tia guessed, the two dogs had discovered food. There was plenty to be found in the ruined huts and the yards and fields with their slaughtered cattle and poultry. Stirred by the tongues of the rabble-rousers the country people had proved themselves as ruthless as any of the Saxon sea-folk on their sudden, summer raids. Soon they, too, would be back. Each year they came earlier and in greater force, and each year more and more of them stayed to swell the ranks of their kinsmen who had made the Saxon shores and the rich corn lands and settlements east of Anderida their own; each year moving farther west with no true leader bold enough to raise arms or banner against them.

The youth beside her began to talk in his sleep. At the sound of the voice Lerg's ears half-cocked and Aesc raised her head. It was difficult for Tia to understand anything of what he said. He spoke sometimes in her own

12

tongue, but it was the rough, slang-filled language of the army auxiliaries, the old language of the barrack blocks and camps, and sometimes he spoke in the true language of the country of which she knew only a few words and phrases. In his voice there was, too, an accent and burr which was strange to her. After a while he slept without talking. Tia sat with him. At midday, feeling hungry, she ate some more of the wheat cake and a piece of the goats' cheese which Tullio's wife had put into her bundle. The smell of the cheese woke Cuna. He stood on his stubby legs and came to her. She broke off a piece for him which he ate and then settled at her feet.

Tia lay back on the grass aware suddenly of her fatigue and her own despair. She had travelled all night blindly across-country fighting always the panic in her thoughts. Within a few moments she was asleep.

★　★　★

When Baradoc woke and came to himself, the sun was halfway down the western sky. He lay for a while watching the dapple of sunlight through the yew branches, aware of the wrack and soreness in arm and shoulder muscles. He raised his hands and looked at the bandages on his wrist. A confusion in his head cleared slowly. Above him appeared the head and shoulders of Lerg. The hound gave a low whine. Baradoc fondled the grey muzzle and then, gripping the dog's neck, eased himself to a sitting position. For a moment his head swam and he shook it to clear his vision, seeing through a blur Aesc and Cuna standing beyond Lerg. Then, as his head swung slowly round, he saw the girl. She was sleeping on the grass, her mantle flung open, the torn edge of her white tunic rumpled above her knees and suntanned legs. Her short, fair hair was breeze fanned across her temples and she lay with her cheek couched in her hand. He looked from her to the dogs and then half turned, wincing with the pull on his strained muscles, and saw the cloth-wrapped bundle on which his head had been resting. Looking again at the girl he saw now that close to her side a small dagger lay on the ground ready to her free hand. He smiled to himself, guessing much of what must have happened, and knowing gratitude; knowing, too, from one look at her face that she was not one of his people. Her red-thonged sandals would have cost more sesterces than any working country girl could have afforded. Unexpectedly his head began to swim violently. He leaned forward, holding it with his hands, fighting off the vertigo. The attack passed and, as he straightened up, he

14

realized that he must have groaned aloud. The girl was awake and, half risen, was resting on her knees and facing him, dagger in shaking hand.

For a moment or two they faced one another without words, and Baradoc knew that, even though she must have cut him down and looked after him, she could have no surety that such an act of charity would be met with friendship or thanks. There were plenty of men in the country today who merited being left to hang for the crows and ravens to pick clean. He looked down at the small dagger which she held in her unsteady right hand, and said, 'You won't need that.' He spoke her tongue. 'The gods were good to send you, and the dogs marking your goodness let you pass. I owe you a life. On my people's sign I swear it.' He pulled the edge of his loose shirt aside and touched his left shoulder.

Tia, fear dying, saw that tattooed on the brown skin was a small, black, crow-like bird with red beak and red legs. She guessed then that he must come from the far west or north for there lived the only tribes who marked their skins so.

She said, 'Who are you?'

'My name is Baradoc. I am from the far west where the land falls into the sea in the heart of which the father of all the oceans sleeps. Who are you?'

'I am Gratia. But mostly I am called Tia. My father was Marcus Pupius Corbulo. He and my mother are long dead. I live with my brother Priscus and his wife . . . ' She broke off for a moment or two and then went on, 'That is, I lived with them until yesterday. They are both now dead — killed by our own farm workers.'

Baradoc let his eyes rest on the bruise on her forehead and then they moved to the bundle on which his head had been resting, to the water-filled cauldron and the beaker by its side and on to the half portion of the flat wheat cake and the broken piece of cheese which lay on a large leaf alongside it. He said gently, 'These are bad times. Men easily turn against their masters. Some do it because there has been a fear in them ever since it was known from General Aetius that there will be no Roman help for us from Gaul. And others because a new fear is growing with every longboat that brings fresh crewmen to join their brothers along the Saxon shore. They fear the new masters and turn against the old.'

Listening to him Tia was surprised at the masterly manner of his speaking, as though his knowledge and authority admitted no

16

questioning. Before she could stop herself, she said, 'When you lay there sleeping you talked in the speech of the camps and the barracks. Now you talk as I do.'

Baradoc smiled. 'I have known many old legionaries, and I talk as they did. But also I was for years a servant of a retired Chief Centurion. With him if I did not speak correctly I felt the weight of his vine staff. I am the son of a tribal chief, taken as slave when I was twelve years old. My master took my education seriously.' He grinned suddenly, deep creases bracketing the sides of his mouth, and added in soldiers' speech, 'My belly grumbles for a taste of that cheese.'

Tia laughed at the sudden transition and, in the midst of her laughter, wondered that she could, with all the darkness which still clouded her life. She handed the cheese across to him. As he stretched out his hand and arm for it she saw him wince at the flex of his stretched muscles. She said, 'When you have eaten I will massage your shoulders and arms. This was something I did often for Priscus in our bath house.'

Baradoc nodded, his mouth full of cheese. Tia, watching him, was sure now that she had nothing to fear from him. There was, too, she sensed, a strength and self-confidence about him which she guessed he could readily

17

muster against trouble.

She asked, 'This master of yours, is he alive still?'

'No.' Baradoc scowled and his face suddenly turned grim. 'The Saxons killed him a month ago. But long before that he had given me my freedom.'

'You are going back to your people?'

'Yes.' Baradoc reached for the water beaker and drank.

'You could have gone before. Since you were free.'

Baradoc smiled. 'I could have done easily. But my master was good to me, and there were many things he taught me. To read and write and speak his language. About farming and fighting, and how to read the stars, and to understand about building and mathematics and geometry and history and about the rest of the world out there.' He waved the empty beaker vaguely southwards. 'So I stayed. I am the son of a chief. One day I shall be the leader of my people. It is right that I should know more than they do and then teach these things to them.'

Tia smiled. 'You will be a very important man, I see.'

Baradoc chuckled. 'Thanks to you, yes — since you came along and cut me down.'

'Who hung you up like that?'

Baradoc frowned and said stiffly, 'Two — that called themselves friends. One day I shall kill them both. But that is no business of yours.'

Tia stood up, suddenly angry at his words and his abruptness. She said sharply, 'True. Perhaps, then, I should have passed the tree and left you hanging there since that, too, was no business of mine!'

Baradoc reached out quickly and caught the edge of her mantle and said, 'Hold now! Don't fly off like a hen disturbed from her night roost. I meant no rudeness. It was just the thought of those two that stirred me up.' He let go of her mantle and grinned, his tanned face creasing. 'You are full of Roman fire and guts aren't you? But that's good — especially in these days. But not good enough to take you safely through this country alone the way things are. So calm down and tell me where you want to go and I will see you safely there.'

'Even though you go west and I should say Eburacum?'

Baradoc laughed. 'Why not? Even though you should say Vindolanda on the North Wall — though that might give us a little trouble. I owe you a life. The longest journey would only be a little paid off the score. So, stop scowling, and tell me where.'

Tia slowly sat down. She said, 'My brother and sister are dead. All that I have in this country now is an old uncle who lives near Aquae Sulis. It is in my mind to go to him.'

'Then let it rest there. I will take you. And I won't pretend that I'm not glad it's on my westward road. But first there are two things to do. Give me your hand.'

'What on earth for?'

Baradoc sighed. 'I shall have trouble with you, I can see, for you are not easily led. Give me your hand.'

Slowly Tia held out her right hand and Baradoc, smiling, took it by the finger tips. Then he turned and said two words in his own language to Lerg. The hound rose from the ground and came slowly forward and stood at Baradoc's side. Baradoc raised Tia's hand and placed it over the eyes of the hound, palm down, and he spoke again to Lerg in his own tongue. This done he called Aesc forward and repeated the ritual. Then, ignoring Cuna, he gave an order to the three dogs and they turned and disappeared quickly into the forest.

Tia said, 'What does all that mean?'

Baradoc answered, 'You will see. Now remember always this word.' He paused and then said softly to her, '*Saheer*. You have it? *Saheer*.'

Tia nodded. '*Saheer* — but what is it?'

'It is my word, and now, for Lerg and Aesc, it is also yours. Whenever you are in trouble, call it as loudly as you can.' He grinned. 'Go on — shout it now. As loud as you can.'

Tia hesitated for a moment and then, taking a deep breath, shouted, 'Saheer!'

Almost immediately there was a crashing in the low forest thickets and Lerg and Aesc came rushing to her and settled one on either side of her, alert and on their legs ready for action, growling and barking. A few seconds later Cuna arrived and began to imitate the action and growls of the other two.

Baradoc gave the dogs an order and they relaxed into sitting positions around Tia.

Tia said, 'They will come — always like that?'

'At any time, anywhere — if they can. And the gods help any man who is near you.'

'Why didn't you give my hand to the other, the little one?'

'Cuna? Because he's young and still a little stupid. But the others will teach him. Some time as we travel I will teach you the other words they know.'

'These are words of your language?'

'Na — these are our words. There is a magic in them because only the dogs, myself and soon you will know them. Can you whistle?'

'No, of course I can't.'

'Then you must learn because there could be times when you might need Bran.' Baradoc put his forefingers to his mouth and let out a sudden blasting whistle that made Tia jump.

Within a few moments a shadow swept across the sunlit patch beyond the bower. Then with a noisy beating of his great wings and a raucous calling of *carp, carp* Bran, the raven, swept under the spreading branches of the yew. He circled twice around Baradoc and then settled on his shoulder, eyes alert, the great ebony beak weaving from side to side.

Drawing back a little Tia said, 'That's Bran?'

'Yes. And when he attacks he goes for a man's eyes. So you must learn to whistle him.' Baradoc reached up his right hand and Bran jumped to his wrist. 'Take a piece of cheese and throw it into the air for him.'

Tia broke off a piece of cheese and tossed it high into the air. Bran made no move to take it and the cheese fell to the ground.

'He's not hungry.'

Baradoc laughed. 'Oh, yes he is. Bran is always hungry. But he will take food from no one unless he, too, is given the word. Throw it up again.'

Tia took the cheese and tossed it into the

air once more and, as she did so, Baradoc
called gently, '*Aka, Aka!*'

Bran swooped from Baradoc's wrist and
took the cheese low to the ground as it fell
and then flew off to the top of a nearby ash
tree.

Tia said, 'So now he knows I am allowed to
feed him?'

'Yes. Though he fends for himself even
better than the dogs. When you can whistle he
will always come to you.'

Baradoc stripped off his under shirt and
rolled over on to his stomach, couching his
head on his arms.

Tia asked, 'What now?'

Baradoc grinned sideways at her. 'You
promised to massage me. My muscles are as
stiff as salt-dry ropes.'

After a moment's hesitation Tia went to
his side and knelt by him. For an ex-slave he
had an abrupt way of treating her at times,
but she guessed that this came from his
self-confidence and his pride in the fact
that he was a chief's son. The women of
the remoter tribes, she knew, were of little
importance except to do the bidding of their
men. Leaning over him she began to massage
and work his shoulder muscles in the way
she had often done for Priscus. As she worked
she pushed from her mind as much as she

could the thought of her brother and his wife. In a handful of savage hours her whole life had changed. Her grief belonged to her. Nobody could share it. The gods had been good to them all for a long time, and now the gods had turned away from them. When she got to Aquae Sulis she and her uncle would make their devotions to the gods of the shades and set up a stone for Priscus and his wife and then . . . ? What would she do then? Her uncle was old and would not last much longer. This country — her country for she had known no other, but not hers in the way it was Baradoc's — was falling apart. Priscus had often talked of selling up and moving to Gaul. But things were not much better there. There was a darkness falling over the land. She could feel the coldness of its shadow touching her heart.

Easing and working the stiff arm and back muscles of the youth, she said, 'How long will it take to get to Aquae Sulis?'

'Who knows? There is no marching these days along the west road like a century of legionaries, quickly knocking off the miles. We've got to take the old tracks and steer clear of towns and villages. It's taken me three weeks to come down from Durobrivae and there's not been a day without smoke in the sky from some villa or homestead going

24

up in flames. Tell me, Tia — what have you got in your bundle? My two good friends, whose throats I'll cut one day, took all my stuff and the pack horse as well.'

'There's not much. Some food. Some clothes. A few cooking things. A little money, the dagger, and a brooch that belonged to my mother.'

'I see. Well, we'll need to acquire a few more things.'

'Acquire?'

'Yes. Steal if needs be.' He rolled over and away from her suddenly and, looking up at her, he said firmly, 'But one thing you've got to remember — if I tell you to do something, you do it — fast! Any bush or thicket can hold a cut-throat. Understood?'

After a moment's hesitation Tia said, 'Yes.'

'And we must cut your hair even shorter. You've got to look like a boy, even if a pretty one. So don't pull a long face about it.'

Although she hid it, there was a flare of anger in Tia at the way he spoke, treating her over-familiarly. Sarcasm edging her voice, she said with a little shrug, 'If that's what the great Baradoc, son of a chief, orders — then yes.' On her knees she made a mock bow.

Baradoc grinned and said, 'Don't give me any of your sauce.' He stood up and began to flex his arms and shoulders and then bent over and touched his toes, loosening up his body. As he did so, he went on, 'You must know this part of the country well?'

'Yes.'

He jerked his head towards the glade. 'Where does the path lead?'

'To the sea. It's not far.'

'Is there a village down there?'

'There was until last year. A longboat raided it and it was burnt. But there are still a few old huts the fishermen use when the shoals come along the coast.'

Baradoc bent and threw open her bundle. He took out a thin woollen blanket, slung it over his shoulders and tied it about his neck. He smiled at her. 'I'm going scavenging. You stay here.' He turned and said something in his own language to the dogs and then walked off. Lerg and the other dogs watched him go. Cuna whined for a moment and then was silent. As Baradoc disappeared through the trees Tia saw Bran lift himself from the ash tree top and slide away on the sea breeze, slanting low over the forest towards the coast.

Tia moved to the open bundle and began to tidy the things which Baradoc had left in disarray. She arranged them neatly in the silk cover but left out the small cauldron and the beaker and her dagger. Before tying the ends of the coverlet together to contain her possessions she unwrapped from a piece of linen her mother's brooch. It was a small gold oval set on a strong pin. On its face, worked in relief, were clasped hands. Around them ran the inscription — *To Januaria Hermia, my dearest. Marcus.* The brooch had been given to her mother on her betrothal by her father.

Holding it Tia was struck by a sense of desolation. Alone now, with no need to cosset her pride or hide her feelings from anyone, she suddenly felt a swift grief and the strange dark knowledge of utter loss possess her. Resting back on her heels she put her hands to her eyes and wept silently, her shoulders shaking, her head bowed.

After a while she felt the warm lap of a tongue caress the back of her hands. Looking up she saw that Aesc had come to her and licked her hands. Behind him Lerg sat upright on his haunches, his great tongue lolling from his mouth as he watched her. She fondled Aesc's silky head and, as she did so, Cuna gave a little whimper, came to her and flopped his head into her lap.

She wiped the tears from her eyes, sniffed a little, and then fondled Cuna's head, setting his stubby, docked tail wagging. The gods took, she thought, and the gods gave. There was no questioning their ways. Yesterday was

27

one life; today another — and one for which she was utterly unprepared or fitted. Well, so what, she thought with a moment's heartening defiance? She must learn to live a new life. And then, almost as though she could hear his voice, a favourite saying of her brother came back to her. *The blackest night must die under the fiery wheels of Apollo's golden chariot.*

She wrapped the brooch in its linen and began to pack up her bundle. Grief for those lost, from now, she would keep locked in her heart. As for herself . . . well, she must count herself lucky. Had she not the son of a chief to guide her westwards to Aquae Sulis? And three guardian dogs and an eye-piercing raven to watch over her? Cocksure and abrupt Baradoc might be at times, but there was, she sensed, far more than that to him. There was a temper and a strength which would hold him to any course he set.

It was close on sunset when Baradoc returned. He came with the blanket slung over his shoulder, bulky with his findings. He carried in his right hand a long, wooden-shafted fishing spear, its socketed three-pronged iron head missing a tang and the two others badly rusted. He dumped the bundle on the ground and, squatting by her, laid out his pickings from the fishing huts. There were

28

some rusty hooks of different sizes; a length of worn hempen rope; part of a circular throwing net with some small stone weights still attached to its skirts; a tangle of old catgut lengths; a sail-maker's needle with a broken point; a small wicker woven bird cage with the bottom missing into which he had stuffed odd lengths of cloth; two wooden platters, both badly cracked; a large lump of beeswax; a raggedly shaped piece of goat's hide as stiff as a board; a thick woollen fisherman's shirt, with a slit down the side, half a sleeve missing and the front coated with tiny, dried opaline fish scales; a well worn piece of striking flint, and a small length of tallow candle with a rush wick.

As he laid all these out, Tia watched in silence. He took no notice of her until he pulled out the last of his finds, a pair of long coarsely woven leggings that reached down to the ankles, stained with rust and pitch marks and with a great hole in their seat. He dropped them on the pile and looked at Tia with a grin of satisfaction.

'What do we want with all that rubbish?' she asked.

Baradoc frowned quickly. He shook his head and said, 'I know the kind of place you come from. Like my old master's. You had servants and maids, fine clothes, and fine table furnishings. Aye, even glass in your windows and worked mosaics on the great room floor. Baths and hot rooms and a home farm that gave you all everything you wanted for the table. You've probably never done a real hand's turn in your life. You've lived soft, wench — but now the world is upside down.'

Tia jumped up and said furiously, 'Son of a chief you may be, but call me 'wench' again and I walk from here and find my own way to Aquae Sulis. My name is Gratia. As a mark of friendship, Tia to you. Name me so and not as a herd or kitchen girl.'

'Whooah! Rein back! I meant no rudeness. Tia it shall be.' He reached up, took her hand and pulled her down. 'Should we fight now — whose side would the dogs and Bran take since they have been given the word for you?'

'I'm sorry. I have a quick temper.'

'No — 'tis pride and that is a good thing. I shall not offend it again — except by mischance for which I ask forgiveness now to save further trouble. So, let's get back to our rubbish which is no rubbish. What one man throws away another can use. A fish spear with two prongs is better than no fish spear. Fish can be eaten but first they must be caught. So, I brought the spear, the hooks, the gut, and the piece of net. I can sharpen a new point to the needle and with threads pulled from the cloth and waxed you can repair the shirt and the long hose.'

'Who are they for?'

'The shirt is for me. The hose for you.'

'I wouldn't wear those filthy things!'

Baradoc was silent. For all that she had recently suffered Tia was far from realizing what change had — if only temporarily — come over her life. Never before had she ever had to think of black tomorrow, of a tomorrow which would be as full of want as all the yesterdays. In this wilderness of place and evil times she was no more able to survive alone than a fledgling, unfeathered, pushed from its warm nest. He could have wished that it had been some simple herd girl who had saved him and who would have needed no teaching. Still . . . she was not. He must learn patience. He said with good humour, 'As you know, the world is upside down and will stay so for a long time, Lady Tia. The clothes can be washed first and mended after. In long hose and the legs gartered you will be a handsome young fellow. And don't frown at me — it must be so for your own safety. Now, do I have to explain the rest as though you were a raw recruit, goggle-eyed in barracks for the first time?' He took the flint and holding the spear head jabbed into the ground struck the stone against one of the iron prongs and brought brief, blue sparks spurting to life. 'Raw fish or fowl cheer no belly. Fire we must have to cook. And have I not brought two cracked platters to go with your cooking cauldron and that wicked little dagger you keep always close to your side?'

'And this — this stinking piece of hide?'

'It's a long way to Aquae Sulis. Those fancy sandals of yours could need new soles in a week. Now — let's get packed up and moving. And Lady Tia — leave the rest of the cake and cheese near the top of your bundle. We shall need them before the night is out. Tomorrow we'll lay up somewhere safe and make a proper meal which will — '

Baradoc broke off in mid speech as Lerg suddenly gave a soft growl. Lerg growled again and was silenced by a sign from Baradoc. At the same time, he took Tia's arm and drew her down flat on the ground so that the screening bushes hid them from the nearby glade. His face close to Tia's, Baradoc whispered, 'Keep down and don't move.'

Pressing herself to the ground alongside him, Tia saw the three dogs slink quietly away from them to disappear into the trees and thickets between them and the glade. At that moment she heard the distant noise of people shouting and singing and the faint thud of horses' hooves beating on the hard ground of the distant pathway.

She lay there with Baradoc's hand gripping her arm. His breath faintly touched the side of her cheek. A few moments later, across the small length of glade path which she held in her view, Tia saw a strange procession pass.

First came two horses ridden by men in loose working smocks. The men carried large leather drinking skins which, as they passed, they up-ended to their mouths, guzzling greedily, wine spilling over their cheeks as they swayed unsteadily on their mounts. Behind them came a rabble of working men and women, shouting and singing. Many of them carried mead and wine jars, and all of them were laden down with household loot and bulging sacks of pillaged goods. Some of the women wore fine silken scarves and pearl-beaded billowing robes while their wrists and necks were strung with loops of amber and coloured glass beads, twisted gold-wire torques and silver and enamelled bracelets. A short, fat, perspiring man stumbled along wearing an old and rusted legionary's helmet topped with a spray of elderberry branch stuck into the plume holder. About his body was wrapped a long white toga sweeping to the ground over which he tripped and stumbled as he pranced by clasping to his breast a large round cheese. An old man hobbled along with a wooden household kist balanced on his bowed back. Children, half-naked, ran wildly in and around the mob, at the rear of which came four youths leading two milk cows and two draught oxen, astride one of which sat a drunken man, shouting and singing who, as Tia watched, fell to the ground and lay there unconscious as the mob passed, abandoning him.

Watching the crowd disappear Baradoc knew that somewhere another villa had been sacked, another farmstead pillaged by these workpeople and servants in whom the quick flowering of long growing envy had been forced by the fast blaze of fear spreading from the east. He twisted his lips in disgust, knowing well the thought that held all these people — *take what we can now before others far stronger come to take it*. Knowing, too, that such a mob had sacked Tia's brother's villa and homestead, he put out a hand and held her wrist, not to restrain her from any rash action but to give comfort. He caught her eyes for a moment and saw them mist with tears before she turned her face from him. One day, he thought savagely, there would arise a leader from his kind who would halt and crush the savagery from the east and bring this country to peace and to a strength and power greater even than had ever been wielded by the Romans.

Slowly the tumult of the mob's passing died away down the valley towards the coast. The drunken man lay in the glade flat on his back, snoring in a stupor of wine.

When the last sound had long died Baradoc stood up, motioned to Tia to stay where she was and went out into the glade to the man. After a while he came back, followed by the three dogs. In his arms he carried a fine cloak of woven goats' hair, a broad leather belt with a bronze buckle which had strapped to it a leather scabbard that held a two-edge dagger, and a small sack half full of oven-dried corn.

He fastened the belt around his waist and handed the cloak to Tia, saying, 'The nights are still cold. Your mantle is a pretty thing but no proof against rain and wind.' He dipped his hand into the sack, showed her the hard corn grains, and smiled. 'Tomorrow I promise you hare or deer meat stew with this to thicken it. A full belly makes a light heart. Now, let us be on our way.'

The Black Raven

During that night's march Tia felt that she was living through a dream. Tired and racked by the want of sleep, her leg muscles stiff from the hard going, there were times when she felt that in a while she must wake from a dream in her own bed in Priscus's villa. She would hear the morning sounds of cattle and poultry from the homestead, the chink of bridle and bit as Priscus saddled up outside to make his early morning rounds, and the creak of the bedroom door as her maid, Tullio's wife, Sabata came in carrying her breakfast of fresh-baked bread spread with honey, a beaker of creamy milk and a dish of fruit all borne on the silver tray which had once been her mother's, a tray embossed with the figure of the god Neptune, the rim decorated with fishes and writhing sea creatures.

The first time they stopped for a rest, she dropped to the ground, pulled the warm cloak close around her, and was asleep almost at once, just conscious of Cuna snuggling up against her side, relishing the softness of the woven goats' hair, before oblivion claimed

36

her. Almost at once it seemed that Baradoc was waking her, his hand firm on her shoulder.

She pulled herself to her feet and swayed a little until he steadied her. For a moment she wanted to protest against being wakened so soon, but the impulse died in her as she saw that while she had slept a full moon had begun to climb the eastern sky and the forest now was a black and silver maze of shadow and light. Baradoc handed her the beaker full of water and she drank gladly, saying nothing but knowing that somewhere near he must have found a spring. To speak was forbidden unless he spoke first. This he had made clear the moment darkness came. She handed the beaker back. He tucked it into the top of her bundle. The bundles had been tied, one to each end of the fishing spear which Baradoc carried fore and aft over his left shoulder, leaving his right hand free to reach for the dagger at his belt. The only thing he had let her carry was the half empty corn sack whose weight as she now set out after him she knew would increase with every step she took.

Her mind clear now that she had slept, she felt a sudden dissatisfaction in herself. She had thought she was fit and strong, but she knew now that real strength and hardihood lay at some point far beyond her experience.

Baradoc had it. He carried his load with ease and seemed tireless. She realized that without her he would be travelling much faster. There was a strangeness, too, about him. Some kind of magic in him which worked without words. Not once since they had started had he spoken to the dogs, and not once since Lerg had gone ahead and Aesc had slid away to their left flank had she seen either dog. Only Cuna — she smiled to herself remembering Baradoc's words, 'a raw recruit, goggle-eyed in barracks for the first time' — stayed with them, trotting between them. Ahead the hardened campaigner, behind the two raw recruits. And, she was sure, somewhere up above Bran would be scouting on sable wings. Priscus had often said that there were men of the tribes who had a power over animals which was beyond belief. Baradoc the magician. Out of her tiredness, she giggled aloud.

Baradoc stopped and swung round, staring at her and in the moonlight she saw his face scowling and full of displeasure. She made an apologetic gesture with her free hand and he turned away and began walking along the track. And that, too, she thought must have something of magic in it. He could not know this forest — the great forest that ran league after league westwards along the south shore

— yet he moved through it as though he had been born in it. Always they were on a path or track of some kind, deer run or one of the ancient trackways made, long before the Great Caesar had come to the country, by the Britons and still used by many of them. And — since the times were now what they were — to be used more and more by them in the days to come.

The days to come . . . The days to come . . . What kind of days would they be? She thought of her uncle in Aquae Sulis. Long, long ago he had been a Chief Centurion in the Second Legion and finally its Camp Prefect but had retired and settled in the country a few years before the Legion left for good. Uncle Truvius, always a bachelor, well over eighty, living for many years now in a villa just outside Aquae Sulis and still hoping that one day its waters would cure his rheumatism. Surely the country would not be so unsettled as far west as Aquae Sulis? She would live with him, look after him. Times would be good again, and one day she would marry. Returning fatigue flighting her mind to wild fancies, she began to think of herself married and with children and the times brought to order again. What kind of man would she marry? A pure-blooded Roman? Blood as pure as her own, though she had never seen Rome? There were not many of such blood left now. No full legions stationed in the country for years. And now only a handful of discontented auxiliaries left. No young men, proud legionary tribunes, no tall, dark handsome cohort commanders or dashing cavalry officers . . . Well, maybe she would have to settle for some nice Romano-British type. After all, that's what Priscus had done, and who could have been sweeter or kinder than his wife, Martina? But then Martina had been born and bred in Londinium where her father had been a wealthy merchant. Who would want to marry, no matter how important his own people considered him, a Celt or — even worse — a Pict or — the gods forbid — a Scot? Fatigue lightening her head and heightening her sense of the ridiculous she giggled silently to herself at the thought of being mistress of some mountain boothy, wearing wolf and bear skin and when the fire failed in bad weather chewing on a strip of dried fish.

At this moment, unmindful of her step, her right foot caught in a half hidden tree root across the path. She tripped and fell forward flat on her face, the corn sack shooting from her hand and catching Cuna on the rump, drawing a sharp bark of protest from him.

Before Tia could stop herself she let fly

loudly a round of her father's favourite army oaths. Baradoc swung round and said low and furiously, 'You stupid, clumsy wench! We might as well march with lighted lanterns and singing! Pick up your feet and watch the path!'

On her knees, half-risen, Tia retorted in sudden fury, 'Oh shut up and don't be so bossy! And I told you not to call me 'wench'.'

For a moment or two Baradoc was silent and then he reached down a hand and pulled her to her feet, saying, 'All right, Lady Tia, I'm sorry I was disrespectful. Am I setting too fast a pace?'

'No you're not. I can keep up.'

'Good.' He picked up the corn sack and handed it to her, saying, 'For a high-born lady you've a nice choice of barrack room oaths.'

They began to march again and Baradoc, without making it too obvious, slackened off his pace a little. In this part of the country there was always by day or night the chance of a dangerous encounter. At any moment one could stumble into the sleeping camp of a party of rogues and thieves or pillaging, cutthroat workers who had taken to the easy pickings that came with the breakdown of law and order. When they got farther west, into more open and, perhaps less unsettled country they might be able to travel by day. But at the moment the forest was best crossed at night. He had Lerg out ahead and Aesc on the seaward flank to give warning of danger. And danger was not only to be feared from humans. There were wolves still in the great forest. True, the packs had grown smaller with hunting, but there were still times — as food grew scarce — when they hunted boldly. Thank the gods that at the moment there were plenty of easy pickings for them amongst the slaughtered and straying cattle.

Hearing Tia moving behind him, he smiled to himself as he remembered the oaths she had let fly. Those he guessed must have been picked up from brother or father. Then, the smile dying, he wondered what lay ahead for her with only now an aged uncle living in Aquae Sulis. The great days of the long Roman settlement of the country were gone. New conquerors were coming in from the east. To be Roman soon would be to be in danger, to be Romano-British little better. The new invaders and the scum and riff-raff of Britons who had served the old masters would have no pity. To curry favour with the new lords, the workers and low born were already turning against the old masters. Only in the west and the north were men true to themselves and their race and determined to hold their own. And amongst them new leaders would be needed. Men who understood what was happening in the world and could shape their courses to meet the thrust of new methods, new weapons, and a new way of life. How many times had he listened to his old master on the subject? A wise old man, wise in wars and learning, who had read to and talked with him, laying out (he could see his stick now, tracing countries and battle formations in the loose sand of the courtyard) the rise and fall of emperors and empires, the onthrust of the races from beyond the Rhine and further east, a great wave rolling slowly but steadily across the western world. Had he not known from some instinct that he had much to learn from him he would have escaped four years ago. His old master had known this, too. He remembered him sitting in the sun one afternoon after he had finished reading a chapter of Caesar's great book on the conquest of Gaul and Britain, and saying, 'The world will always have its Caesars, boy. Some good, some evil. One day this country will spawn one . . . some Celt living or yet to be born who knows that in the heart and the brain there is no true man who can live and be called slave. It is because of this that I know if I freed you today you would not yet

43

turn westwards with Lerg and Aesc.' And that had been the truth. But now the old man was dead and he was going westwards — even if it were with a Roman girl dragging at his heels. *Aie!* that was ungrateful since but for her he would have still been swinging from an oak all spark gone from him and his carcass drying up like an empty, sunbaked wine skin. The gods give her thanks, her gods and his gods. He had made her a promise. To Aquae Sulis. Long before she got there she would be marching twenty-five miles a night without turning a curl of her pretty fair hair which tomorrow would have to be cropped as close as a boy's.

Marching, he watched the moon and the stars in their slow swings, and shaped his course, but even in pitch darkness the magic compass in his mind would have served him, though less finely. Once or twice he heard an owl call, and now and again came the harsh screech of a hunting nightjar. The forest was alive with Nature's hunters whose skills were more precise than any man's. Now and again either Lerg or Aesc would come from the darkness to his side for a few seconds and then disappear to their posts once more. Towards morning, with daylight like a grey wash of cobwebs through the eastern trees, he sent Cuna out to the right flank. Of all the dogs he and his old master had bred for export abroad, there had been none to touch Lerg or Aesc. They had been kept jealously for the household. Cuna would learn the wordless signs in time. Of all animals the gods had gifted dogs with a magical kinship with man, but only to some men the gift of the words and signs that held them coupled in understanding and loyalty.

*   *   *

It was almost mid-morning before Tia woke. There was a fresh westerly wind blowing and the sky was full of low, rolling grey clouds. She sat up and looked around her. She had only the vaguest memory of the last stretches of their march and the moment when Baradoc had halted and said they would make camp. She had been conscious of him stirring around in the moonlight and shadows, unloading their bundles and spreading covers on the ground, of herself dropping to the ground and the last memory of him throwing the warm goat-hair cloak across her.

She stretched her arms, yawned and rubbed the last of sleep from her eyes. The camp had been made on a high bluff which rose clear of the forest, in a small ravine whose sides were a jumble of broken stones.

45

Behind her the rock face rose sheer and smooth like a fortress wall. The sound of running water reached her ears. Away to the left a thin stream dripped down a moss-covered cleft of the rocks and was gathered into a small gravelly pool from which it seeped away down the hillside in a marshy slope bordered by primroses and blue-starred periwinkle growths. There was no sign of Baradoc or the dogs, but Bran sat on a spur of rock above her beak-combing his flight-feathers and scratching himself about the head as he made his morning toilet. Tia smiled to herself and decided to follow his example. Her tiredness was gone but she felt dirty and tousled.

She went to the pool, stripped off her tunic and took off her sandals. Wearing only her short woollen drawers, she splashed and washed her face, the top half of her body and then her legs. There was a blister on her right foot where the sandal had rubbed her during the march. She wiped herself with a corner of her bundle cover and dressed, and shivered a little until her clothes began to bring back warmth to her body. For a moment or two she thought of the villa bath house, of hot water and Sabata bringing her clean clothes after her toilet. Soft living . . . those days were gone for the time being.

Then, seeing close up against the rock face the contents of their bundles which Baradoc had opened up, she picked up the dirty old seaman's shirt and the filthy pair of long hose. There was no sign of the fishing spear. Baradoc, she guessed, was away with the dogs hunting for the pot. At the thought of food, she felt her belly empty and hunger bring saliva to her mouth, and she knew that she had never been so hungry before. Well, Baradoc must see to that. Each to his own duties.

She took the shirt and the hose to the shallow scoop of pool, threw them in and then began to tramp and knead them underneath her bare feet. The water flowed away muddy.

From above Bran watched her. She pounded away with her feet, and then knelt at the poolside working the clothes with her hands, spreading them out and beating them with a small heavy length of stick, talking and grumbling to herself. Bran turned his head away. He had seen many women pounding and beating away like this before. His eyes followed the dark-crested, rolling spread of the forest top away to the south. Distantly there was a glimpse of a thin arc of the sea, iron grey and still, and away to the west a sudden fall in the trees to a narrow edging of marsh and grasslands biting up into the forest. Through this valley coiled and looped a wide, slow moving river.

Moving slowly up the river, a good five miles away, was something else which Bran had seen before, a longship, the oar blades dipping and flashing rhythmically. The saffron coloured sail had been half-struck and loosely furled. Bran watched the swing of the rowers' backs and arms, saw three men standing in the raised stern, and a solitary man perched high in the prow who now and again swung a weighted sounding line overboard to read the depth of the river. As the long ship moved into a broader reach of the river, the stern steering oar was put hard over and the ship slowly swung round in a half circle and in to the left bank. Oars flashed with waterruns as they were lifted and shipped, and from stern and bow men jumped ashore with mooring ropes. As the ship was made fast a party of men moved out from the forest that fringed the river meadow and made for the ship. There were ten or twelve of them, helmeted and armed with swords and spears, and with them came four pack horses laden down with loads slung across their backs. That, too, Bran had seen before. Had he been free he might have launched himself on his broad wings and swung down valley, quartering against the cross wind, and taken a closer look, for anything that moved excited his curiosity. But the freedom was denied him because he had been given the word to mark his place by Baradoc before he had left with the dogs and the fishing spear. Bran ruffled and then ordered his feathers, shuffled to a new grip on the rock ledge and settled down to wait.

Below him Tia wrung out the shirt and the hose and spread them over the steep rock face, weighting them down with stones. They were a little cleaner, she thought, but not much. Looking at the roughly woven hose she made a wry face. Before she got used to them they would probably chafe and rub her legs raw. Still, Baradoc was right. For her own safety she had to turn from a well-bred young lady to a ragged country youth — but, thank the gods, only until they got to Aquae Sulis. She stood for a moment thinking of her uncle's beautifully furnished and decorated villa, and the soft silk and cotton covered beds with their mattresses of swan and duck down. Then she put the thought from her and, taking her dagger, went back to the pool which had now cleared. Leaning over it, she began to saw and hack at her fair hair. The wind took strands of it away like floating cobwebs and some fell into the water, drifting away on the slow current. Once as she worked, the dagger slipped and the sharp edge nicked the side of her thumb. Without thinking she used her father's favourite curse word and sucked her thumb. Then she grinned to herself. Why should she not curse and condemn the bloody knife and the bloody times to the darkness of bloody Hades? They were a man's words and she was now a man — albeit a very good-looking one.

An hour later Baradoc arrived back with the dogs. Tia was sitting with her back to the rocks, pulling threads loose from a piece of cloth and drawing them through the lump of beeswax which she had warmed in her hands. One moment she was alone, frowning over her work — and then there was Cuna at her feet, Lerg by the pool and Aesc on a rock ledge above him, with Baradoc at his side. The suddenness and silence of their appearance startled her, making her heart thump quickly. But almost immediately she realized how glad she was to see them all, feeling the comfort of their presence warm her, admitting to herself for the first time that she had not relished being alone.

Baradoc said something softly to Bran, and then jumped down to the poolside and came across to Tia. Bran lifted himself from his perch, beat upwards in a slow spiral towards the grey sky which was now showing an occasional break in the clouds, and then he drifted away southwards. He was free now to do his own foraging. There would be something to be picked up down by the river where the crewmen of the longship were now busy setting up a shore camp. Such men ate until they were full and then tossed their leavings over their shoulders to make easy prizes for any ready scavenger.

★　★　★

From his shoulder Baradoc dropped the hind of a young deer to the short grass. Then, from the inside of his shirt, he pulled out a handful of different fungi.

Squatting on his hunkers he took out his dagger and began to skin the leg, looking at Tia for a moment with a smile and saying, 'Fill the cauldron, Lady Tia, with water, and then search around for dry grass, dry twigs and some of that crumbly dry moss from the rocks.' He paused and nodded at the clothes she had washed. 'I see you have been busy. Turn your head.'

Tia slowly turned her head so that he could see her cropped hair. She said with a note of sarcasm in her voice, 'I hope it meets with the great Baradoc's approval.'

'*Aie!* but 'tis a pity to see such a fine flow of

golden locks go. Still, a few weeks in Aquae Sulis will see them back and you'll be able to look in your mirror and admire yourself again.'

Rising to get the cauldron, Tia said, 'You are in a good and teasing humour.'

'Why not? The hunt was quick and easy. The dogs have already eaten and I brought only what we might need for a while.'

'How did you catch it?'

'One day soon when your wind and legs are stronger I might show you. Now fill the cauldron and tip into it a few handfuls of our corn and the toadstools.'

'Are they good to eat?'

Baradoc sighed. 'Would I have brought them else?'

Tia filled the cauldron and did as she was bid by which time Baradoc had skinned the meat and cut off four fair-sized portions. Then he gathered the little heap of kindling and tinder-moss together which Tia had gathered and carried them to a dry flat stone at the foot of the rock face. As he arranged them he said, without looking at her, 'Bring me the spear and the flint and your mantle.'

It was no order. He just said it as though it were the most natural thing in the world to order her around without thought of resentment from her. So, she told herself, if she wanted to get to Aquae Sulis it must be. When he did something he did it wholeheartedly, his absorption in his task leaving him no room for niceties to others.

He took the spear and jammed the two prongs into the ground at the edge of the stone, easing the dry grass and moss close to it. Then, taking up the flint, he said, 'Drape the mantle over me and hold the edges so that no wind comes in.'

Tia, knowing this was no moment to resent being ordered around, drew the mantle around the spear haft and covered Baradoc, holding the edges of the material close together to keep out the draught. Standing there she heard him begin to strike the flint against one of the tangs. Again and again she heard it strike and sometimes she heard Baradoc muttering to himself in his own language. The thought crossed her mind that he was probably swearing to himself in his own tongue. Once or twice she heard him blowing gently, only to break off with another bout of mutterings. It was then that she realized how much she had taken fire for granted in her own life. Fire and light at night had always been with her, fire for the room braziers, fire for the furnace that fed hot air into the house warming system, fire for the corn drying racks and the cooking holes of the raised hearths, and light from the tallow candles flickering in their lanterns and from the oil-soaked wicks of the elegant wall lamps of the villa. But the gift of the great god Vulcan, maker of Jove's thunderbolts, once let die had to be won from the earth again by the clash of flint and metal. Suddenly, the thought of meat stew thickened with corn and fungi made her mouth water, and there was an impatience in her for Baradoc to make fire.

At last when her arms were aching from holding the tented mantle around Baradoc she heard him blowing gently without stopping. Then a thin trickle of fine blue smoke seeped through the edges of the mantle. Baradoc lifted away his covering and put aside the spear. On the flat stone little tongues of flame were working through the dried grass and twigs.

Baradoc, face covered in sweat, said, 'Now build it. But remember only dry wood. We want no heavy smoke from damp stuff. What little there is this wind will whip away from the top of the bluff. The fire and the cooking is all yours.'

'All mine?'

'Why not?' Baradoc was genuinely surprised. 'Did you think you would ride the whole way to Aquae Sulis lolling on a litter and not a hand to lift for any comfort or food?'

'But I've never cooked in the open. In fact I — ' She broke off.

Baradoc grunted. 'In fact, you've never cooked at all. Well a late start is better than none. I've brought you the meat and the flavouring and made the fire. Would you sit by and see me do woman's work? True, I owe you a life. But at the moment you owe me a meal.'

'And what are you going to do?'

He held out his blood-stained and dirt-streaked hands, and said brusquely, 'Take a bath, of course. It's a habit my master beat into me. When that's done, I'll grind a new point to the needle, and wax some more threads — so that you won't be left idle after we've eaten.'

Tia looked at him in silence for a moment or two, and then said evenly, 'What you say is fair, though not gently said. But — ' her voice began to rise, ' — don't think, son of a chief, Baradoc, that I can't do as well as any tribe woman with greasy hair and dirty face. I will do all you ask of me, but speak me fair — or I will set Lerg at your throat and claim the life you owe — barbarian!'

Baradoc stared at her round-eyed with surprise. Then he burst out laughing and said, 'I am sorry. I was wrong to give you offence. Now, *please*, do as I ask. And also — ' a twinkle came into his dark eyes, ' — since I don't want to offend you again keep your eyes from the bath house. I haven't washed for three days and I'm going to strip.'

He strode away towards the pool, and Tia turned back to the fire and her duties. As she worked she heard the splashing of the pool water and his cheerful low whistling as he washed himself. There were times when she liked him, and times when she could kick him for his cocksureness. Still, whatever he was, she needed him to get to Aquae Sulis. How many more days would that be? Already the moment when she had come into the forest glade and seen him hanging from the oak seemed an age away. She fed the fire with more sticks and picked up loose stones and rocks to build a guard around it which would hold the cauldron. Her belly grumbled suddenly with hunger. As she crouched there Cuna came up and pushed his head against her thigh. She fondled his muzzle briefly and then smiled to herself. The raw recruits . . .

Two hours later they ate. When they had finished Baradoc cut the rest of the raw deer flesh into flat strips. Laying them on the hot cooking stone, he put another flat stone on top of them and then raked the hot embers over the stones and covered these with slabs of turf cut with his dagger. By the time they were ready to move off at night the meat would be cooked dry and easily carried as emergency rations. Then, in the fitful sunlight which now came between the lifting and breaking clouds, Tia began to mend the shirt and hose with the waxed threads while Baradoc with a piece of grit stone — on which he had repointed the needle — began to burnish and hone the tangs of the spear to put an edge and point on them.

As they worked, in answer to a question from Tia, he explained that in normal times they could have walked the distance to Aquae Sulis easily in six or seven days. But now the journey would take longer because they must pick their route to avoid large towns and settlements and the old Roman-built main roads. He said, 'The only people on these high roads will be armed parties, able to look after themselves, and not always to be trusted to give a true greeting to a couple of strangers.' As she sewed, his spear head finished, he drew in the loose gravel for her a map of the southern and western parts of Britain, marking in roughly the towns, rivers and forests and the areas of bare downs. He showed her where they were now — to the west of Anderida, a quarter of the way towards the next coastal town of Noviomagus. He stabbed the gravel with a stick, reciting the names of the towns like a litany . . . Portus Adurni, Clausentium, Venta, Sorviodonum and Lindinis. Tia smiled to herself for, though she recognized most of the names, she knew that quietly Baradoc was showing off his knowledge. As she sat now, so must Baradoc have sat many times at the feet of his master learning the geography of his own country.

She asked, 'And where is your country?'

Baradoc's stick swung far to the west, and he said, 'Down here, beyond Isca, beyond the Tamarus river, on the north coast two days' march from the Point of Herculis, in the valley of the great rocks. Away further, right at the end of the land, is Antivestaeum where the sea stretches away to the edge of the world.' As he finished speaking. Baradoc reached for the unwashed cauldron and ran two fingers round the inner rim to collect the grease gathered there. Without looking at her, he reached for Tia's blistered foot and spread some of the grease over the red, chafed skin. Then he tore a piece from one of their collection of rags, bound it round her foot and tied it in place with a couple of waxed threads. This done he looked up at her and smiled, saying, 'In the days of the legions a man would get a beating and lose a week's pay for neglecting his feet.' He stood up, holding the cauldron, and began to move away.

Tia asked, 'Where are you going?'

'To scour the cauldron for you.'

'Woman's work?' Tia grinned, pulled a thread tight and bit off the end.

'I see no woman around here — only a crop-headed Roman lad sewing up a rip in the backside of his long hose.'

Tia watched him kneel at the pool and begin to scour the cauldron with sand and pebbles. He could be angry and bullying at times — perhaps that came from an exaggerated pride in his own powers and the knowledge that he was the son of a chief and destined for high office one day. But a little while ago his hands had been gentle and adroit, salving and bandaging her foot. There were two Baradocs. She liked most the gentle, thoughtful one. But she knew that at this moment it was the other Baradoc she needed most for he was the only one who could take her safely to Aquae Sulis.

Baradoc brought back the pot and said, 'I leave Aesc and Cuna with you. There is something I saw early this morning which interests me.'

He turned away and began to climb up to

59

the top of the bluff and was soon lost to view. Although he spoke no word nor seemed to make any sign, Lerg went with him. The other dogs remained, stretched out beyond the fire. A dark shadow swept across the ground and Tia looked up to see Bran come to roost on one of the high rock points.

★ ★ ★

At the side of the river stood a lone alder tree, its lower branches still festooned with the jetsam and flotsam of the past winter's floods. Baradoc was wedged in the fork of the trunk close to the top where he commanded a clear view of the river downstream. Below him the banks were broadly fringed with reeds that gradually gave way to the new growth of this year's meadow grasses. Lerg sat at the foot of the tree. Below Baradoc the muddy river flowed southwards, looping and coiling its slow way to the sea. Along the rush fringes coots and grebes busied themselves with their mating and nest building. A flight of duck went downstream, the air whistling with the cut of their pinions. A marsh harrier dropped from a slow hunting foray into the reeds and rose holding a large water vole. The air was full of bird song. Out of the corner of his eye Baradoc caught the high crescent-shaped silhouette of a falcon poised for the stoop and kill. But his real interest lay downstream, a quarter of a mile away.

There, moored against the same bank as the alder tree, was a longboat. The saffron sail had been lowered and was now stretched the length of the mid-deck over its own boom to make a tented canopy. There was some large black design painted on the canvas, but because of its folds Baradoc could not make out what it was. He had seen longboats before and he knew it would be some device to give recognition of its sea warrior master to others of his kind, green, red or black raven, a whole gallery of sea eagles, sea dragons, rising suns or silver moons, great hands holding aloft broad, two-edged swords, and sometimes multi-coloured serpents coiled in great circles over the whole spread of sail.

It was no Saxon ship. It was the long keel of a far north sea-raider, of a race that sought no foreign soil to hold, no land to conquer. These men looked only to plunder and slaves and to the easing of the deep salt itch in their blood which was only stilled as the seas rolled under their keels and the winds of all seasons filled their great emblazoned sails of finely dressed skin. These men loved colour and bold designs as they loved the sea and their bloodthirsty raiding, as they loved fighting

61

and, after the slaughter, loved eating and drinking until they fell from their boardseats bloated and stupefied.

On the bank two hide shelters had been set up and the smoke of cooking fires rose into the air. Men were carrying supplies and loot aboard and other men worked round the fires. When the work was done the feasting would begin. Somewhere along the coast or in the leagues of forest that rose beyond the water meadows, he knew, there would be ruined huts and homesteads, burning barns and byres, and the fly-clouded corpses of men, women and children.

That morning, returning from his hunting, he had seen one of their raiding parties moving down the river path and with them they had been leading four sturdy ponies carrying their bundled loot. The loot meant nothing to him. But the ponies had made his eyes glisten with desire. With one or, better still, two of them, he and Tia could make faster time to Aquae Sulis and — when he had delivered her to her uncle — a pony would bring him home that much quicker; and home he longed for now with a longing which was a great thirst in him.

The ponies were in his sight now. The four of them had been loosely hobbled and were grazing in the meadow grass not more than a spear's throw from the first slopes of the forest. Within an hour all the crewmen, he guessed, would be drinking and feasting and soon have no thought in their minds for the ponies which they probably planned to slaughter for meat to ship aboard with them the next day.

Baradoc watched as the sun began to slide down the sky. The shipmen had stowed their gains aboard and were now gathered ashore around the cooking fires and the rough tables set up outside their skin tents. Their voices, as they ate and drank, became louder and were broken by great gusts of laughter and now and then the lusty, roaring of a song. Baradoc marked a spot on the westward crest of the forest and, when the sun touched it, and the alder threw a long shadow across the rushes and the meadow, he slid down from the tree. He picked up the fishing spear which he had left at the bottom with the length of salvaged rope. He looped the rope about his waist and, keeping to the rushes, he went back up the river side with Lerg following him. When he was safely out of sight of the ship he swung away across the meadow grasses and into the skirts of the forest at the bottom of the hill. He worked his way through the trees until he was almost opposite the place where the ponies grazed. The shouting and drunken singing of the men came clearly to him now.

He wet a finger and tested the wind. It was quartering up stream and towards him. He made a half circling hunting sign to Lerg and the hound moved off into the tall grass. It was the sign he used when he wanted to send Lerg or Aesc upwind of deer or game to drive them down to him. Marking the slight crest movements of the long grasses, he watched Lerg's progress until the hound was between the ponies and the longship and upwind of the animals.

Baradoc slipped to the edge of the forest and crouched behind the dark cover of a holly bush. For a moment or two the ponies grazed peacefully. From the river came the sounds of the feasting men. Then Baradoc saw first the farthest pony and then the others lift their heads and cease grazing. Coming downwind to them was the scent of Lerg, and the body smell of Lerg from near ancestry was more wolf than dog, but not so much wolf that it immediately panicked the ponies. It made them restless and puzzled them so that they moved slowly away from it, awkward in their gait from the hobbles they wore. Then they settled to graze again. But after a while their heads went up as Lerg, belly to the ground, slid nearer to them through the grasses, and they moved closer to the trees.

Three times Lerg moved the ponies forward and the third time the leading pony, a sturdy, rusty red mare with a pale golden mane, was almost within spitting distance of the holly bush. Gently Baradoc began to make soft clicking noises with his tongue. The pony looked towards the bush. Baradoc began to talk softly to it in his own tongue, calming it with words whose magic lay not in their sense but their sound. *Aie! you red and gold beauty . . . Aie! who is it with the eyes like dark crag pools and the soft mouth, softer than the dove's breast? 'Tis you, my handsome, my proud, with the taste of sweet grass like honey on your breath. Come away, then, come away . . .*

As he spoke the mare came to the side of the holly bush and Baradoc, talking low still, rose with an unbroken, slow movement, stepped smoothly forward and put his hand on the pony's muzzle and then ran it up the long cheek and caressed one of its ears. The pony stood for him as it might have stood for its unknown master.

Baradoc, talking to it still, unslung the rope from his waist and looped it over the mare's head making a rough halter. He drew his dagger, crouched, and cut the hobble between the forelegs.

He led the pony slowly into the shelter of

the trees, took his spear from where it rested against a tree, and turned to lead the pony up the forest track. As he did so, a man stepped from the cover of an oak trunk less than six paces ahead of it. Baradoc halted and checked the movement of the pony with his hand on the halter. He cursed himself that he should have been caught with the fishing spear in his left hand.

The man standing slightly above him on the slope of the narrow track smiled, swayed a little, and then said gently in the Roman tongue, ''Twas well done, lad. And bravely done with my crew only a few cables' lengths away and you, risking your guts to garter their trews if they'd spotted you — and all for the sake of a pony! You understand my talk?'

Baradoc shook his head.

The man gave a low, tipsy laugh. 'Your ballast has shifted, lad. Your brains must be lopsided or you would not shake your head to say No if you did not understand my talk. O brave lad who can talk strange love talk to a part-broken forest pony, a lad who wears a soldier's cast-off sandals, and a lad who has not turned tail in fright like a startled hare, and even now stares me boldly in the eye when one sight of me would make most Britons void their bellies with fear. Speak me fair, for you understand me, or I will take your head off and fillet you from throat to vent like gutting a cod. Why do you steal my pony?' He hiccoughed.

From his manner and speech it was clear to Baradoc that he was someone of authority, someone who was used to command and to be obeyed. The odds were that he was the master of the longboat. He was bare-headed, a tall, powerfully built man, wearing a saffron-coloured, flared tunic with a wide whale-skin belt from the left side of which hung a broad sword in a decorated scabbard. His thighs were bare to his knees and his legs were wrapped in saffron-coloured cloth and bound with black thongs down to his black sandals. Across the front of his tunic was embroidered a spread-winged black raven. But the most unexpected thing about him was that he was no ruddy complexioned Northman. His skin was black, as black as the Aethiop auxiliaries who had been with many of the legions. In his right hand he held a short-hafted throwing axe. The whites of his eyes rolled now, as he hefted the axe in his hand and said impatiently, 'Answer me!' and hiccoughed again.

Baradoc said, 'How can I steal from you that which is not yours?'

For an instant the man's face tightened with sudden anger. Then, unexpectedly, he smiled, and said, 'By Odin, you've a bold tongue to speak so saucily when in the blink of an eye I could split your skull.' He tossed the throwing axe lightly in the air and caught it deftly.

Baradoc answered, '*Aie!* You could throw your axe and kill me. It is a skill I know your kind have. But you would not live long. There is one who stands behind you who would tear your life out by your throat before you could shout for your men.'

The man's smile broadened and he shook his head, swaying a little. 'Oh, no, my gamecock. You think that I, Corvo, master of the Black Raven, am to be fooled into turning by such an old trick, and give you time to use your spear? Now, toss down your spear and turn the mare shipwards. We've lost two men. We can use a good pair of slave shoulders and hands on the rowing benches. The rope's end and leg and neck irons will soon take the fire out of you. Around with you, and thank your country's good mead that you still live.'

Baradoc who, under his courage, knew fear and was not fool enough to fancy yet that any advantage was his, said, 'No, Captain Corvo, my way lies past you. And I do not try to fool you.' He threw his spear to the ground. 'Now, look behind you.'

Corvo blinked at Baradoc for a moment or

two, and then slowly turned. Five paces behind him stood Lerg, the great, grey shaggy body tensed, the powerful, long head lowered, jaws parted showing his long fangs, the breath easing from him in a sudden low growl as his eyes watched Baradoc. Slowly Corvo turned back to Baradoc. Anger and admiration fought a battle across his face. Baradoc guessed that the temper of this man was not to be trusted. Anger and drink might spur his recklessness and he might risk all. *Aie!* and might succeed. The thrown axe could take Lerg first and the sword himself after. Few along Britain's coast had not heard of Corvo and his reckless courage. With drink that courage would have no limits.

Suddenly Corvo gave a loud laugh, spun the axe again into the air, caught it, and said, 'Bacchus is on your side, lad. The drink runs smoothly in me and your daring teases my humour. Take your pony. That marks the two of us as thieves. But since you must know who I am, it is just that I should know who you are.'

'I am Baradoc, son of a chief of the Dunmonii. I travel far westward beyond the Tamarus river and for this need the pony.'

'Which you now have got. Aye, I know your country and have sailed beyond it, past the Blessed Isles where the natives eat only fish and sea birds and their women have scaly tails and from the rocks sing songs of love to tempt wife-and-sweetheart-hungry crews. So, what think you of the great Corvo now you have spoken face to face with him?'

Baradoc said, 'First, that it is well that you were no Saxon for I would have put the hound at your throat long since. I hate them all.'

Corvo laughed. 'Aye, and so do I for they are land-grabbing coast-crawlers that risk the sea only on summer waters. You do well to hate them for they mean to swallow this land. Now, answer — what think you of black-skinned Corvo?'

For a moment Baradoc hesitated, then with a frank grin he said, 'That he is a man with a dark skin and a darker reputation, but that there is a goodness in him which comes not from drinking mead.'

Corvo shook his head. 'You are wrong, boy. Two horns less of mead or two more and I would have chopped you and the horse for dog meat and forced your great hound to eat it. Now go, lad, before my gentle humour leaves me.' He stepped back off the path and made way for Baradoc to pass. 'And when you next pray to your rough gods, make your thanks that you found me mellow at the time of our meeting.' With that he turned his back on Baradoc and went down through the trees to the water meadows, singing quietly to himself.

Baradoc, knowing there was no certainty that the man would not send a party after him, led the pony quickly up the rough track through the woods to return to Tia. But when he got back to her he knew that he would say nothing of his meeting with Corvo. What she did not know of the dangers around them could not upset her. As he marched, he recalled the many tales that were told in the country about the man. It was said that his mother had been an Aethiop slave of a wealthy British family near Lemanis who had been captured while a young girl by the sea-raiders and taken to their country where she had conceived Corvo by her master. Corvo, born coloured, had as a youth saved the life of his master and father and had been given his freedom and thrown in his lot with the longboat men, raiding, pillaging and fighting with his father's people, but choosing for crew ex-slaves, outcasts, any riff-raff of any race that caught his eye and earned his accolade for their valour, seamanship and ruthlessness. He called no man chief but, while he still lived, had grown into a legend. Half the stories which were told of him came from the fearful fancies of the eastern and southern tribes he plagued along the Saxon shore. Baradoc smiled to himself as he remembered his old master speaking of Corvo; *Child of a black slavegirl, fathered by a seawolf. The gods gifted his birth with the stuff of legend. The destiny of such a man can only be dark for his spirit seeks always to revenge his birth, and to forget it in the heat of battle or drink.*

Well . . . either from drink or some lingering goodness the man had attempted him no harm.

Hunter's Dream

That evening they made a start long before darkness came. Baradoc gave Tia as reason for this that it was a bad part of the country and the sooner they crossed it the better. It was on the tip of Tia's tongue to point out that if this were so, surely it would be better not to move until night came. Something in Baradoc's manner made her hold back the words. She was no fool. Not for a moment did she believe that he had found the pony wandering loose in the river meadows. He had stolen it, she guessed, and in the stealing there had been trouble which made him anxious to be on his way. It was a sturdy pony with a mild nature and gentle manners, placidly taking a handful of their corn from her as it stood to be loaded with their two bundles slung as saddle-packs across its back by the hempen rope. Since Tia now had her goats' hair cloak they folded her mantle over the rope to make a small riding pad to prevent her being chafed.

'When it gets dark,' said Baradoc, 'you can ride and we shall journey faster.'

Meaning, Tia knew, faster than if she were

stumbling and tripping along at the pony's heels in the dark. Well, why should she grumble? The pony was strong and would take her weight easily.

She said, 'The pony should have a name now that it has joined the party.'

Baradoc, standing at the animal's head, ready to lead it off, smiled and said, 'Then, as you're going to ride it, you name it.'

'Well, she's red and gold, so it is no hard thing. She shall be Sunset.'

Baradoc nodded. 'It's a good name. Come on, Sunset!' He gave the halter he had made for the pony a jerk and began to move off.

Without any sign or sound from Baradoc Tia marked that Lerg and Cuna moved ahead of them swiftly and disappeared over the rocky bluff top that sheltered their camping place. Aesc dropped back at her heels, and Bran flapped lazily away out on to their left flank and was soon lost to sight.

They travelled for two hours and in all that time few words passed between them. Baradoc stayed at the head of the pony and Tia brought up the rear with Aesc. Their path lay through high woodlands which every few miles dropped into steep little valleys cut by narrow streams and rivers. Tia noticed that Baradoc kept their course as much as he could into the eye of the westering sun. North by west, away from the coast, that was the way to Aquae Sulis. At least, Tia — her memory now of Baradoc's map a confused one — hoped it was. Once there this Baradoc of many moods, this son of a chief of a half-savage tribe, would leave her and go on to his home grounds, perched on the edge of the endless seas where Neptune and his conch-roaring son Triton ruled, and she would never see him again. That would be no loss. Still, when he brought her to her uncle safely, she would get the old man to reward him well, and after she might for a while remember him in her vesper prayers.

She walked behind Sunset letting her thoughts roam idly, banishing them only when they turned to the cruel things that had happened to her brother and his wife and the villa and farm. The air grew chilly as the sun dropped and she pulled a fold of her great cloak over her head because the breeze cut coldly around the nape of her neck where her hair had been shorn. Her rough hose, cross-gartered up her legs, was still slightly damp and the harsh material made her skin itch. Although she had washed the garment as well as she could, she hoped that she would not catch some skin disease from it.

Ahead of her Baradoc halted the pony. She saw that he was looking at the loose sandy soil of the track they had been following through the trees. On his knees he examined the ground for a moment or two. Then he rose and led Sunset on. As she came to the spot Tia stopped and looked at the ground. Part of it had now been disturbed by one of Sunset's hoof marks. But, still clear in an untouched part of the track, was the imprint of a sandal. It was obviously a man's heavy sandal from the depth of the print, the outer edges of the sole showing a rim of deep stud marks. In the centre of the sole, studs which had been hammered into the leather made a pattern of a five pointed star in the sand. Well, that was not unusual; many sandals, for men and women, were often soled with fanciful stud patterns. But somehow she had the feeling that Baradoc's attention had quickened as he had examined the print. When he had risen he had glanced back at her and his tanned face had gone wooden, signalling emotion even as he sought to show no trace of it. Why did he have to be like that, she thought crossly? So self-important and secretive. If she let herself forget some of the nice things about him, she could easily bring herself to dislike him completely. Well, she supposed some people were like that. They tried to make themselves impressive by keeping things to themselves. Something, she was sure, *had* happened when he had found Sunset. He had come back grim-faced and had just started packing up, hardly throwing her a word until they were ready to go. Well . . . if he thought she cared a fig he could go to Hades. She pushed all thought of him from her mind and began to think about Aquae Sulis and her uncle's villa which lay a few miles outside of the town. She had stayed there many times with her father and then her brother. Always she had the small room with the wall paintings of naiads bathing in splashing brooks and waterfalls. The real sound of falling water came from the courtyard outside. Here, her uncle had planted flowers and grape vines and cosseted two olive trees which had been grown from the stones of olives eaten at his farewell banquet when he had retired from his prefecture of a cavalry cohort. She sighed at the thought of it . . . a lovely villa, full of treasures acquired by her uncle in his many campaigns all over the empire. Part of the covered walk beyond her room was an enclosed aviary where he kept his collection of exotic birds. Having no children, he treated them as such so that they came to his hands to eat and their colours flashed through all the hues of the rainbow as they flighted free about the great courtyard when the weather was fine ... And the food at the villa! By the gods, it made her belly feel empty to think of it! And the soft, soft bed with the alabaster-carved lamp at its side!

Her left groin began to itch and she scratched at it, Aquae Sulis going from her mind. Fleas or lice for certain, no rough scrubbing with cold water killed them. Or, maybe they had come from one of the dogs. Aesc was always scratching. Well, it was no good complaining. Baradoc would probably tell her that a flea had every right to take its living where it could. For certain he and his greasy tribespeople would never give them a second thought.

Baradoc halted Sunset suddenly. Tia, engrossed with her thoughts, walked straight into the pony's hindquarters and was brought to the present by the sharp switch of its long tail against her face.

Without thought, she shouted, 'Pluto take you! Why don't you give warning when you're going to stop?'

Baradoc turned, eyed her, and said mildly, 'Why don't you keep your eyes on where you're going instead of day-dreaming along? And shout a little louder, then if there's anyone around they'll get a real chance of knowing we're here.'

Cross with herself for her show of temper,

Tia mumbled, 'I'm sorry.'

'That's all right.' He chuckled. 'Nobody likes walking into the backside of a horse.' He patted Sunset's neck. 'Luckily, she's good tempered or she might have kicked out.'

He began to re-arrange the bundles on Sunset's back into a saddle pack.

Tia asked, 'What now?'

'It's getting dark. It's better that you ride. Up you get.

He bent down and made a cup of his clasped hands for her to mount. Tia climbed on to Sunset and made herself as comfortable as she could with her legs dangling behind the bundles, her hands taking a loose loop of the halter. She looked down at Baradoc through the darkening gloom and said, 'There was a print on the path some while ago. Does that mean someone is close ahead of us?'

'No,' said Baradoc. 'The print was not made today.'

'I had a feeling the star pattern meant something to you.'

'You're right. You have quick eyes. But for now, stop trying to read my thoughts and hang on tight.' He moved forward and Sunset followed with Tia swaying on her back.

The next few hours were mild agony for Tia. Baradoc set a good pace. The going was rough, up and down the forest and valley tracks, with the occasional switch of a loose branch flicking across Tia's face so that she had to pull the cloak close about her head to protect herself. Within a mile the inner skin of her thighs was chafed, all feeling had been bumped out of her bottom, and her arms ached from hanging on to the halter. Curiously enough the hardship — since nothing could be done about it — served to lift her spirits, making her forget the biting of the fleas which attacked her from the old hose. Aquae Sulis lay ahead — hot rooms and warm baths and her uncle's old maidservant to massage her body with oils and perfumes . . . and clean clothes. To reach all that comfort and security, what could a few days of dirt and discomfort matter?

When the moon rose, long past midnight, they stopped in a small clearing where years before the trees had been chopped down and the ruins of a woodman's hazel-latticed shelter still stood.

Baradoc helped Tia down from the pony. As she stood bow-legged he smiled at her and said, 'The stiffness will soon go. Did you never ride before?'

'Yes, of course. But not bareback.'

'In a couple of days you will think nothing of it.'

He took the cold deer tack from one of the bundles, the last of their cheese and wheat cake, and they ate, lying on the ground with their backs propped against a moss-covered fallen tree trunk.

He said, 'There's no water nearby. But we'll drink at the next stream we cross.' Then, as though she had asked him a direct question, he went on, 'The star pattern comes from the sandal of one of the two who strung me up to the oak. He is of my tribe — my cousin — and journeys westward as I do. The other was a wanderer who had joined us. They could have killed me but that, because of the laws of our tribe, is forbidden to the wearer of the star-sandals. So they strung me up to let death come without any dagger thrust.'

'Why is it forbidden?'

'Because I am the seventh son of my father. The last son, too. None of my brothers is living. The gods will give no gifts, nor long years to any who kills, except in fair fight, the seventh son of a family. But to leave me to die was different.' He shrugged. 'It's a nice point of morality. But when I reach home there will be a fair fight and a killing of my cousin — thanks to you.'

'So, I save one life in order that another shall die.'

'The gods have thrown their dice. They fell that way. I tell you this much to excuse a hardness that is sometimes in me. The two ahead will soon take a different path from ours. I'll take you to your uncle and then my debt will be paid. He smiled and rubbed his hand over his beard-fuzzed chin. 'Maybe your uncle will give me the use of his bath house and the loan of a razor to smooth my chin. With my people no man may grow a beard or long moustache until he is married.'

'Is there a chosen girl in your tribe that you will marry?'

'No. My cousin and I were only twelve and gathering shell fish along the shore when we were taken by sea-raiders and sold together as house slaves, first to a Phoenician trader and then to my master in Londinium — where he then lived.'

'Your people must think you are dead?'

'No — the word was passed many years ago. But under the law there was no way of buying our freedom. Nor did either of us need it, for we are much alike in many ways and knew there was much to learn and a sheaf of years ahead.'

'But this cousin — '

'No more of him.' Baradoc sat forward and tossed a piece of deer meat to Aesc.

Tia, not wishing to break their talk, said,

'What are the girls of your tribe like?'

Baradoc laughed. 'Like all other girls. Some fat, some thin. Some beautiful, some plain. At your age many of them are long married and have children. Sometimes I see in my mind's eye the girl I will marry.'

'Tell me.'

'How can I since the picture changes so often? Sometimes her hair is a dark flame, richer than the stag's coat when he stands in the full light of the new morning's sun. Sometimes it is blacker than the raven's wing spread against the year's first snows. And sometimes her skin is warm and polished, brown like a harvested hazel nut, or creamier than the finest goat's milk and blushing with the glow of a bright ember.'

Tia teased him. 'Her eyes, too, will be no ordinary eyes?'

'Why should they be? Dark as a black sea pebble with the green of waving tide-wrack reflected in them. Or bluer than the brooklime flower and dancing with a brightness as clear and crystal as a hill stream over white sands.' He turned to her and, matching her mood, said, 'You wish me to go on? Her teeth, her arms and legs? The way she walks and runs and swims? Her voice like a dawn blackbird's when she sings.'

'Spare me. I've had enough poetry.'

'*Aie*, that is true. But there's always room in each day for a little — otherwise living is as flat as stale wine. We're not barbarians, my people. We have our songs and our stories, and there's not one of our kind who doesn't learn them from first talk and pass them on. So, even with death, they are not lost. Their magic cannot die so long as men have ears.' He stood up, sucked noisily at a fragment of deer meat lodged in his teeth, and said, 'It's time to move.'

He turned away from her abruptly and went across to the woodman's shelter. He came back after a while carrying an armful of bracken which he had found there, the remains of a rough bed. He bound it into a soft roll within their piece of fish netting and then wrapped it in her mantle to make a large, soft saddle. Without a word he helped her to mount.

Riding after him Tia was touched by his rough, silent courtesy. Yet when he needed words he could find them. Then, thinking of his dream of some girl waiting for him, she was amused that he had given no place in his thoughts for a fair-haired girl like herself. Maybe there were no fair-haired women in his tribe, but she doubted it. Amongst the Britons of the south and east there were plenty. Strange Baradoc, rough and kind, withdrawn one moment, then easy with talk the next. And one day — for she guessed the intent lay in him as hard as a stone — he meant to kill his cousin for the wrong done to him. She shivered a little at the thought. There was too much of killing already in this land.

* * *

Early the next morning they made camp beyond the fringe of the forest in a small willow grove on the edge of a clear stream that flowed down from the distant line of the almost treeless uplands which rose away to the north. They ate and then slept while the dogs kept watch. When they woke Baradoc went down to one of the stream pools and with willow stakes fixed their piece of net across the narrow gullet through which the stream fed into the pool. Then he called to her to help him, telling her to take off her long hose and sandals, and to roll up the skirt of her tunic and pin it tight with her mother's brooch. Tia noticed that although he was concerned she should keep her leg-hose dry, he seemed heedless of wet or discomfort. He just walked into the water wearing his leather short trews and his shirt. Rain or shine, wet or dry seemed to make no difference to him.

A few paces abreast they waded up the pool, beating the surface with branches. The trout and grayling in it went upstream to escape through the gullet and some of them were entangled in the stretched netting. Baradoc pulled them out, killed them and tossed them on to the bank.

When they waded out together, Baradoc picked up the fish, strung them on a slip of branch through their gills and handed them to her, saying, 'If you have not done it before you cut their heads off, slit them down the belly and shake or scrape their innards out. The ones with the big fin on the back are grayling and smell of dried thyme. The others are trout. We'll eat them before we move off.'

'Women's work, my lord.' Tia said it with a straight face.

Baradoc nodded, unsmiling. As Tia took her dagger and started work, Baradoc went to one of their bundles and ferreted about in the pile of old rags he had found in the fishermen's hut. He sat down and laid out a long narrow piece of cloth before him.

Tia, her hands slimy and scale-covered as she gutted the fish, asked, 'What are you doing?'

'Making a throwing sling. There are duck farther downstream which I can kill and Aesc will retrieve. The fish will serve us for today.

The duck we can cook and carry for tomorrow in case nothing else turns up. I will make a fire when I come back.'

He rolled the long ends of the cloth into thin grips, binding them with pieces of catgut. The centre of the cloth he thickened into a pad by sewing on top of each other three squares of extra cloth. Then he gathered a handful of smooth small stones from the stream verge.

Coming back to Tia he dropped a stone into the padded loop of the sling and said, 'Watch. The top of the far stake I set up for the net.' He swung the sling gently in a circle at his side to get the feel of the weight of the stone. 'It was with such as this that the first of my countrymen over four hundred years ago gave a welcome to the great Caesar.' He whipped the sling around and let the stone fly.

'You missed,' said Tia.

'I expected to. With a new sling one must get the feel and the balance.'

He slung another stone and this time only narrowly missed the stake. With the third stone he hit it a hand's span from the top.

Tia clasped her slippery, fish slimed hands and said mockingly, 'O Mighty Baradoc!'

Baradoc shook his head at her, smiling. 'You should not be too pleased. When I come back you will have a duck to pluck and gut.' He tucked the sling into his belt, thrust a handful of stones into the front of his shirt and walked off downstream with Aesc following him. Tia went on with her work. Sunset, tethered by a long head rope to a willow, cropped at the young grass. Bran flew down from a willow perch and took one of the trout heads. Cuna lay sleeping in the sun, and Lerg lay on the ground, head raised, watching the direction in which Baradoc had disappeared.

When Tia had finished the fish, she covered them with leaves against the sun and then washed her hands in the stream. She took off her tunic and spread it in the sun to dry. Wrapping their woollen blanket about her she wandered around the willow grove collecting dried wood for the fire, and gathered a small pile of dried leaves and grasses so that Baradoc should have tinder for starting a flame.

Half a mile downstream Baradoc crouched, hidden in the rushes at the riverside with Aesc lying at his side. The river was broader here and ran in two channels around a long island fringed with mace reeds and low alder growths. Coming downstream he had put up several pairs of mallard and teal, but with no chance of hitting them. This was the courting and mating season and he guessed that the island would be a favourite nesting place, for the weed-thick shallows around it made good feeding grounds. He and Aesc crouched, still and watchful, hidden in the rushes. A dog otter came upstream, rolled like a porpoise, sun and water silvering its flanks, and dived to appear in a few moments with a large trout in its forepaws. It lay on its back and let the current drift it downstream while it ate the trout. A kingfisher fished from a low, overhanging branch at the top of the island. The life which Baradoc had disturbed when he took up his hiding place began to come back. Grebe and moorfowl fed and went through their courting rituals below the island while overhead a pair of buzzards circled high, their mewing calls coming faintly to him. Beyond the river and the far grassland, the forest trees rose in long swelling waves of changing greens. Distantly, above the farther tree crests, Baradoc marked a thin plume of blue smoke coming from some solitary fire. He guessed it to be some hours' march away. Now and again the smoke thickened to a dark, breeze-ragged plume. Whoever tended it, he thought, was well-armed or foolish. These days men and women held close to their homesteads or villages for safety. The forest held only the spoiled or the spoilers. The dark face of Corvo came back to him and with it a quick stir of concern about Tia. Yesterday he had left her for a while and there had been trouble, trouble which he had kept from her. He decided that if no flighting duck came in soon, or mating pair appeared from the island reeds, he would go back. Not even Lerg could protect her against some odds.

He smiled to himself as he thought of the way she teased him now about 'women's work', and the flashes of angry spirit she showed from time to time. He guessed that she must long for the security and comfort of her uncle's villa at Aquae Sulis. That was her kind of life. She had lived sheltered and lived soft, her family wealthy and with servants to come to her call for all her needs. In his time with his master he had known many such families and households. These Romans, most of whom had never seen Rome, lived in the dying radiance of the empire's glory, and called this country their own. And so many of them, even now, did not understand that it had never truly been their country and that slowly now the strong hand of another race was closing in on it. Tia, he thought, might find lasting shelter and plenty at Aquae Sulis, a haven that would last out her days may be, but he doubted it. Men like Corvo were only carefree raiders who lived from day to day and for each day's plunder and each night's drinking and feasting. But back in the east, now far beyond Tanatus and Rutupiae, spreading north and south of the Tamesis river, encircling Londinium, their eyes looking ever westwards to the rich lands of the Atrebates, to Pontes, Calleva and Venta, were the Saxons, driving forward slowly and holding every mile of ground they took and making serfs of common folk and culls of British chiefs, Romano-British merchants and town dignitaries, all those of power and wealth who had lived soft too long. Only among the men of the north and west on mountain and moor and wild cliff top and deep river fronts the dream still lived of dominion over all the land. It lived with him, too, like a slow peat-burn waiting only the right wind and the right season to start the hidden embers to flame. His old master had known his dream but had denied its truth, saying that there was no going back to old glories, old times, that the gods gave men dreams but shaped their destinies, and the fate of their nations, into patterns the human mind could not foresee.

Aie, if he believed that, then he would never have stayed slave to learn and listen and watch for so long. He would have run

and been back with his people years ago
. . . back and married to some maiden who
would have given him other dreams and other
cares to fill his days. Thinking this, he smiled
again to himself, remembering Tia asking
him about the girls of his tribe and how
— although there were fair-haired ones
amongst them — he had described no such
maiden, knowing he held back yet not
knowing why in truth. Bright hair like the
gold of the marigolds in the marshes, and
eyes under pale lashes, their colour misted as
the faint sea-haze softened the sheen of the
turquoise slow-heaving seas of summer.

Two heavy splashes brought his attention
back to the river. A pair of mallards, duck and
drake, had planed in, furrowing the water as
they landed. Baradoc watched them as the
drake began to display to the duck. Beside
him he felt the faint tremble of Aesc's body as
the dog watched too. Under the sun the drake
shone as though it were a jewelled bird,
yellow bill and glossy green head flashing as it
bobbed and dipped, the great white and
purple wing patches opening like a fan as it
preened its wings and rattled its quills while
the duck, head lowered, slid away pretending
lack of interest, but never going far. Baradoc
fingered the set of his stone in the sling and
slowly stretched the length of cloth even, held

in both hands at his side ready to throw when he rose. *Aie!* it was a pity to kill when the day was so bright and the birds moved to the dance of love. But an empty belly drove all thought of beauty and poetry from the mind. The slate-backed peregrine would rove and stoop and kill untouched by sentiment, and the questing vixen would scatter the bronze and green and white feathers as she shook her clamped jaws to break the long neck to carry food for her cubs. The gods gave dreams of a paradise where none killed, man nor beast nor bird — but they shaped the destiny of them all differently. Taking a deep breath and holding it, Baradoc tensed himself for the move which would bring him upright with the long sling already circling to take the drake, his left hand already holding the second stone for the duck.

He stood swiftly, smoothly, and the sling stone hummed like a hornet as it sped across the water and took the drake with a vicious blow on the right shoulder, breaking the wing joint. Baradoc whirled the sling again and aimed at the duck which with a beating of wings and strong thrusts of its webbed feet had jumped into the air for flight. The stone narrowly missed the duck which disappeared up the river calling with alarm. By the island the drake circled helplessly on the water, thrusting uselessly with one wing to find flight. Aesc, knowing her moment, slid into the stream and swam to retrieve the bird. She brought it back to Baradoc who killed it quickly with a twist of the head which broke its neck. He pushed it into the front of his under shirt, looped the sling over his belt and turned to leave his cover, to hunt further downstream away from the disturbance he had caused.

As he reached out his hand to take the fish spear which he had thrust into the mud of the bank a voice said, 'Touch it — and you get this through your head.'

Standing full in the centre of the break in the reeds through which Baradoc had made his way to the river was a tall youth, dark-haired, his skin brown from dirt and sun, a straggling growth of beard covering his chin. He wore old, tattered woollen breeks to the knees, the rest of his legs bare. From his shoulders hung a brown cloak held tight about his waist with a broad leather belt from which hung a deep fringe of rusty, finely linked ring-mail to form a short skirt. On one side of the belt was looped an unscabbarded short broad sword, rusty and blunt-edged. Hanging from the other side was a leather quiver full of short arrows. His arms raised, he held a charged bow, the arrow aimed at

Baradoc. He was flanked on one side by a lank-haired young woman with a long, ill-humoured face, an old scar deeply marking her right cheek. She wore strings of coloured beads around her thin neck, the long loops falling across a dirty, ragged, long-sleeved white stole striped with red and green diagonal bands. At his other side stood another youth who, small and sturdy, dressed in a belted tunic of furs, heavy sandals on his feet, carried a light throwing spear.

Baradoc, making no attempt to touch the fish spear, said calmly, 'You need not hold the arrow on me. I mean harm to no one. I hunt and kill for the pot alone.'

'You live around here?' The tall youth spoke with the flat accent of the eastern Cantii. Many such, dispossessed, roamed the country now.

'No. I make my way west to join my people. I have been working up-country.'

'You had a master there?'

'Aye. But he is now dead.'

'He was good to you?'

'He was. He gave me my freedom.' To name himself once a slave, he thought, could do him no harm with them.

The youth spat suddenly. 'No masters are good. So you were a slave?'

'I was.'

The young woman said impatiently, 'Leave him, Atro. Take his spear and sling if you will.' She laughed. 'His clothes, too. And those good sandals and trews and the dagger at his belt. But leave him. We have better work at hand.'

'Shut your mouth, Colta.' Atro spoke roughly without looking at her. Then to Baradoc he said, 'Come here.'

Baradoc moved through the reeds on to the grass and Atro stood back from him, the arrow still levelled.

Colta said, 'Now what is in your mind, Atro?'

'That we have to live. That he means nothing to us. That there is no tie between us except poverty. These days that tie is a cobweb broken by a breath. So — ' his mouth twisted angrily, ' — he is a freed slave. But who should take his word for it? There are those in Clausentium and Venta who will buy without questions — and crop his ears to mark their property. Enghus, tie him.'

But for the arrow tip a few feet from his head Baradoc would have made an attempt to escape. The iron-tipped arrow could not be denied. It would split his skull like an eggshell. Then the thought of Tia left alone stirred him to make a plea which came hard to his lips. This Atro spoke of poverty with

96

hard, personal anger. Yet under his ruthlessness there might be some common sentiment
to wake good feeling.

Baradoc said firmly, 'Shared poverty holds
no value these days. But we are of the same
country and we have the same enemy. If
you sell your own kind to slavery what can you
expect for yourself when the new masters
come? And come they will unless we hold
together in a kinship bigger than this country
has ever known since the old queen put
Verulamium and Londinium to the sword
and flame.'

Atro shook his head. 'Now you talk big and
fancy. Such talk means nothing. Old kings
and queens or new ones mean nothing. Today
it is each for himself. Bind him, Enghus.'

Enghus, giggling, danced round behind
Baradoc while Colta knelt to a travelling
bundle that lay on the grass at her feet and
brought out rope lengths. She handed these
to Enghus. Then, taking his light spear, she
pressed the point against Baradoc's neck,
saying, 'Now, Big Talker of the good times to
come, put your hands behind your back and
stand calm. What matters it to you if you are
sold as a slave?' She scratched the tip of the
spear lightly across the skin of his neck and
laughed. 'There is always escape to another
frcedom.'

97

Baradoc put his hands behind him. Enghus bound them tight and with another cord roped his arms to his body, grunting as he jerked at the knots.

Atro lowered his bow and withdrew the arrow. He reached forward and jerked the dead mallard from the inside of Baradoc's shirt and tossed it to Colta.

'Take it. Tonight you shall roast it at the shrine keeper's fire. Eh, Enghus?'

Enghus gave a giggle of pleasure and jerking his head to the west said, 'But not until we have roasted him first to make him sing. The old fool, he burns his garden weeds, filling the sky with smoke as though the whole world moved at peace.' Then he shook his spear and pleaded, 'But first, brother Atro, promise, let me tease him a little with this to put him in the way of true speaking before the fire touches him.'

Atro laughed. 'Maybe, Enghus, maybe. Just to make you happy my little blood-thirsty brother.' Then, to Baradoc, he went on calmly as though there could be no hard feelings between them, 'Enghus is my brother. When he was born the gods touched him with a happy madness. Even when he feels like weeping he laughs. He laughs at his own pain and the pain of all others. But my wife Colta, my beautiful Colta, she is gentle and good

— unless the mood takes her otherwise! Then sometimes even a kind word will have her turn on you like an angry adder. Now, since you know us all, tell us your name.'

'My name is Baradoc.'

Colta, now holding the fish spear, came up to him and touched his cheek and gave a sudden sharp tug to the beard growth on his chin. 'If you were my slave I would beat you daily to take that proud look from your face.'

'Enough of that,' said Atro. 'We move.' Then looking round, he asked, 'Where is the dog?'

Enghus said, 'It moved off a while ago. And such a pretty colour. I could have made myself a hood from its skin and a belt pouch from its ears.' He laughed to himself, jerking his head up and down.

Atro said to Baradoc. 'Call the dog.'

Baradoc shook his head. 'It would not come. It is a stray that joined my company only this morning. But someone has trained it well.'

'So I saw when it took the duck. A dog like that could have been useful.'

Baradoc shrugged his shoulders and made no answer. Atro turned abruptly away and began to walk down the river bank. Before Baradoc could move he was pricked none too lightly from behind with the point of Enghus' spear. He began to follow Atro with Enghus giggling behind him.

Baradoc knew that Aesc would return to Tia. What she would do now that she was alone he could not guess. But one thing was certain. If he did not manage to escape from this ragged, broken-down band soon and return to find her the dogs would leave her after a few days and come seeking him. Beyond that point he shut his mind to her fate. Before he could help her, he must first help himself.

Ahead of him Atro marched now with his bow slung over his shoulder, the ring-mail skirt swinging about his thighs, the rusty links making a soft whispering music, the battered old broad sword bumping at his side. The sword was Roman and uncared for, and the bow, an old one, but serviceable still, was of the kind which in the old days the Parthian auxiliaries had used, cunningly made of alternate strips of wood and bone. To have been taken by these three wanderers touched his pride sharply, but he could understand how it had happened. When a man hunted all his mind was on his quarry. Lost in a hunter's dream, he had crouched in the reeds, all his senses concentrating towards the moment of the kill — even Aesc had shared that dangerous isolation — and had allowed Atro to move up behind them.

He raised his eyes to the far side of the river valley, where the forest rolled upwards in green sweeps. Over a distant crest rose a plume of yellow and purple smoke to be taken by the wind and swept raggedly away.

★ ★ ★

When Aesc returned, still damp from the river, Tia expected Baradoc soon to follow. But time passed and he did not appear. She got up, walked out of the willows, and found a rise in the ground where she could look down the river. There was no sign of Baradoc. She went back and carried on with the work she had taken in hand which was to repair a large slit in one of the bundle cloths made by a broken branch or thorns during the previous night's march. But when Baradoc still did not appear, she began to grow uneasy and troubled. For the first time the black thought touched her that something might have happened to him.

Almost as though this fear, newborn in her, had been some mysteriously understood signal for which the dogs were waiting, she heard Aesc whine. She looked up from her sewing.

Lerg had risen and stood near her, his head

101

low, the grey-brown eyes full on her. Aesc moved restlessly to and fro behind Lerg, whining gently, while Cuna lay still on the ground his eyes watching the other dogs as though he were trying to read the meaning of their change of mood. Only Sunset seemed untouched. Tethered to a slim willow trunk on a lengthened head rope, she cropped the sweet green grass, flicking her golden tail occasionally against the flies. Tia saw that Bran had flown down to the ground and sat now on an old mole hill, plumage fluffed out raggedly, head and beak drawn down between his shoulders, a picture — so her imagination prompted — of unhappiness.

Resolutely, pushing her fears from her, she went on with her work. Almost as though in protest Aesc gave a sharp bark and moved to the edge of the willow glade and back. Lerg waited, unmoving, his eyes on Tia.

Tia went out of the willows and began to walk down the river. Aesc ran ahead of her, nose to the ground, and she turned to see that Lerg and Cuna were following her. She walked a couple of bowshots down the river but could find no sign of Baradoc. When she turned back the dogs came with her reluctantly. It was this behaviour that put firmly into her head that they knew that something had happened to Baradoc.

In the willows, she stood undecided for a while. The afternoon was wearing away. It was not often in her life that she had had to make important decisions for herself. Always there had been someone to turn to, someone who would decide for her. The conviction came strongly to her that something *had* happened to Baradoc. Without him she would never get safely to Aquae Sulis. The selfish thought made her immediately angry. Baradoc might be in real trouble . . . even dead — and she thought only of herself. She had to find him. If Aesc had not come back alone she would not have been worrying. But Aesc *was* back and all the dogs were uneasy and had returned to the willows reluctantly. Suddenly she decided that there was no sense in just staying in the glade while fears mounted in her.

She began to pack up the camp. It took her some time to stow all their possessions and lash the bundles across Sunset. As she did so Aesc and Cuna fretted around her, but she threw them a sharp word and quieted them. When, finally, she led the pony out of the willows Lerg ranged himself at her side and Aesc, followed by Cuna, ran ahead. Tia followed the line which Aesc took.

Half an hour later Aesc stopped at the break in the river reeds where Baradoc had taken the mallard drake. Tia saw at once in the muddy soil the marks of footprints.

As Aesc sat whining in front of her she waved the dog on. Aesc, head low, began to move down the river bank. There was no doubt in Tia's mind that the bitch was following Baradoc's scent. A little later she found proof that she was following Baradoc and that he was not alone. From that moment the anxiety in Tia changed to a real fear, but not a fear that robbed her of resolution. She had to find Baradoc for her sake and for his.

She stood on a sandy beach where the stream shallowed to a ford. In the damp sand at the edge of the water were the clear marks of the studded sandals which Baradoc wore. With them, some confused and some clear, were the marks of other prints though she could not decide by how many people they had been made.

Across the river was a narrow strip of wild meadow and sedge-land from which rose great terraces of dark forest.

Leading the pony Tia forded the river which nowhere came more than knee high. Cuna alone had to swim in places. On the far bank were more confused prints.

Aesc, head lowered, was already moving across the marshy meadow towards the woods. As Tia followed Bran came flying up from behind her and with a sharp *cark, cark* beat his way over the trees and disappeared.

The climb through the forest was hard and slow going. Aesc was clearly following a trail which was fresh. But the way, while it led sometimes along narrow tracks where the going was fairly easy, often headed off into the low tangle of scrub and bushes under the trees where Tia and Sunset had to force a path. That others had done the same before her was obvious from the broken branches and downtrodden growths. Sometimes Aesc disappeared ahead of her, impatient with her slowness, but always she came back whining gently and insistently. Lerg stayed with Tia all the time, content to match her pace. Looking up at the sun, Tia realized that the afternoon was fast wearing away. The thought of the coming darkness frightened Tia. And the thought that she might never see Baradoc again, perhaps never get to Aquae Sulis put a dryness in her throat and a weakness in her body that made her despise herself. Silently she cursed herself for her weakness and her selfishness for she knew that the strongest desire in her was to get safely to Aquae Sulis. If she could have been magically spirited there now, leaving Baradoc to whatever was to be, what would she have decided, she wondered? She escaped any answer from herself by cursing, stringing together all the old army oaths she could remember — and finding a strange comfort in them.

She stopped twice to drink at small streams and to rest herself. Her arm ached from tugging and leading Sunset who faced some of the thickets reluctantly, and there was now a persistent nagging pain in her right thigh where she had slipped and twisted her leg.

The sun was tree-top low in the sky when Aesc, who had disappeared ahead, came back and lay down on the track before her, panting, her long tongue lolling over the side of her jaws. She waved the dog on, but Aesc refused to move.

Puzzled Tia looked ahead along the narrow trail they were following. The trees had begun to thin a little. Twenty or thirty paces ahead the track disappeared over a thicket-crested outcrop of stony ground. Looking up Tia realized that the tall plume of smoke which now and again she had glimpsed in her march was very close. As her eyes came back from the smoke Lerg, who had never gone more than a couple of paces ahead of her so far, slowly began to walk away on his own. When he reached the bottom of the rocky rise, he stopped and sat back on his haunches.

Tia hitched Sunset's halter round a branch

and walked forward. Neither Aesc nor Cuna made any move to follow her. The behaviour of the dogs puzzled her. Yet at the same time there was a strange comfort in their behaviour. She had a feeling that they knew — even Cuna — what lay ahead and, by their actions, obeyed some sure instinct. Tia moved up towards Lerg. When she was with Lerg she stopped and looked back. Aesc and Cuna lay on the ground close to Sunset who was cropping at the low leafy branches of a tree. Bran, who had shown himself only now and again during the march, dropped through the trees and settled on the ground near the dogs and began to peck at the dirt and grit of the narrow track.

Tia had an uncanny feeling that the dogs and Bran now waited on her, that in some way they were all linked in an understanding into which she could and must enter. Between them and Baradoc, she knew, there was always a silent flow of knowledge and command which linked them magically even when they were not in sight of one another. With a quick pulsing of blood and nerves, she felt suddenly that somewhere close ahead was Baradoc — and that he knew they were all here, close to him, coming to help him.

At this moment from beyond the outcrop there came a high half-groan half-scream of pain that was followed by a burst of almost demoniac, giggling laughter. Lerg's hackles stiffened and the long ridge of his back was furrowed with the slow rise of his pelt. The hound turned and he looked at Tia.

As fresh laughter and a cackling of voices came from beyond the ridge, Tia, full of fear, but refusing to let it hold her, began to move forward.

The Keeper of the Shrine

Baradoc lay on the ground on his side. A few feet behind him were the nearest trees. His hands were still tied behind him but now, too, his legs were bound at the ankles. Before him, sloping in a shallow bowl, was a clearing which rose on the far side to a crescent-shaped ridge with large rock outcrops showing through a growth of brooms, gorse, and brier tangles. At the foot of this ridge, and cut into it, was a narrow doorway framed on either side by upright slabs of stone with a thick wooden crosspiece at the top. In the centre of the clearing a large patch of ground was cultivated, the dark earth now marked with new bean growths, rows of young cabbages, a line of vines, a patch of young barley and a bed of glossy green-spiked spring onions. Beyond the garden an apple and a fig tree stood close to a low-roofed, long wooden-framed hut, the roof and sides thatched with rush bundles. At one end of the hut was a small wattle enclosure in which a cock and half a dozen hens foraged. Nearer Baradoc a small spring welled from the ground and ran in a thin rill through a marshy channel to the far slope of the forest. Between the stream and the hut a fire burned, a fire piled now with new kindling so that fresh flames leaped from it and the blazing wood crackled and spat sparks and black ash that rose in the air like a cloud of flies. Close to the fire stood Atro and Colta, each holding an arm of a tall, thin-bodied old man whose long, girdled brown robe had been stripped from the top half of his body. Standing in front of the old man was Enghus, holding the light spear. Already he had scored the man's bare chest with the spear point and now he thrust the spear head almost fully into the man's left hip. Both arms already ran with blood from previous thrusts. From a new-found fortitude or numbness from shocks already received the old man made no sound.

Baradoc watched, sickened and angry with disgust, as Colta striking the old man's face with her fist, spat at him, shouting, 'You old fool — talk!'

Enghus raised the spear to thrust again, crying, 'Yes, talk, talk, talk! Where is the treasure?'

Atro swung his free hand and sent Enghus spinning away. 'Enough, Enghus! Enough!' Then to the old man he said, 'Listen, father, be sensible and talk, and then we will leave you in peace. But if you don't we will surely

110

kill you.' He reached out, took the old man's long dark beard in his hand and jerked his head up. 'Talk! Where is the treasure?'

Baradoc saw the slow bracing movement of the man's thin, bony shoulders as he drew breath. His dark eyes opened and he stared at Atro and his lean, weather-bitten face was stony with stubbornness. He said nothing.

Enghus lowered the spear point and held it against the old man's belly. 'Let me, Atro. Let me!'

Atro shook his head. 'No, he's had his chance. But now — you shall make him talk.' He laughed gently. 'Roast him a little. That'll start his tongue to wag.'

'Yes, yes, roast him a little . . . ' Enghus dropped his spear and began to dance around, beating his hands in joy, like an excited child, chanting, 'Roast him! Toast him! That'll make his old tongue waggle!'

At this moment, long before he caught the downwind scent of the hound, Baradoc knew that Lerg was close to him. And with Lerg would be the others . . . Yes, even Tia, for he knew the dogs would never have left her so soon. He slowly turned his head and looked back at the near trees. The group around the old man were too busy with their own business to pay any attention to him now.

Enghus had taken a dry branch and was

holding it in the fire, the end of it flaming in a great yellow and blue tongue. He whipped it from the fire and swung it around to kill the flame and fan the thick end into a living red coal. The moment it glowed well Enghus danced in, cackling with delight, and drew the red end slowly across the old man's chest. The old man, his body jerking violently, threw his head back and screamed, the echoes of his cry beating back from the surrounding woods, setting pigeons flighting from the far tree-tops.

Near him on the fringe of the trees Baradoc heard the shaking of a bush and a quick breathing as someone moved behind it. Slowly he turned his head. Momentarily the sunlight flashed on a scrap of fair hair. As another scream from the old man rang in his ears, Baradoc sat up so that the top half of his body would cover any approach from behind. All he wanted now was to feel the dagger thrust at the thongs of his wrists, and then to have the dagger in his free hands to slash his ankle bonds.

The old man screamed again. Baradoc watched Atro and Colta supporting the long, thin frame and Enghus dancing back to the fire to heat up the brand for a fresh assault. Anger burned in him at the wanton savagery of the three. Then he felt his left arm grasped, heard Tia's heavy breathing, and took the warm body smell of her into his nostrils. He strained at his wrists to stretch the thongs tight as, lying full length, hidden behind him, she sawed at them with her small dagger. When they came free, he said quietly, 'Stay where you are.' He took the dagger from her and brought his right hand round quickly and began to cut away at his ankle bonds.

Across the clearing Enghus stepped back from the fire, whirling his brand to make it glow. Colta was pulling at the old man's beard while Atro supported him as his legs sagged. The light spear lay on the ground, unheeded. Atro's bow was slung across his back, the quiver and broad sword hanging at his belt.

Baradoc's ankle binds came free. Dagger in hand, he began to rise swiftly. The movement caught Atro's eye. He turned full towards Baradoc, let out a loud warning cry, and began to fumble to free his bow from his back.

Through the courage Tia had forced into herself to crawl to Baradoc raced a sudden surge of fear as she saw Atro beginning to unship his bow as Baradoc ran across the clearing. Then Tia heard the racing Baradoc shout, '*Saheer! Aie! Saheer!*'

Lerg leapt from the thicket behind her and

113

with him went Aesc and Cuna. Before Baradoc could reach the group at the fire, Lerg was past him and leaping at Atro as the youth freed his bow. They went over in a roaring, growling mêlée of arms and legs and twisting grey body. A long shriek of pain cut through the air. Colta let go of the old man and he fell to the ground. Enghus threw his burning brand at Aesc as the dog rushed in and bit and snapped at his legs as he tried to reach his light spear. Colta raised her fish spear and ran at Baradoc, but before she could reach him Bran dropped from above in a threshing of spread wings, his talons raking at her head, his beak thrusting at her eyes. Colta screamed, dropped the spear and ran for the woods covering her face with spread hands. Enghus ran after her, away from the snapping, savage attack of Aesc and Cuna, abandoning hope of gaining his spear.

Baradoc shouted to Lerg and the dog drew back from the fallen Atro. Baradoc picked up the light spear and stood over him as Colta and Enghus disappeared in the woods. Tia ran forward and, hardly knowing she was doing it, pulled the old man away from where he had fallen so close to the fire that the hood of his gown was burning. She beat out the flames with her hands.

Baradoc stood over the fallen Atro, spear

and dagger in hand. Blood was pouring from the side of the youth's neck where Lerg had taken him.

'Make one move,' said Baradoc, 'and I'll put the hound on you.' Spear poised for action, he bent down and picked up the Parthian bow and threw it behind him. Grimly, he said, 'Stand up and keep facing me.'

Holding his hand to his neck, Atro rose to his feet. Then with a slow shrug of his shoulders, he smiled and said, 'What need is there for all this? The talk of selling you as a slave was not in earnest. You should join us. Together nobody could face us.' He nodded towards the old man. 'There is treasure here. Everyone around knows it. We have only to make him speak and then share it.'

Baradoc pressed the point of the spear against Atro's breast, pressed it hard so that it reached his skin and made him wince away. 'Undo your belt and let it drop. And give me no more talk. After all I've seen — a wrong word could yet move me to kill.'

Slowly Atro brought his hands to his belt buckle. The belt fell to the ground, an arrow slipping from the quiver, the heavy sword ringing against the stones.

'Now go,' said Baradoc harshly. 'And remember this — you are marked by me and by the hound. To see you again means a killing. Go!'

Atro, tight-lipped, faced him for a moment or two and then turned and began to walk to the trees. Behind him stalked Lerg and when Atro passed into the trees Lerg still went with him.

★ ★ ★

They took the old man into his hut, stripped the gown from him, and laid him on his bed which was made of long, rough-hewn boards without over or under covering. He lay there, breathing faintly, making no move, his eyes shut.

Baradoc nodded to an earthenware jar by the door. 'Get some water. Wash his spear wounds and find some cloths to bind them. Don't touch the burns.' He went out of the hut, gathered up all the weapons and brought them back. Then, carrying only the light spear, he went towards the low crest above the hillside doorway.

Tia filled the jar with water. As she did so she noticed that Aesc and Cuna had stationed themselves on the forest edge of the clearing. Back in the hut she washed the old man's wounds and bound them as well as she could with some of the rags which Baradoc had found in the fishermen's hut. Since the rags were dirty she tore strips from her short undershift, which was reasonably clean, to go next to the wounds. When the dressings were done she made a pillow from the old man's gown, propped his head up and fed water to him from her beaker. The old man, eyes closed, drank a little and groaned sharply when her arm touched one of his burns.

Baradoc came back after a while carrying two handfuls of leaves and herbs. With a stone he began to pound some of them into a pulp on a platter and said, 'There's a hen run at the side of the hut. Get some eggs.' He said it without looking at her, pounding away at the leaves. As she went out she was glad that he was there. He knew what he had to do and acted swiftly. For the moment she existed only as someone to help. The old man was all his concern. She found four eggs in a bracken nest in a corner of the run and brought them back. She saw that Lerg had returned.

Baradoc broke them over the pulpy herb mass and stirred them into it to make a paste. When the paste was well mixed he took handfuls of it and spread it over the old man's chest burns. Although he did it gently the old man twitched and groaned at his touch.

Over his shoulder Baradoc said, 'Find

something to cover him.' Except for a rough loin wrapping, the old man had been naked under his coarse woollen robe.

'There's nothing here. I'll have to fetch Sunset.'

'Then get her. There's no danger. They won't be back to face Lerg.'

Leaving the hut, there was no resentment in Tia at Baradoc's brusqueness. There was still burning in him the anger and contempt which Atro had raised. He had held back from a killing with difficulty, she guessed. His cold look, stern and rejecting, she knew would live for long in her memory. Tribesman, ex-slave he might be — but the moment had ennobled him with authority and power . . . the power of life or death.

As she left the clearing, Lerg rose and went with her without any sign or word from her.

When she came back with Sunset she unloaded the two panniers and freed her brown mantle from the saddle rope. In the hut she spread the mantle over the old man, covering him just short of the lowest burn on his chest.

Baradoc said, 'We must take turns to watch him. He's not in his proper mind and may try to pull the salves away.'

'How do you know about such things?'

'By not running away from my master.

118

From his words and from his books. And much from my own kind. Although the old man burns, water will not put out his fire. It is the air which gives us life which feeds a fire. The burns must not be allowed to breathe. Did you not know this?' He looked up at her and then, unexpectedly, smiled

'There are many things I don't know. And some things I have only learnt in the last few days. It seems there is much that is missing in me.'

Baradoc stood up. 'But much that I am grateful for. You can be fearful but not lose your courage. I owe you a life already. And now I owe you my liberty. Those devils would have sold me to slavery and this time my ears would have been clipped and I would have been shackled.' He reached out, took her hand and held it between the palms of his own, pressing it firmly.

'Why do you do that?'

'As a sign. While we stay together nobody can harm you until my own power is broken.' Releasing her hand, he grinned. 'There is nothing missing in you that cannot be easily learned. And there is much in you that many will never have. You came to me here, and I am free. Because of you, too, the old man lives and will live.'

Tia shook her head. 'I came because the

dogs brought me.'

'No. Without them you would have found a way. There is the mark on you. I know it and the beasts know it. They read your thoughts and know your heart. Before we reach Aquae Sulis I will teach you how to speak to them without words. Already the gift is in you. Now — ' he turned to the hut door, ' — let us get unpacked and settled in. It will be many, many days before we can safely leave the old man to himself.'

'Many days?'

Baradoc laughed. 'Now your face grows as long as Sunset's. But 'tis far prettier. Do you think the old man will recover by tomorrow? He will be long on his couch and longer before he can work his garden and care for himself and his shrine.'

'But that means — ' Tia broke off suddenly, ashamed of her own selfishness.

Baradoc said easily, 'Aquae Sulis will not run away. A little more rough living will make it seem like paradise. But if you wish you are free to go and to take Sunset with you.'

Tia's face stiffened angrily. Then putting out her hand, she said, 'This hand you took in gratitude has an itch to smack your face!'

Baradoc shrugged his shoulders. 'Good. That means you will stay. Now, let us get things to order.' He laughed, took her arm and tugged her gently towards the door, saying, 'You have forgotten to bring the fish and I have lost the duck you were going to pluck. But don't be disappointed. We will wring the neck of a hen and you can prepare that. The old man will be better for a good broth to help him heal.'

Looking back at the old man Tia said, 'He's very old. Might he not die from the burns?'

'He is old, yes. Just skin and bone. But he will not die.'

'How can you know that?'

'Because we are here. Because Atro took me in a hunter's moment of dream. Because you found your courage greater than your fear. Because the gods, yours and mine — *Aie*, and his — joined together to weave the pattern that way. Now, come and I'll show you how to twist a hen's neck.'

★　★　★

For the next few hours as the tree shadows lengthened across the clearing they were both busy. Baradoc killed the hen and Tia sat outside the hut and plucked it. The dogs drew back to the fire, and Sunset was tied on a long halter to one corner of the hut. Baradoc carried all their belongings inside and emptied the bundles. He made up two rough beds on the floor with cut rushes from a pile he had found behind the hut. Tia's bed was at the far end of the hut, next to the adjoining fowl run. Baradoc set his just inside the low doorway. All the arms were laid out in readiness. Holding Atro's broad belt with its sword and arrow quiver, Baradoc promised himself that the next day he would sharpen the sword and make himself familiar with the bow. It was a long time since he had used bow and arrow and he looked forward to it. The bow was an old one but strongly made and Atro had fitted it with a new drawstring. Atro and the others, Baradoc guessed, would not come back. By the time they had found new weapons their minds would be set to fresh mischief. There had been a moment when he could easily have killed Atro. He was glad now that he had held back, not only because he sensed that there was some hidden goodness in Atro which, given time, might grow to mastery in him, but also for the old shrine-keeper's sake. He would have wanted no killing, no matter the injuries done to him.

Sword in hand, standing over the old man, he looked at the wall above the bed. Hanging there was a rough tablet made of three pieces of board held in a frame. Painted crudely on it was the portrait of a beardless young man with a halo round his head. Above his head was the Christian Chi-Rho monogram. The shrine in the hillside was a Christian one, and the old man its keeper. There were many now in Britain who held to the new religion, worshipping the Nazarene and his holy father. Baradoc felt that it was the religion of slaves, no matter what its virtues. For him the gods of his people could never be replaced. Anyway, the world and the hereafter were wide and big enough for all religions. There was room enough for all the gods to live in peace. That most of the wealthy landowners and merchants of Roman and mixed Roman and British blood and their servants and workpeople had adopted the new religion meant nothing to him. The old gods were his gods and would always be so. Unholy and unlawful it was to kill for one's own gain. But if any sought to take one's life or to conquer one's country then it was simple justice to kill them. The fast dying Roman Empire had long made the new faith its own, but here in his own land there were few among the proud tribes of the far west and north who had turned from the true gods of their fathers.

He went out and began to help Tia around the fire with the cooking of their meal. They ate it in the fading light outside the hut doorway. Tia fed the old man with some broth, but he took little, most of it spilling down his chin and neck, matting his beard so that she had to wash it clean afterwards.

Coming back to Baradoc and sitting cross-legged on the grass near him, watching the hawking flight of martins across the darkening clearing, the sky paling to a faint marigold glow from the dropping sun, she said, 'Why did they treat the old man so badly?'

'Because they believed he had a great treasure hidden here.'

'Has he?'

'Who knows? He is a Christian shrine-keeper. A holy man. The country around will know him. He probably wanders about preaching. His kind are always talking of laying up treasures in heaven. Simple people get things mixed in their minds.' He took a chicken leg from his platter, chewed at it until it was near clean, and then tossed it to Cuna. He went on, 'Tomorrow I must hunt for the dogs and ourselves. There is a little store of old corn in the hut and a grinding quern. You can mill it and we can bake bread. If we are to stay here we must make a store of provisions quickly so that we won't have to go far afield each day.' He smiled at her. 'Once the old man starts to recover he will heal quickly. Although he's all skin and bone there is a strength and health in him like seasoned oak. A few weeks will see you in Aquae Sulis.'

They went to bed by the light of the small length of tallow candle which Baradoc had found in the fishermen's hut. Lying in the darkness Tia now and again heard the old man moan, and from time to time he talked to himself briefly in some language she could not understand. The dogs slept outside. Once in the night she woke to hear the far-off howl of a wolf. In the silence that followed there came the restless padding of one of the dogs circling the clearing. There was no fear in her. The hut around her seemed a fortress. Baradoc guarded the door and the dogs stood sentinel. She drifted into sleep again.

She woke to the sound of the cock crowing in the hen run. First light came weakly through the open door. She got up and ran her hands through her hair. The old man slept, and his breathing seemed easier. Baradoc's bed was empty.

She went out and saw that only Cuna remained in the clearing. He trotted behind her as she went to the spring and washed herself. The fire she noticed had been banked with new kindling. The wood was dry and burnt low and bright with little smoke. She collected eggs from the run, filled the little cauldron with water and set it by the fire to have warm water to dress the old man's wounds. Some of the herb plasters on the man's chest had cracked and fallen away in the night. Baradoc would have to renew them and would need the eggs. She would also hard-boil some for themselves. In the hut she tidied their beds and then began to take stock of the place for the first time with real attention.

It was poorly furnished but clean. A hazel twig broom for brushing the floor stood inside the door. On a shelf rested the few simple items of the shrine-keeper's crockery and earthenware. There was also a big bronze skillet pan. In one of the earthenware jars she found three round goats' cheeses. Another robe like the one the keeper wore hung from a peg at the end of the bed, but it was much cleaner and the edges were trimmed with the white fur of winter hares. The grinding quern stood on the floor in a corner. Looking at it she was taken back to the great kitchen of her brother's villa. For a moment a pang of grief touched her, but she pushed it away. Grief would come back when she reached Aquae Sulis and there, with her uncle, it would be given its full term and they would make the obsequies. Until then she lived another life.

She stood in front of the bed and looked down at the shrine-keeper. Outside the forest was stirring with bird calls. Blackbird and thrush she could pick out but none of the others. Baradoc, she guessed, would know them all. The sunlight, strengthening, flooded through the door and lit up the painting over the bed. She had seen many such portraits and mosaics in the houses of some of the friends of her brother. The young face with the shining halo, and the Greek letters behind it, had a tranquil yet slightly sad expression. Although none of her family had adopted the new Christian faith, she had sat often through the talk of her brother with others when they had discussed religion and had been without real interest. In fact, it seemed to her now, that she had sat, or walked or idled through many times, great stretches of her life, without interest in anything except herself and her pleasures, taking to herself only the lightweight knowledge which girls of her class came by easily in their idleness and luxury. She looked at her hands with their now broken nails and the grained skin, and her mouth twisted wryly. They were fast becoming the hands of a servant . . .

The old man stirred and she saw that his eyes were open. For a moment the shadow of a smile touched his lips. With a slow movement he raised a hand. She took it gently in hers and felt his grasp tighten.

He said hoarsely, 'You are?'

'Gratia.'

'And the other?'

'Baradoc.'

'In my memory their sounds are ever joined . . . like the links of a golden chain . . . ' His voice faded and his eyes closed. Tia lowered his hand and turned away.

When Baradoc came back he brought with him, slung over his shoulders, a young roe buck which Aesc had hunted downwind into the reach of Lerg who had caught and pulled it down, holding it until his master had come to kill it with a spear thrust to the heart. In his tunic front he had a store of fungi and roots which he had gathered on the way back. As he gralloched and skinned the deer, he nodded at the fungi and roots and said, 'There's little in the old man's vegetable patch yet ready for pulling. Today I will show you where to find the fungi and roots which are good to thicken broth. We must make a hanging bag for the meat we do not eat today. Even so — ' he grinned, ' — a few bluebottles will find a way in, but their eggs can be washed away.'

Tia made a grimace of disgust. 'You say that to turn my stomach. And so you do.'

Baradoc shook his head. 'There's much

that goes into a rich man's kitchen would turn anyone's belly. But at table it is eaten with pleasure. How is the old man?'

'He sleeps. But for a moment he came back and asked our names. I have dressed his wounds, but some of the plasters have fallen away.'

'When this is done I'll make fresh salves.' Baradoc went on cutting up the carcass. He threw each dog a portion, and each dog carried its share apart and fell to eating.

So began the run of their days in the clearing. Baradoc hunted when their meat and game fell low, and Tia learned the herbs for the plasters and tended to the old man's burns and wounds. She cooked and looked after the poultry, opening their run in the morning and closing them in at night. Between them, with an old wooden hoe and a rusty mattock, they kept the weeds from the garden; and all day long and at night the dogs watched and roamed the edge of the forest. Bran, who was sociable only when he could find no food for himself, was seldom seen but never far away. Nobody now came to make offerings at the shrine or to bring small gifts to its keeper. The nearest homestead and village was some miles away. Honest people hugged their own hearths and stayed together for safety. This was not the first wave of unrest and violence which had swept across the south reaching as far west as the fringes of the countries of the Durotriges and the Belgae. Many said that it would pass and times would settle again and people would be at peace to travel the roads without fear. That was the hope of most. Something in Baradoc told him that already that hope was an addled egg no heat could hatch, but he said nothing of this to Tia who now worked hard and learned fast and who, at night, often stiff and sleep-logged, would think of Aquae Sulis and carry the thoughts into her dreams.

But it was true that she learned fast. She knew soon the herbs and roots and fungi. She knew how to broil and roast and baste meat with wild boar fat (a young sow of that year's early farrowing, run hard by the dogs, had been killed with two bow shots from Baradoc) and to mill the corn between the quern stones and to bake the bread in the small stone oven Baradoc built and over which the hot fire embers were scooped and piled using flat slabs of shale for shovels. She learned to ignore the weather, going lightly clad in the sun and meeting the rain with indifference if her work took her into it, finding that the best way to dry wet clothes was to go on wearing them.

Also, and this pleased her most, she began

to learn how to talk to the dogs without word or look. As Baradoc had guessed, there was in her a little, waiting for growth, of the magic he commanded so easily. She learned how, without seeing Cuna, Aesc or Lerg, though they rested nearby on the forest edge, to put one of them into her mind like a small picture. Then with a concentration, almost like holding her breath until she would choke, though she went on breathing easily, she would force herself into her own mind, making a picture of herself within herself and there give a silent word of command or direction. Not always it worked, but as the days went by it became easier and more often successful and she knew that with practice she would soon always be able to reach them. But with Bran she could do nothing, though Baradoc could. When she questioned this he laughed and told her that Bran, named after one of his people's gods, would only serve a woman when it suited him and that was not often in simple day by day matters. Only danger stirred him to chivalry.

With each day, too, the old shrine-keeper grew better, but it was to be seven days before he could safely take to his feet. For those first days Tia dressed his wounds, plastered the healing burns, nursed him and helped him with his washing and toilet as though he were a baby, often wondering to herself that she could do this, the work of the lowest slave or infirmary servant. But slowly she came to think it of no more account than serving his broth or changing the rushes on his bed boards. The old man, she guessed, however, had a shame from this. Although he was clear in his head now, he spoke little, withdrawn from them both into some other world, as though to escape the humiliation his body put on him. Yet each night as Tia settled him comfortably for sleep, he would take her hand and squeeze it gently then turn his head from her. With Baradoc, when Tia was not there, he was a little freer and made his thanks for all they had done and were doing, and told his name, saying 'Asimus is my name. Not Father or Brother, but a simple servant of our Lord Jesus Christ who sent you to me, knowing I waited for you but — ' he smiled faintly, 'choosing the moment of your coming to remind me of my own weakness and pride.'

On their first day Baradoc and Tia had gone into the shrine. Beyond the rough stone and wood door with a plaited hanging rush curtain covering the entrance was a small, natural cave which ran a few yards back into the hillside. Hanging from the rock face at the end of the cave was a long wooden cross.

Below it stood a table made from a wide slab of loose rock raised on two rough boulders at either end. Worn in the loose earth of the floor before this simple altar were two shallow depressions where Asimus and his visitors had knelt for prayer. On the table itself was an odd collection of gifts and tokens which had been placed there in thanksgiving: a string of blown birds' eggs, bronze and iron nails, a folded linen napkin, a small wooden model of a farm cart drawn by two yoked oxen, a little statuette of an angel made from beaten lead, some curiously shaped stones with coloured veins of quartz and minerals running through them, a bunch of dried thistle heads, an old slave whip, the worn leather thong-tails spiked with rusty iron studs, their points broken and blunted, some cheap wire bracelets and bead rings . . . a dusty, odd collection but each object, Baradoc guessed, symbolizing or commemorating some accident or turning point in the lives of the givers which had brought or linked them with the worship of the Christian god. So, too, did his people lay their like tokens before the gods as gifts and the value of the gift lay not in itself but in the heart of the giver and in the all knowing mind of the god.

Tia said, 'It's cold in here.'

'True, were it not a shrine it would make a good place to hang our meat.'

Shocked, Tia said, 'You shouldn't say that.'

'Why not? 'Tis but the truth.'

'But this is a holy place.'

'Then there is room for truth here.' He smiled. 'Now — if I were to hang the meat here then there would be blasphemy, and that I offer to no god, mine or any other's.'

At the beginning of their second week when Tia woke one morning it was to find Baradoc already away hunting, for their store of meat had grown low. She washed herself at the spring and then went to the fire and began to warm up some broth for Asimus's breakfast. Squatting on her heels by the fire as she watched the pot, she listened to the steady sawing notes of a chiff-chaff coming from the top of a tree beyond the clearing. With help from Baradoc she was now coming to know more and more of the bird songs and calls, and through him, too, her eyes were becoming sharp and observant. The way the wind swayed the tall grasses or the hanging branches of bushes she knew as natural, but any break or change in the rhythm awoke an instant awareness in her. She could pick up the overhead passage of a squirrel or the quiet foraging of Cuna in the sedges and rising bracken growths of the shrine hillside, and sometimes the overbowed tip of briar or hogweed where some harvest mouse or wren or bluetit swung unseen at first searching for insects and grubs. Until now, it seemed to her that she had passed through life hardly aware of this ever-present stir and change of colour and shade, of animal and bird movement and the shifting cloud patterns. She had begun to have a nose for the smell of rain and even a developing sense of coming wind changes. More than that, too, the sense had grown in her of knowing when she was being watched. This had come first from Baradoc who had sometimes returned silently to stand hidden just inside the flanking forest growths to watch her work, staring unseen at her until slowly she had become aware of the feeling of eyes on her. Because of this, one day she had looked up slowly and, after a while, had made out the sharp-pointed features of an old dog fox, drawn by the smell of meat she had been cutting up for the pot, merged against the background of last year's russet bracken growth. Her ears had sharpened, too, so that at night she could tell the clumsy sound of an arrogant wild boar noisily pushing and rooting his way through the hillside tangles of the forest slopes a bowshot away, knew when a dog padded round the clearing which one it was, and when a little owl or nightjar called suddenly sensed at once from where and from how far the cry came. She was learning fast to know also the differences that marked real from imagined danger. Going to the spring early one morning she had cried in alarm for Baradoc at the sight of a snake sliding through the small pool. When he came he had picked up the snake by the neck, its long length curling like moving bronze clasps round his brown arm, and told her it was a harmless grass snake, pointing out its markings to her and, later that day, bringing her a viper he had killed and showing her the difference.

Sitting now by the fire, the broth almost ready, she was suddenly aware that she was being watched from behind. But there was no fear in her. She turned her head and saw Asimus, his brown habit drawn closely about him, standing in the hut doorway, leaning a little sideways as he supported himself on a staff.

He smiled at her, waved her down as she started to rise, and then began to walk towards her, stiffly but steadily. He came and sat down near her, upwind of the thin fire smoke.

He said, 'The smell of the broth gave strength to my legs.'

'You should have let me bring it to you.'

'No, it is time I began to fend for myself again.'

Tia filled a bowl of broth for him. He held it in his hands, blowing at it for a while to cool it, and then began to sup with an old horn spoon which Tia had found in the hut.

He said, looking at his garden which they had tended, 'The beans have grown, and the weeds are hoed . . . all while I have slept and dreamed and found strength. You and the young man have been good to me at a time when there was little goodness to hope for in this land. Is he your brother or perhaps betrothed to you?'

Tia laughed. 'Neither.'

Asimus frowned a little. 'There is no tie between you?'

'Only that we are now both making our way to the west. He goes back to his tribe and I to my uncle in Aquae Sulis.' Without emotion, for the recent past was a memory now imprisoned as surely as a fly in amber in her mind, Tia went on to tell him what had happened to her and how she and Baradoc had met. She finished, 'When we get to my uncle, he will go on to his own people. I shall never forget him and my uncle will reward him well. But there is nothing between us.'

The old man shook his head. 'You saved his life and now he guards you to your uncle.

Such acts of charity put ties between people which can never be broken, neither by time nor distance. While I live there will be no day when my prayers will not include you both. Thus, you see — ' he smiled gently and the dark eyes were soft in the bearded face, ' — you will always be linked together by me until the good Lord closes my days.'

Made a little embarrassed and uncomfortable with this talk, Tia asked, 'Is it true that you have treasure hidden here?'

The old man finished his broth, set the bowl down and then, shaking his head at her move to help him, rose awkwardly to his feet with the help of his staff. He looked down at her, one hand gently teasing his beard, and there was a slow twinkle in his eyes.

'You are a practical, forthright young woman. That is there for all to see. So, to talk in riddles to you would make you perhaps impatient. Each day that God gives us — or that your gods give you — life and freedom to worship them is a treasure. Is that not enough?'

Tia, puzzled, shrugged her shoulders. 'That kind of talk is beyond me. You know what I mean by treasure. The kind those people would have wanted to find. Silver, gold and jewels.'

Asimus laughed quietly. 'Practical and

frank. Then so will I be because a dream and a prophecy have come true. Yes, I have treasure here, treasure you could sell in the market place for a few gold coins. But their weight set in the scales against it would be nothing. You would need the whole weight of the world against it to make the beam tilt. But when you go, you and your friend shall take the treasure with you.'

Tia, feeling he was teasing her, grinned and shrugging her shoulders said, 'Well, I just hope it won't be too heavy. We have to travel light.'

Asimus shook his head at her, giving her up, and then turned and began to make his way slowly towards the shrine.

Tia filled a bowl of broth for herself and sitting cross-legged watched the old man go into the shrine. Priests and holy men were all the same, she thought. Riddles and mysteries — particularly when they were faced with awkward, straightforward questions. She tipped the bowl to her mouth to drink and, over its edge, saw Bran sitting on the top of the hut slowly preening his flight feathers. It would be good, she thought, to be a bird, to be able to spread wings and fly to Aquae Sulis, to hot baths and fine table ware, to soft sheets and clean, comfortable woman's clothes . . .

The Centurion's Cup

From that day Asimus made an ever-quickening return to health and he would take no more personal service from either Tia or Baradoc. He gathered and pounded his own herbs and worts to make into salves for his burns and he kept his half-healed body wounds clean but refused all dressing for them, preferring to sit in the clearing by the fire letting the air and the sun work on them. If Tia had not fought him over it he would have insisted on helping with the preparation of food and cooking. But she stoutly scolded him away from the fire and such tasks and he would retreat chuckling gently to himself. At night, depending on the weather, they would sit outside the hut or just within the door to catch the last of the light and talk.

It was, at first, unmarked by Baradoc or Tia that the talk was little about himself, but always brought around to one or other of them talking about the past, of their homes and experiences and — more often from Baradoc than Tia — the way their minds worked about the state of the country, of the ills it suffered and the remedies they could

140

suggest for shaping the new times coming into an acceptable and civilized form. He was never without questions to Baradoc about his old master and the things he had taught him. His face would be masked with a grave, yet almost amused cast when Baradoc (who never lacked words or wild flights of fancy) turned towards the east sometimes in his excitement, shaking his clenched fist as though he held a sword in it and with one swing could annihilate the threat from the Saxons who sought to swallow up the whole land, and bursting with emotion cried, '*Aie!* their time will come!' and Tia noticed that he showed no shadow of his own thought, no sign of whether he agreed or disagreed with Baradoc.

It was this that one evening made her say quietly in a pause, as Baradoc stopped talking, 'Master Asimus, these last nights you have turned us both inside out as though we were chests stuffed with trifles and odds and ends of our lives and opinions that serve only to brighten your eye like a magpie's or to raise a smile under your whiskers as though you were a cat who had been at the cream. Is your own chest empty?'

Baradoc said sharply, 'Tia. That is no way to speak to a holy man.'

'No, no,' said Asimus, 'she is not to be

scolded. First, because I am not a holy man. Only an indifferent servant of our Lord, Jesus Christ. Also, too, it is true that I am like a magpie or a well-fed cat, for the brightness and richness of your minds give me joy . . . aye, and hope. Though none of these can escape the shadow this world casts on them from time to time. So — ' he smiled at Tia, ' — you would know what I have to show? And so you shall and so you should. I was born in Antioch. My father was a steward in the household of a general officer in the Imperial Army. Later, I worked in the household too and became the personal servant of a young son of the house. He was called John and was ten years younger than myself. He wanted none of the Army and studied law and I went with him when he left his father's house. But when he was little over thirty he turned from the law, became a Christian and joined the clergy in Antioch. I became a Christian, too. We had bad times and good times, and with the passing of the years my master became archbishop of Constantinople and people named him John Chrysostom, John of the Golden Mouth. And his mouth was golden always with words in defence of the needy and in condemnation of the intrigues in his own church. Aye . . . he had a mouth with a tongue of gold when he praised and preached the teachings of our Lord, and a tongue like the whip of a fiery lash when he faced wickedness. I will not empty the whole of my chest for it would take too long. My master, the good John, died well over twenty years ago at a place you will never have heard of, near the river Irmak in Asia Minor, and I was with him at his death, which was a lonely one.'

'Then how did you come to this country?' asked Tia.

'Because of a gift he gave me the day before he died, and because of a dream he sent me after his death.'

'If all this happened over twenty years ago you must be very — ' Tia broke off suddenly embarrassed at her own impetuousness.

Asimus smiled. 'There is no shame in age. I have seen far more than eighty summers. My only sadness is that I did not come earlier to the service of the Lord.'

Baradoc said, 'I believe in dreams. But the understanding of them is often difficult.'

Tia said, 'Bother the dream. Tell us about the gift first.'

'Tia!' Baradoc frowned at her.

Asimus smiled. 'There is no call to scold her. She is the practical one. Things must be clear and in the right order in her mind. It is no scolding fault. I will tell you about the gift when I give it to you, and then of the dream — but neither until the day you leave for Aquae Sulis for that too was part of the dream and — '

At this moment Baradoc jumped to his feet. Turning his head towards the forest, he said sharply, 'Listen!'

For a moment or two the three of them were silent, listening. The fire burned low like a small red eye. The feet of the trees around the clearing were lost in black shadow, and beyond the fire the three dogs were alert, facing away from the hut, watching the forest. Through the stillness of the evening came the sound of a low, long sighing throat rumble from Lerg and then Cuna whined sharply once. Then suddenly from beyond the stony, bush-clothed rise that held the shrine came a sharp, racking burst of deep roaring. There was a silence for a while, and then the spasm of roaring broke through the night again and this time it was much closer.

Baradoc turned to Asimus and Tia and said quietly, 'Get inside the hut.' He reached down and pulled Tia up and then helped Asimus to his feet.

As they moved to the hut Tia said, 'What is it?'

Asimus put his hand on Tia's arm and led her to the door saying, 'There is a time for questions — but it is not now.' Then he turned and said to Baradoc, 'I have heard the sound before — twice. The only thing you can use is a bow. A spear would — '

Baradoc broke in impatiently, 'I know. Now, into the hut.'

He went in with them and took up his bow and strapped on the belt with its quiver of arrows and went back into the clearing, closing the rough door behind him, though the door, he knew, would hold no protection against the attack to come. That had to be met and held before the bear could move across the clearing to it. The racking, angry roar split the still night again and the dark wall of trees sent back its thunder in searing, pain-filled echoes. Only once before, while hunting with his old master, had Baradoc ever heard the sound but the memory lived with him and he knew that the beast which was coming their way moved now in a frenzy of pain and hatred for all of the kind who had lodged that pain with it. Somewhere in the forest recently, he guessed, a party of hunters, eager for meat, for the rich bear fat and the warm skin which would ward off winter cold, had attacked one of the last few of the great brown bears that roamed the southlands. Avoided and left to themselves they were no threat to human life, content to live on honey from wild bees' nests, on leaves and forest fruits and grubs and insects. But attacked and not killed, escaping with broken spears and arrows in its body, such an animal turned killer, savaging with blind anger and pain-goaded fury anything that crossed its path, following the scent of homestead fire, of any human or animal body that came downwind, seeking only a berserk killing to assuage its own agony.

Baradoc went to the fire and stood with it between him and the rocky rise. He called the dogs to him. Only in desperation would he send them in against the bear, and then only to harry and not to attack for not even Lerg could stand against such an animal. He slipped two of the short arrows from the quiver, held one in his mouth and fitted the other to his bow. When the bear came over the rock rise, following upwind the smoke and human scent, it would be outlined clear against the sky. The bear would see him and come straight for him . . . and he knew that he would have to wait until it reached the foot of the rise before he loosed the first arrow at the farthest killing range.

Behind him Cuna whined gently and from the corner of his eye he saw Lerg stretch his great jaws in a slow, wide defiant gape and he knew that while fear ran in him, drying his mouth and lips, there was no fear in Lerg. One silent signal would send the hound in.

The bear roared and as the sound beat into the air, the animal appeared as though by magic on the crest of the rise. It stood for a moment on all fours, its great head weaving and swinging. Then it rose on its hind legs, raised its head to the sky and roared its anguish and fury once more. It stood almost twice as high as Baradoc and against the long line of its belly he saw the heavy milk-full dugs . . . a she-bear, her cubs now killed to swell her fury . . . and from the right side of her thick, pelted neck stuck out the splintered shaft of a great spear, and another broken spear shaft showed in her left flank, the blood from the wound thickly matting her fur.

The animal, seeing Baradoc and the dogs, dropped to all fours, roared, and began to lumber down the slope. As it did so Baradoc saw that an unbroken spear shaft stood upright in its back. He raised the bow and drew it, sighting along the arrow, knowing exactly where it must lodge, through the long fur a hand's span in from the top of the left foreleg to smash through bone and sinew and find its heart. To shoot at its head would have been to shoot at a rock. As he covered the lumbering downhill approach of the bear the pony tethered to the back of the hut whinnied and neighed suddenly with fear and then Baradoc heard the thud of her hooves as she reared and bucked in panic. At the foot of the rise the she-bear, hearing Sunset, stopped and swung her great head towards the sound. For a moment the beast's left shoulder was wide open to Baradoc.

He let the arrow fly, heard its hornet flight across the clearing and saw it bury itself deep in the bear's shoulder. The animal roared with pain, rose full height and, its jaws flecked with white foam, the red mouth gaping, the great teeth flashing ivory dull in the lowering sunlight, came on in a lumbering run towards Baradoc. And Baradoc stood his ground, for there was only death in flight; and standing his ground he cursed himself that he had not practised more with the bow at close range. It pulled to the left but the nearer the target the less it pulled. All this swept through his mind as he stood, marking the spot which the bear must reach before he fired again; and, as he held the tensed bow, he prayed to the gods that they would put virtue and cunning into his hands and eyes to humour and direct the arrow in a true flight to the small target inside the left shoulder.

When the bear was two spear-lengths from the fire, Baradoc loosed the second arrow, saw it find its mark, heard the heavy sound of its strike as the short length of shaft bore into the beast's body until the flight feathers were only a finger length from the rough pelt. The bear roared, dropped to all fours, and still came on. It charged across the small patch of garden and through the low burning fire, scattering ashes, red embers and hearth stones, and Baradoc, as he fitted another arrow, knew that the gods had deserted him, for there was no time to draw and fire.

At this moment Cuna barked sharply and ran in at the bear. He ran from the side, jumped for the furred throat of the animal, and got a grip on the side of its neck. The bear, pausing in its forward movement, rose to its hind feet and with one sweep of a forepaw brushed Cuna from its neck like a fly. Cuna flew through the air, yelping high, and landed in the soggy ground around the pool. Then, as the bear still came on and the signal was moving from Baradoc to send Lerg in, the great beast swayed sideways, halted, roared to set wild echoes ringing around the clearing, and then dropped to all fours and collapsed on its side on the ground at his feet.

Baradoc stood unmoving. From the poolside Cuna barked sharply and then came limping towards Baradoc. Lerg went forward slowly and his great muzzle dropped to the bear's head. He stood, hackles risen, and then turned away. Baradoc knew that the bear was dead, the second arrow had done its work. Then, feeling Cuna rubbing against his leg, he bent and picked him up, fondled him, and then felt his limping leg and found that no bones were broken. Silently he thanked Cuna because but for the pause the bear had made to brush Cuna away he might have been crushed and mauled beneath the bear in its dying seconds.

He went towards the hut and Tia and Asimus came out to him. Tia ran to him and for a moment held his arm, anxiety still high in her.

'You are all right?'

Baradoc nodded. 'But we have lost Sunset. The smell of the bear made her panic and she broke loose. It is growing too dark now to go after her. If she doesn't come back I'll search for her tomorrow.'

Asimus, looking at the bear, said, 'God give you good days for your courage.'

Baradoc said, 'Those who hunt should always kill. To leave a beast alive and full of broken spears would mark the name of any of my tribe with shame. A man should fetch fresh spears, take the trail and finish the killing. But now the bear is dead it is your gain, father. I will skin and butcher it and Tia can smoke the meat and fill your jars with bear's grease, and the skin you can use for a bed cover on winter nights. So do the gods, out of their wisdom, arrange bad and good into their own patterns.'

Suddenly Tia said woefully, 'Without Sunset I shall have to go afoot to Aquae Sulis. I give no thanks to the gods for that!'

Baradoc and Asimus, seeing the half angry, half rueful look on her face, eyed one another and then burst out laughing.

Asimus, chuckling, said, 'Maybe your gods, seeing into the future, have their reasons.'

And Baradoc said, 'Sunset did not break the tethering rope. The knot was pulled free from the hut post. Who was it that tied the knot?' He looked at Tia.

* * *

Sunset did not return and the next day Baradoc went with Aesc in search of her. He found her in a small valley under the craggy face of a cliff that blocked its end, but before he saw her he knew that she was dead. When he was half a bowshot from the foot of the crag with Aesc well ahead of him a cloud of carrion birds rose into the air. For a while the valley was full of calling and wheeling birds, the wide ranging, keen-eyed scavengers who came to pick clean the killings of man, wolf

151

and fox, the air patterned with the spiralling sweeps of kite, buzzard, white-tailed eagles and a ragged black swarming of crows and ravens. Standing over the fly-swarming carcass Baradoc could guess that a hunting wolf — for the packs were broken now for cub-raising — or a rogue band of dogs had driven her up the valley to make their kill under the crag. He left the halter rope length on her and when he returned to the clearing he told Asimus and Tia that he had found no trace of her. The lie was guessed at by Asimus but he knew that it was told for Tia's benefit. That Baradoc should have this consideration for the young girl pleased him and heartened the faith he had in the dream he had dreamt so many years ago, lying under the cold winter stars by the river Irmak, waking with the sound of his beloved master's voice still alive in his memory though his master lay dead in the small riverside chapel outside which he, in keeping vigil, had slept.

A few days before Tia and Baradoc left Asimus two young men from the nearby village came to the clearing to have news of the holy man to take back to the village. They brought with them bread and a milch goat which had long been promised to Asimus, and brought also the news that the country roundabout was quiet. For days there had been no sign of sea-raiders and the rebellious town and country bands had moved away along the coast towards Clausentium and Portus Adurni in the hope of stirring up more of their kind there to a new rage of plunder and destruction against the masters and merchants and estate holders. It was this news that made Baradoc decide that, when he and Tia left and headed north-west beyond Venta and to the more open country that ran from Sorviodunum almost to Aquae Sulis, they would travel by day. When the two saw the great bear skin with the head still on it, pegged out on an upright frame of poles, the inside of the skin already three-quarter scraped clean by Baradoc and Tia, their jaws dropped.

After they had gone, Asimus, who had sat by as Baradoc had told the story of its killing, said, 'Now the story will grow in their minds with every step they take towards home. So begins the rise of a legend. Baradoc and the bear. In years to come in Venta and Noviomagus . . . aye, and Calleva, there will be a drinking house or hostel called the Bear of Baradoc. Some too will come here to see the skin on my bed and to hear the story. And when they have heard it — ' he smiled gently, ' — may be some will stay to hear the story of Jesus, the holy one, who died on the cross for the sins of men and the salvation of their souls.'

Tia, running her fingers through the hair on the nape of Cuna's neck as she sat by the fire said, 'Here is the real hero, little Cuna. The drinking shops should carry his name too. I take no praise from Baradoc, but Cuna should have his share.'

Baradoc grinned and said, 'Give him no praise. It will turn his head. He is so foolish still that he thinks he is a Lerg. But when I tell the story to my people he shall have more than his full due.'

'You see that you do.'

Looking down at her, her short golden hair stirring in the breeze, her blue eyes alight with the pleasure she took in teasing him, the glow of the lowering sun touching her cheeks with the soft blush of a blooming peach, Baradoc said without thought, 'If you doubt that I will — then journey west with me and do the telling yourself.'

Tia rocked on her heels with sudden laughter. 'The gods save me from anything like that! No power on earth will get me further west than Aquae Sulis!'

Baradoc laughed, and Asimus, smiling as he turned away to go to his shrine to make his evening prayers, thought that there were many gods, hers and Baradoc's, and his own.

And had not the Son of his own said that in his father's house were many mansions? Perhaps there they all met together from time to time to sort and settle the destinies of mankind.

On their last evening with Asimus, after they had eaten, Baradoc and Tia were sitting by the low fire when the old man came to them from the shrine where he had been saying his evening prayers. In his hands he carried a well-worn doeskin bag gathered at the mouth with a draw-string. He sat down with them and put the bag on the ground at his feet. Then, quietly and without any emotion, he began to speak to them.

'In this country, as you know, there are many people who are Christians. And in the old Empire which is slowly dying there are many many more. Neither of you are Christians. And both of you, as I have learned while you have been here, know little of the martyrdom of the Lord Jesus Christ who was crucified at Golgotha. Before he died a centurion of the crucifixion guard dipped a sponge into a cup of vinegar and sprinkling it upon a spray of the hyssop plant put it to His mouth before He died. And when He was dead, but to be sure of His death, the same centurion thrust a spear into His side and the life blood ran from Him. The blood ran down

His body and some of it dripped into the vinegar cup which had been put at the foot of the cross. All this happened long over four hundred years ago and the story changes and changes in the mouths of men as they retell it, but the real truth never departs from it. It is said that as He hung on the cross two black birds, common in the country and around its shores, perched on the cross and their feet were covered with the blood from His pierced hands. When they tried to preen the blood from their feet with their beaks then they too were covered and the bloodstains have stayed with all their kind since. There are many such birds all around the eastern Mediterranean.' He reached forward and pulled back the opening of Baradoc's rough shirt and exposed the tribal tattoo on his skin. 'You are marked with such a bird.'

'It is our tribal bird,' said Baradoc; 'and it is the bird of our sea cliffs. We call them choughs, but there is a secret tribal name which I cannot speak to you. It means the red crow of enduring. To kill one is punished by death, for as long as the choughs live so will our people.'

Tia said, 'What is in the bag, father?'

Asimus picked up the doeskin bag. 'It is the gift I have promised you. It is the little cup or chalice which stood at the foot of the cross holding the vinegar. It is made of silver, now old and battered, and it has been lost and found many times, and by some is still much sought after. The good John Chrysostom gave it to me on his death bed. It is said that warmed in the hands of a man or woman who is marked for great and noble duties, someone whose name will live forever, to be praised by all true and just people, the inside of the chalice, though now unmarked, will slowly begin to glow with the crimson stains of our Lord's blood.'

'Have you seen that happen?' asked Baradoc.

'No. Nor have I tried it myself for I know my own worth. But it is my gift to you both, for that was the command I received from the good John in my dream.'

'You mean you dreamt about us . . . all those years ago?' Tia's brows furrowed with a frown.

'So it would seem.' Asimus smiled, knowing her scepticism. 'My master's voice said that I would be in a wild place, in a country far to the north and in a moment of great peril to myself there would come two people to save me. One would be a youth bearing the sign of the red crow and the other would be a fair-haired maiden dressed as a youth who wore as a fastener on her torn tunic a silver brooch bearing a design of clasped hands.'

'You really dreamt that?' asked Tia. 'Before we were born?'

'If the good father says he did then he did,' said Baradoc sharply. 'Why should not the gods and the spirits of the departed send such dreams? How else speak to us and be sure that the memory of their words lasts long and true?'

'But,' insisted Tia, 'what's the good of giving it to both of us? We part at Aquae Sulis. To whom does it belong then?'

Asimus smiled and shrugged his shoulders and then handed the doeskin bag to her. 'I do not know. You will find some way to settle that. I obey only the dream, and now tell you the last words of my master. The gift being made the bag must not be opened before me, and the dream being told must not be told again until one comes to hold it and the inside glows crimson with the ghost of the Saviour's blood.'

'Does that mean it won't glow for either of us?' asked Baradoc.

Tia laughed. 'Poor Baradoc — did you want to be marked for great and noble duties, your name to be praised for ever?'

Before Baradoc could speak, Asimus said with a smile, 'She teases you, Baradoc. That you must bear, for that is the duty and nature of women.'

Baradoc said stiffly, 'For the work I have to do I need no magic chalice. One needs only — '

'Spare us!' cried Tia. 'Father, by now you should know that he goes back to his tribe to be an important man, to do great things. And so I hope it will be — but I wish he wouldn't talk about it so much.'

Baradoc stood up. He was getting used to Tia's flattening remarks now, and could see, too, that they were often deserved. Though what could a man do if that were his nature and destiny? Then, with a warning look to Tia not to interrupt, he said to Asimus, 'Father, we thank you for your gift and for your words. How the gift will be settled between us at Aquae Sulis I do not know. The gods will decide. But this I say for both of us, will be cherished and protected until the right hands come to warm it to crimson life again.'

And Tia watching and listening to him thought, the certainty strong in her, that one day he would lead his tribe, the dignity and strength and courage now in him would grow . . . and perhaps, now that so much of the old life was falling apart, that was a good thing. The power and protection of her own people who had taken and civilized this country over four hundred years ago was dying, almost dead. Only Baradoc and his kind were left now to gather their forces in the west and north and then to turn eastwards to meet the waves of savagery and conquest reaching farther and farther across the country. She suddenly shivered against the cold night air . . . Aquae Sulis at the moment would be safe. But for how long?

★ ★ ★

The morning of their departure from the clearing a soft drizzle was falling, the slow swathes of fine rain swaying before a mild southerly breeze. From his hut Asimus watched them go, taking the narrow path around the northern edge of the rocky bluff and soon disappearing into the massed trees of the far reaching forest. Both of them carried heavy bundles over their shoulders, the heavy sword thumping at Baradoc's side, his bow tied on top of his bundle and in his hand the heavy fish spear. Tia carried the light spear and the cowl of her mantle was hooded over her fair hair against the rain. Asimus smiled to himself as he watched her ungainly walk. The soles of her light sandals had worn and Baradoc had repaired them with pieces of hide, stitched on with sinews

160

taken from the dead bear. Cuna stayed at her heels, the two other dogs went ahead and, for a fleeting moment, Asimus saw Bran the raven, with the southerly breeze under his tail, swing high into the rain and disappear over the far crest of the trees.

Asimus turned away and went into his shrine to pray for them and for a safe journey to Aquae Sulis. As he knelt to the ground and bowed his head he saw at once that there was a new offering on the stone table. It was the arrow which had killed the bear, the head and part of the shaft brown with dried blood. Tied in a small bow just above the feather flights was a piece of bright braiding which he knew Tia must have cut from the loose end of the belt that she wore about the waist of her tunic. He closed his eyes and began to pray.

The soft drizzle lasted until nightfall. Tia and Baradoc marched through it and their clothes and bundles grew heavier with the weight of water soaking into them with each hour that passed. A quiet misery took Tia as she plodded along. But it was a misery she could carry with the same fortitude as she carried her bundle because with each step she told herself that she came nearer to her uncle. But marching was at first awkward because she had not become used to the weight of her new-soled sandals. Now and again she would trip and sometimes curse aloud only to hear Baradoc give a soft chuckle from up ahead. At midday they ate cold meat and hard corn cake, washed down with barley mead that Baradoc carried in a small leather skin slung at his belt — a present from one of the young men who had visited the clearing.

Through the afternoon the country began to change a little. At times the forest broke away into bare heathland over the high tops and the path was overhung with tall bracken growths and drooping new-flowered switches of broom. Here and there were patches of long-stemmed foxgloves, the lower buds on their towering stalks already in bloom. Once or twice Tia heard a cuckoo call and she remembered, but held all feeling down, how often she had stood on the terrace of her brother's house and heard the same call from the hazel copses that lined the near fields, and how from those same hazels — where she had so often gathered the filberts in autumn — she had heard at night the liquid notes of the nightingales. All that seemed now a lifetime ago.

Late in the afternoon they came to a main road. It was banked up on a small causeway. As they came up on to the road Baradoc stopped and Tia halted behind him. A bowshot to the left a man and woman stood on the high agger crown of the road. In one arm the woman carried a child wrapped in a blanket and with her free hand held the halter of a small pony. Below the shoulder of the road, in the broad scoop ditch from which the material for the road had originally been taken, was a small two-wheeled cart lying on its side. Thinly through the drizzle came the cry of the child which the woman held.

Baradoc said, 'Stay here.'

Tia dropped her bundle and sat on it, and watched Baradoc move down the worn surface of the road. It was, she knew, for she had seen many in her life, one of the old military roads. But it was many years since anyone had bothered to repair it. With Baradoc went Lerg. Aesc and Cuna sat at her feet and she fondled the stiff wet fur of Cuna's nape. She watched Baradoc go up to the couple and begin to talk to them. After a while he turned and beckoned to her. Tia plodded down the road, splashing through the puddles in its broken surface. No legions, she thought ruefully, would ever swing down this road again, the eagles carried high, the studded shoes of the legionaries thudding out their heavy rhythm.

The woman was young, wrapped in a russet-coloured gown, its skirt edges torn and muddy. Rain shone on her long dark hair and her face was drawn and thin and she held the child to her right breast suckling it. The man was much older with a rough skin surcoat belted over a green tunic, his legs and feet bare. In the belt about his surcoat was thrust a small axe. He held his left forearm with his large dirt and work engrained right hand, his face twisted with pain. But as Tia came up and Baradoc said something to him in his own language the man laughed briefly and there was a flash of pleasure in his dark eyes.

Baradoc said to Tia, 'They are from Calleva on their way to Durnovaria. He is a fuller but there is no work for him in Calleva and he goes back to his people with his wife and child.'

'What happened?'

'He slept as he drove and the cart went off the road. His left arm is broken. Even with his wife he can't one-handed get the cart back on the road. They are good people — but maybe a little stupid to take the risk of travelling the old road.' He smiled. 'It is all right. They do not speak your language.'

Tia said, 'You and I can get the cart back, can't we?'

'Easily.'

They went down into the ditch and cleared the cart of the few goods still in it and then between them they righted it in the ditch.

With Tia pushing from behind and Baradoc setting himself against the cross bar of the yoke pole which was designed for two horses or oxen, they ran it up onto the road. While they did all this the man and woman stood on the road and watched them as though they were rooted to the ground by some numbness of spirit which froze their bodies.

As Baradoc took the pony and yoked it to one side of the pole, he said, 'I think they both still live in a nightmare. They say Calleva has been half burned. They fled at night. They have a son of six but lost him before they left. If they ever reach Durnovaria it will be only at the gods' wish.' He patted the lean flank of the pony and then dropped down into the ditch and began to hand up the couple's belongings to Tia who put them in the cart. As she did this Tia, eyeing the two who watched them, suddenly felt angry with them for their helplessness. She felt like shouting at them to wake and stir themselves from their apathy . . . but then the feeling went. She saw a town burning, flames arching over the night sky, people screaming and shouting, panic reaching through the streets and houses and, somewhere, a small boy lost and frightened, crying for his parents. And she remembered her own panic, numbness and helplessness as Tullio and his wife had done everything for

165

her, sending her blindly off into the night from her brother's burning villa.

Before the two drove off Baradoc made a rough arm sling from a strip of cloth for the man. He made a remark in his own tongue and the man smiled and laughed again and now Tia realized that it was truly the laugh of the simple-minded. The man said something and then the woman laughed.

As they drove away Tia asked, 'Why do they laugh?'

Baradoc shrugged his shoulders. 'Because they have gone beyond tears and weeping.'

'Was his arm truly broken?'

'It felt like it. But it will heal with time and Nodons' help.'

'Nodons'?'

'Yes, Nodons'. He is our god of healing, the god with the silver hand.'

'Did they say who burnt Calleva? Oh . . . it was such a nice place.'

'They don't know — but not the Saxons. There are plenty of loose-footed tribal bands in the country who would be greedy to loot such a town simply out of old hates against your people and the legions that made it. I think maybe they could have been people from Cymru, from beyond the Sabrina river . . . kinsmen of my own people who would do better to keep their spears and swords sharp

166

for the real enemy. One day — '

'Oh, no.' Tia laughed. 'Not that again, Baradoc. This is no day to stand in the rain dreaming and speech-making.'

For a moment Baradoc frowned, then he smiled and said, 'You're right. Let's content ourselves with the day that is.'

As they left the road, however, he was thinking to himself that one day these old roads would serve again for the marching of armies, but for armies from the west and the north. The men who had built them had long gone, but they were good men, true soldiers who knew discipline and purpose. Men with such qualities were needed again, but next time they would carry no imperial eagles, they would come under the banner of Badb, the goddess of war, and with the blessing of the great father Dis.

★ ★ ★

They slept that night in a charcoal burner's open-fronted lean-to. It had been built between two ash trees facing a small dell in which were the remains of the old slow fires which had not been used for months. Weeds and grasses grew now over the litter of charcoal shards and stick ends. It still drizzled and the rain dripped through the broken bracken-and-twig thatched roof. It was too wet to try and make a fire. They ate cheese and brittle bread, fed some of their meat to the dogs and then lay down on the hard-packed floor making themselves as comfortable as they could on their bundle covers and piling all the spare clothes they had over themselves. In a very few minutes Baradoc was asleep, but Tia, the dampness of her clothes and coverings reaching right through to her skin, twisted and turned for a long time before she drifted off. She woke some time during the night and felt, before true consciousness came back to her, that she must have fallen asleep in her brother's warm room while bathing. Her body was damp and hot and, for a moment, she felt too that someone had bound her arms and legs. Then she realized that to her left Lerg and Cuna had stretched close to her, and on the other side Baradoc and Aesc had moved up against her. She was being baked with the press of bodies. She lay for a while debating whether to struggle free. It rained still, and the roof drips fell monotonously through the darkness. If she moved away there would be no escape from the wet that reached her body and she would grow cold. It was better to stay warm. Before sleep took her again, she smiled to herself. The whole mass of dogs and humans must be steaming in the dark like a mass of dirty clothes in a washing cauldron. She turned over to give herself a little more room and Lerg grumbled in his half-sleep and, his back to her, Baradoc muttered something in his sleep. Tia drifted into sleep herself.

When she next woke it was daylight. The rain had gone and a pale sun showed now and then through a drift of high clouds. She sat up and rubbed her eyes with her hands to clear the last of sleep from her, then yawned and stretched her arms. Her body was wet and stiff and she shivered a little against the freshness of the morning. Looking round she saw that Baradoc and Lerg had gone. Aesc sat outside the lean-to and Cuna slept at her side. In the dell there was a sudden yellow and green flash as a woodpecker flighted across it. A blackbird called from the trees and a yellow butterfly with brown tips to its wings went erratically across the grasses like the moving reflection from a broken mirror. The bright movement made Tia groan to herself as she thought suddenly of mirrors and combs, of warm scented baths, of her body's stiffness being massaged away by the skilful hands of her maid ... of comfort, cleanliness and clean dry clothes. Let Jupiter, she thought, throw his bolts and strike every

169

Saxon in the land dead. She said it so fiercely and loudly that Cuna woke with a start and was immediately on his short feet, pugnaciously prancing to the front of the lean-to and barking his head off. The dog's reaction was so sudden that Tia laughed and Cuna, giving her a puzzled look, came to her and she fondled his ears.

At this moment Baradoc moved into the clearing with Lerg. He came over and squatted before her. In his hands he held a rough platter made of large dock leaves on which was a large piece of honeycomb.

He said, 'Honey for breakfast.'

Tia looked at the crushed mass of comb-wax and honey and then said, 'Look at the grubs in it. I couldn't eat that!'

'You don't have to eat the grubs. Take them out.' He picked out some grubs from the honey and then crooked his finger into it and sucked it.

Tia, after a moment's hesitation, did the same. The honey tasted delicious. Then, grinning, she said, 'You look like a Nubian. Your face is covered in charcoal dust.'

'What do you expect if you sleep in a charcoal burner's shed? Your face is the same. But we'll have to stay dirty. There's no water around here. Later in the day we'll find a place to wash and clean ourselves.' He looked up at the sky. 'The clouds will soon lift and the sun will dry all our stuff.'

Tia, taking more honey, suddenly greedy for its sweetness, said, 'How did you find it?'

'I followed a honey bee. The nest was in a hollow trunk of an old willow.'

'But didn't you get stung?'

'Why should I? I told the bees that we were hungry and that the goddess Coventina would bless them.'

'So, they didn't sting you?'

'No.'

'Then what are those red lumps on the side of your face?'

'Ah, those. Well, those came from a few hasty bees who attacked me before I mentioned Coventina.'

'And who is Coventina?'

'The goddess of wells, lakes and springs and of all things that fly but have no feathers.'

Seeing the humorous twist to his mouth, Tia said, 'Son of a chief Baradoc your words are as crooked as the finger you dip into the honey. But if you are so close to this goddess then ask her to lead us to water soon. I'm as grimy as a bath-house stoker.'

Baradoc shrugged his shoulders and said nothing, but the smile on her face and the way she tipped her head at him and the light in her blue eyes reminded him of a girl he had known in Durobrivae . . . the handmaid of a visitor to his old master, a girl who had brought a lump to his throat and a bumping in his heart every time he had looked at her, and a girl, sadly, who had taken no notice of him at all.

The Circle of the Gods

Midway through the morning they left the forest and moved into a country of heath and smooth downland, some of whose slopes were cut with the long rectangles of fields and cultivation. Some of the fields were being worked and from the hollows of shallow valleys there rose here and there the smoke from the hearths of homesteads and villages. But although the land seemed at peace here Baradoc kept always to the high ground. Behind the face of peace there was no telling what might be hidden. Even honest folk could give a hasty, hostile greeting to strangers. To pass through or near such places these days travellers had to stand and call from a distance, to show themselves and then wait while the men gathered and came to question them. There were many that travelled these days who carried a hunting horn to blow when they came down the road to a settlement or moved out from a forest fringe above a valley farm or village and, the horn sounded, stood and waited to know whether their way would be barred or opened.

Topping the smooth crest of a down they saw the land falling away below them to a river valley. Alders and willows fringed the river and the grass grew long and lush in a ribbon of pastures along its banks, and nowhere was there sign of human beings or their work.

The rain had stopped now and from the clearing sky the sun's warmth beat down against their damp clothes. Seeing the river below and the sheltering groves of trees that marked it here and there, Tia thought longingly of stripping her wet garments off and plunging into the water to clean herself. Never in her life had she felt so damp, dirty and stiff. But she said nothing to Baradoc. He was the master and he would decide.

As he moved down the slope a few paces ahead of her he stopped suddenly and waited for her to catch up with him. He dropped his bundle and put a hand on her arm.

'Listen.' He stood looking up the narrowing valley.

Tia looked in the same direction. At first she could hear nothing unusual.

'I can't hear anything.'

'You will soon. Look at the birds.' Baradoc pointed up the valley. Clear to his ears was a faint rustling noise overlaid with a thin half-squeaking, half-grunting, almost complaining sound. A couple of bowshots up the valley the air was slowly filling with the movement of birds, circling and wheeling low over the ground and gradually edging their way down the valley.

Tia said, 'I can hear it now. Like a lot of tiny puppies whimpering in their sleep. And what are all those birds?'

'They follow the army of the little furred ones. Have you never seen the march of the shrews and mice and voles before?'

'No.'

'Suddenly they all move. Nobody knows why. Perhaps the seasons have been good to them, the litters have increased and then, one day, there are so many of them they begin to move, looking for more living room, more food. As they move all the hunting birds follow them, the birds of day and the birds of night. Look, see them!'

He pointed up the valley and picked out for her the birds that wheeled and hovered and stooped and dropped into the tall grasses. Tawny, brown and barn owls swept low on silent wings. Kestrels hovered and drifted along the line of the march, sparrow hawks, merlins and hobbies cut and dashed through the air, and above them hung a ragged cloud of kites, ravens, crows and peregrines, and all of them in their own fashion dropped from the air to plunder and ravage the advancing army.

And now Tia could see the vanguard of that army and hear clearly its noise as the small brown and grey bodies rustled and squeaked and chattered through the grasses. It passed them on a wide front a few paces below them and stretching down almost to the river edge; voles, mice, shrews, all leaping and scuttering forward, calling and complaining in tiny voices that melded together grew into a low, surging of sound like the slow roll of a wave over fine gravel. Like a wave itself the brown and grey mass flooded over the ground, twisting and breaking and overleaping itself, moving always onwards; and as it went it left the tall grasses broken and flattened and filled the air with a sharp, pungent smell. Following, overshadowing and harrying it, went the preying birds of the night and the day and now they struck and killed but never stopped to feed as though, already long sated, some of the madness in the little creatures below had taken them so that only the instinct to kill was left alive in them.

Together Baradoc and Tia stood on the high slope and watched the living flood pass, and with them stood the three dogs, set back on their haunches, quivering, their eyes on the moving mass. No sound came from them, except from Cuna who, his body trembling with excitement at the sight of an occasional rat that fled by, whimpered as he longed for the chase. Of Bran — the lone one — there was no sign but Tia could guess that he was with the other birds and would stay with them until he tired of the sport. As though Baradoc had read her thoughts, she heard him say, 'The gods have linked all dogs with man. But the fish that swims and the bird that flies choose always their own paths.' He nodded at the last stragglers of the passing horde, and went on, 'They move like a people driven from their own worked-out land by hunger. So move the Saxons seeking new tilling and cattle grounds — and there is none to stop them among our peoples until the day of the new leader comes . . . until the day when that god-gifted man arises and turns sword in hand to face the east and its fury. May Dagda, the lord of perfect knowledge, send that day soon and Tentates, the god of war, strengthen every sword arm.'

Tia smiled to herself as he spoke. At that moment she knew that he was oblivious of her. He spoke seeing himself as the leader. She was well used now to these sudden heroic moods which carried him away. She suspected that underneath it all he enjoyed the fine passion of his own oratory. Maybe his old master, too, had smiled at times without showing it. Maybe the old man had divined something in him that even rhetoric and speechmaking could not hide. Son of a chief, Baradoc, one day to be the leader of the people of the enduring crow, one day to be . . . what?

She said quietly, 'That day will come. But at the moment it is this day that has to be lived. I want to get these wet clothes off. I want to swim and clean myself in that river — and then I want to eat cooked food and not hard-tack cold meat.'

Baradoc turned and grinned at her. 'As the good Asimus said — Lady Tia, the practical one. All right, so you shall. We'll catch some fish and maybe, I can find a clutch of duck's eggs in the reeds.'

At a place where the river divided into two channels they waded across the shallows and set up camp on the small island between the streams. They took off their clothes and laid them with their other possessions in the sun to dry. In the cover of a low willow Tia wrapped her shift about her loins and knotted it at her waist and then bound a cloth about her breasts before she joined Baradoc, naked except for a loin cloth. The far channel was deep and they swam together enjoying the mild bite of the river's spring-fed water on their skin. Tia washed her face and body with a piece of cloth, shutting from her mind all thoughts of warm bath houses, and scrubbed her hands with the fine river-bed gravel and then sat in the shallows and cleaned her broken nails as well as she could with the point of her small dagger. But even when she had finished they looked, she thought ruefully, like the hands of a kitchen servant. Massaging her feet to clean them she felt the soles harder than she had ever known them, and the sore place on her toe had healed to a hard callus.

Between them they caught three of the thyme-smelling grayling and a fat trout. Baradoc made fire and they broiled the fish on a green willow branch over the fire into which Baradoc threw wild sage and water mint leaves to flavour the flesh. All that was lacking, thought Baradoc, was salt to spark the full taste of the flesh and in his mind's eye he saw the salt pans cut in the flat land at the side of the river estuary near his home, with the white crystals glistening like frost as the sun evaporated the water. There had been some seasons when the traders would give almost the weight of silver for the harvest in his tribe's salterns, and other seasons when no traders came and the salt rotted. And thinking of the traders he did not know whether to be happy or angry, for it was a

Phoenician trading captain who had taken his cousin and himself from the lonely beach and had sold them as slaves in Lemanis to a dealer from Londinium. Which would he rather have had happen — to stay free with his tribe and be there now with so much of the world's knowledge closed to him still or to have known slavery, albeit he had been kindly treated at the last, and the teachings of his old master? Only the gods knew, for he had no answer. He smiled to himself, watching Tia at the fire. Without slavery he would never have met her, never be here now and never seen the slight raising of her eyebrows and the look of mocking amusement on her face when he became too self-important and full of himself . . . *Aie!* she was not like any of his tribe's girls or women. Her beauty came truly from her own race. He eyed her now as she squatted by the fire dropping pale bluey-green mallard eggs into the pot to boil them hard for the next day's journey. Her face and arms had browned, but the rest of her body was as white as a swan's and her loose, short hair shone under the sun like the rich gold fire of his own cliffs' ragged tansy blooms.

At that moment a dragon-fly hovered close about her face and she put up a hand and brushed it away. The dragon-fly darted jerkily away and began to hover and hunt over the running silver of the river. Without thinking Baradoc spoke aloud in his own tongue.

Tia turned and asked, 'What did you say?'

Embarrassed for a moment Baradoc answered, 'It was nothing.'

'If it was nothing why say it in your own tongue?'

'You would laugh if I told you.'

'Then make me laugh. There's nothing wrong with that.'

Baradoc shrugged his shoulders. 'If you truly want to hear.'

'I do.'

'Well, seeing you wave away the dragon-fly I spoke poetry in my own tongue.'

'Then speak it to me in my own tongue — if you can.'

Baradoc hesitated a moment and then, as well as he could, he spoke the poetry in her tongue.

Over the silver stream hunts the four-
    winged fly
Each eye holds a thousand eyes
But he sees not your beauty

Tia was silent for a moment. From Baradoc, she thought, always something new. Then, turning to drop more eggs into the boiling water, knowing that she was hiding her face from him, she said, 'Which of your tribal bards said that?'

Baradoc laughed. 'None of them. There is no man of my people who cannot say such things. The tongue speaks what the eye sees.'

Tia, her eyes on the boiling eggs, said, 'And did you hear me laugh?'

'No.'

'Nor should I. The words were good.' She turned to him and her mouth was wreathed momentarily with a teasing smile. 'And poetry is a change from warlike speeches about the future of this country. Now come and eat.'

But after they had eaten and Baradoc had gone off with his bow and Aesc at his heels to get a wildfowl for the next day's pot, Tia lay back on the grass and let the warmth of the sun flood across her bare body and thought about Baradoc. Even against his tanned face she had caught the flush of his embarrassment when he had spoken his lines. In herself there had been not embarrassment but a quick flush of pleasure to which she was no stranger. At her brother's villa there had been many visitors and friends from the neighbourhood and among them young men that she knew were attracted by her. Some she had liked and some she had avoided but, like or dislike, she was always pleased when she was complimented, when she was feasted with a string of flattering words. Why not? She was a woman . . . well, almost, and one day she would marry . . . Dreamily, she tried to imagine Baradoc as one of her own kind. But it would not work. Dress him in no matter what clothes or uniform there was something utterly unRoman about him. Not even could he be taken for Roman-British. He was a Briton, a tribesman, and it stood out all over him like the true grain of his own country's oaks. Chance and tragedy had brought them together. She liked him and was grateful to him and she thought nothing now of the roughness of some of his ways, but in his heart she guessed that there was only one love, greater than any he would ever give to any woman. She sat up shaking her head in silent sympathy with that woman somewhere in the future who would be his wife. He would honour, protect and cherish her — but she would never have a full entry to his heart. One thing above all others ruled his mind — to be a man and with full authority and the might of a united people behind him live for that day when with a great shout the swords of the tribesmen were raised east-wards and the dust began to rise under their marching feet.

She leaned forward and picked up from the ground, where their belongings were spread to dry, the doeskin bag which held the chalice Asimus had given them. Baradoc, she guessed, since he knew that it would never glow with the soft crimson of the ghost blood for him to mark him for greatness, had no interest in it. Not once since it had been given to them had he mentioned it or shown any care for it.

She opened the bag and took the silver chalice out. It was no larger than a drinking goblet with handles each side curved and worked in the form of rams' horns. One of the horns was badly bent. The bowl itself was pocked here and there with dents and there were scratches on the fluted base. Around the outside rim ran a continuous Greek key pattern and on one side of the body of the bowl, worked in relief, was a large round boss in the shape of an almost circular wreath of bay leaves enclosing the simple outline of a human eye. For a moment or two Tia was tempted to encircle her hands about it to see what would happen. Then she put the thought from her mind. If it glowed for her — even though Asimus had said it would not — she would be scared stiff because she had no wish to become a great leader. Anyway, there was no true belief in her heart for his story. Still, if Baradoc did not want it

... well, cleaned up — for it was dirty and tarnished inside and out — it would make a nice ornament for her bedroom in her uncle's villa, and would look pretty with flowers in it.

She rose and went to the river carrying the chalice. She had nothing to do until Baradoc returned and they started on the rest of the day's march. She squatted in the river shallows and scooped up a handful of the fine silver sand and began to clean the bowl, working the sand lightly over it as she had often seen servants working fine pumice stone dust over her brother's silver. As she worked a dragon fly came upstream and hovered low over a drift of white-starred water crowfoot. Tia smiled to herself. *Each eye holds a thousand eyes: but he sees not your beauty.* One day, she thought, some woman, some tribal maiden, would be won by his poetry and find herself only a shadow against the power of his dreams and ambitions.

★   ★   ★

For the next two days the weather was fine and they travelled north-west at a leisurely pace. Now and again, and always approached with caution, they met singly or in small groups travellers like themselves, some going north, some south and some west, but none

185

going east. From them they heard many stories whose truth it would have been idle to try to unravel. This year the Saxons were coming ashore in even greater strength and spreading and settling through the eastern countries. And with their coming all over the country many of the common folk, touched with a madness born of their fears and their deep-seated, generations-old resentment of their masters, had turned to pillage and murder. It had happened in other years, and it would happen again in the future, for as each wave of invaders swept farther through the eastern breeches and across the country so the fear and resentment would strengthen. They told, too, of rumours that the far western Cymric hill tribes, the Dobunni and the Ordovices, and the Silures from beyond the Sabrina were moving down from the mountains in raiding parties, bolder even now than they had ever been in the days when the ranks of the legions had thinned in the garrisons and forts, eager to take and hold what they could before the tide advanced to the foothills of their own homelands. The rumours, Baradoc knew, would be exaggerated, but the truth beneath was ugly enough. Until this phase passed, safety now for ordinary folk lay in the bigger towns where law and order still held, where men still kept to their businesses, paid taxes and travelled well armed and in strength, and where slaves still served them because there was no true freedom to be found in running away. Much of all this came to him in his own tongue and much of it he kept from Tia or trimmed down in the telling. Although Aquae Sulis lay on the banks of the Abona river which flowed north-west little more than twenty miles to join the Sabrina, the place was large and would be well-organized. No raiding party of free-booting tribesmen could touch it. All these tribes were tied by blood and history and common origins to his own people, and like his own people they were torn and divided by internal rivalries and feuds and had long forgotten how to stand together against a common enemy. Although they sang the virtues and valours of their ancestors who had faced the Fourteenth, Twentieth and Second Legions in the early days of the coming of the Roman invaders, they were a rabble now under many quarrelling chiefs, their destiny to be conquered unless they learned to hold rank and order disciplined battle skills against the new invader and dedicate themselves and their swords to a single leader and follow him without question or greedy turning aside for private plunder and rapine.

Of the people they met there were many he sensed, particularly among the women, who looked at Tia and must have guessed that she was no youth. Their eyes would turn back to him full of questions to which they gave no words, for curiosity about others was dangerous and their own plight swept such curiosity quickly from their minds. Tia, he knew, thought no farther ahead than Aquae Sulis and her uncle. When he left her the months and years would shape her and her life the way the gods willed. By then the gods would have shown him where his way led. Tia would live only in his memory, fading into the grey mist of the years, and be as hard to picture in fine detail as was now the image of the laughing handmaiden who had made his heart beat fast in the house of his old master.

On the evening of the second day they came up from a river valley, followed the track of an old ridgeway for a while and then climbed the bare, grass- and thorn-covered shoulder of a rising down full into the light of a low westering sun. Black against the blood-red glow of the sun were silhouetted the circular double ranks of great rising stones, three times the height of a man, many of them joined together across their tops with long stone lintels and caps. A handful of wild sheep cropping around the stones galloped away from them as they came near.

Tia said, 'What is this place?'

'A great henge of stones. There are some in my own country but not as big as this. This may be a place my master often talked of.'

'Men raised these stones?'

'No. They were raised in the days before man — when only the gods walked the earth. They raised them as a temple for man to use when he came, as a place for worship and sacrifice. Only priests are allowed to go inside the circles.'

'I don't believe all that.'

Baradoc smiled. 'I don't ask you to. But I do. And we do not go inside. We can camp on the far side, away from the ridge road.'

Tia, looking at the stones towering from the ground, their shadows long and black across the grass, gave a little shiver and said, 'I don't want to go inside anyway. All I want to do is to put up our shelter and sleep.'

That night, before they slept, as they lay under the meagre cover of a canopy made from their goats' hair cloak and a blanket, tied over hazel poles which Baradoc had cut, Tia said, 'How many more days before we get to Aquae Sulis?'

'Three or four. Tomorrow or the next day we should come to the headwater of the Abona river. Then we can travel down it.

Does your uncle live in Aquae itself?'

'Oh, no. In the country. About two miles outside.'

'Which side?'

'I don't know. Just outside.'

Baradoc sighed. 'You mean once we get to Aquae you still couldn't find your way to the villa?'

'No, of course I couldn't. I've only been a few times and I was taken by my brother. We used to go in two carts with servants. But I remember the road. Up to Calleva and then down the legionary road through Cunetio — we used to stay there a night — and then on through Verlucio and so to Aquae.'

'And when you got to Aquae — was the villa this side, or did you go through the place to the south, west or north?'

Tia yawned. 'Oh, we always went into Aquae, but after that . . . how would I know which direction? But it makes no difference. All you have to do is to ask for the villa of my uncle and anyone will tell you. Everyone knows him.'

Baradoc said nothing. It was useless to expect too much of a woman. But how could you go anywhere and not afterwards remember the road you took? How could you, even if the gods whipped you up and set you down in the dark of the darkest night without stars

190

to see or wind to smell, still not raise your hand and point to the north? To do that was as natural as breathing.

Suddenly out of the darkness Tia said, 'You think I'm stupid, don't you?'

Baradoc laughed quietly. 'No, I don't. You learn fast. You can shoot a bow well, you can silent-talk the dogs, you can make a day's march and carry your load, and you can now strike fire from flint and iron. But you only learn when you have to. You don't learn because it is good just to learn.'

'Women aren't supposed to. Anyway, what a lot of fuss over my uncle's villa. It is called Villa Etruria, and that because he was born in Etruria. In Aquae we just ask for it and we shall be told. And the sooner I'm there the better. And for you, too, because my uncle will show his gratitude for the way you have looked after me. And anyway, you wouldn't like it if women were as clever and good at things as men. Though sometimes I think, the way things are now and man having made them so, it's a pity that they aren't.'

Indignantly Baradoc said, 'The gods made man to fight and rule and to reason, and they gave him woman to bear his children and to keep his hearth, though sometimes, when a nation needs it, they give a woman the heart and brain of a man and then we have queens

191

like Boudicca who your people — ' He broke off for from Tia had come the sound of a gentle snore. But he knew that it came not from sleep but from good-humoured teasing and to stop his speech-making. He lay back with his head on his hands and watched the night sky through the front of the shelter and, seeing the shapes of the standing stones against the pale night sky, he knew what he must do at first light. He had not known that they would come to the great stone henge. Surely the gods had directed his feet this way with a purpose, maybe to show that they were with him. He heard a dog fox call across the downland beyond the stones, and a vixen answer and felt Cuna, who lay against his leg for warmth, quiver aggressively in half sleep. Then from his left came the genuine sound of Tia's slow, long-paced sleep-breath as night claimed her.

Baradoc woke at first light. He slipped quietly out of the shelter without waking Tia. He strapped on his sword belt and moved away over the dew-drenched grass followed by the three dogs. He turned and looked at Cuna and the small dog, after a moment's hesitation, went back to the shelter. Northwards from the stone circle the downs rose and fell in gentle swells, marked here and there with clumps of wind-twisted thorns. A light breeze came full into his face. In a little while the sun would be rising, but now the light was a pearl-grey, muting the colours of trees and grass. A couple of bowshots away to his right he saw a flock of great bustards. For a moment or two he was tempted to go after them, but then he knew that he must have a truly ritual animal. The bustards, seeing him and the dogs, moved away, running awkwardly, and then took off heavily, flying low, their slow wing-beats stirring up the dust and dead grasses below them until they gained height and wheeled away out of sight over the crest of the downs.

He sent Lerg and Aesc ahead and for a while they were lost to his sight. Then downwind came the clear sharp barking of Aesc. Baradoc whistled and dropped to his knees on the ground. After a moment or two he heard the thud of hooved feet and he whistled again. Over the low swelling of downland ahead of him suddenly appeared the close-packed ranks of a handful of wild sheep, heading downwind towards him, moving fast away from the dogs who had circled behind them.

As the dogs appeared over the sky-line behind the sheep, Baradoc stood up and marked quickly the beast he wanted. Seeing him the small flock swerved caterways across the face of the down. Before Baradoc could whistle, Lerg raced along one flank and turned them back on their old line and Aesc came in on the other flank. The flock slowed, made an attempt to break away, but was held by the dogs. The old ram leading them stopped and the rest of the flock bunched behind it. The ram lowered its head and stamped angrily with its forefeet, the thuds ringing across the hard ground.

While the dogs held the flock on the flanks Baradoc moved forward slowly. The closer he came the tighter they bunched with the old ram at their head. Baradoc went step by step without hurry towards them, his eyes on a young ram he had already marked as the wanted beast. He whistled gently to Aesc with her own slow trilling call and she crouched watching the flock. Lerg moved in closer from the other side The sheep, packed tight now, moved uneasily, waiting for the signal from the old ram to break from the flock pattern and scatter in all directions. The young ram pushed out to the side of the flock and faced Lerg. Following the fashion of the old ram, it lowered its head and stamped. From the way the sheep stood and their slowness in breaking into a wild panic rush in all directions Baradoc knew that they were not truly wild. This was a flock made of strays and abandoned animals, the sight of dogs and man still without the full force of danger for them. As the young ram stamped again and tossed its head in threat towards Lerg, Baradoc whistled high and shrilly and made a quick movement of his hand.

The flock broke wildly in all directions and Lerg moved in fast and leaped at the young ram, knocking it over and then holding it down by the grip of his great jaws on the loose neck fleece and the weight of his body.

Baradoc ran in, pulling a long hide thong from inside his shirt front. Seizing the immature horns of the ram he swung the beast on to its back, clamped his knees around its forequarters and with a few quick movements looped its front and hind legs together and knotted them securely. The ram lay on its side, its back arched, its feet pinioned. Baradoc picked it up, slung it over his shoulders, the strong, aromatic smell of its dew-wet fleece sharp in his nostrils, and turned back towards the stone circle.

As he neared it the lip of the sun came over the eastern ridge of the downs and the dew on the grass was suddenly fired with its red glow, the shadows of the stones reaching long and black over the ground.

He carried the ram up to the circle. To one side of the entrance a grey, lichen-stippled stone lay on the ground. Baradoc dropped the ram on to the stone and stood back with Lerg and Aesc on either side of him. He drew the broad sword from his belt and holding it before him by point and hilt looked up at the great arc of the stones, their eastern faces flooded by the fiery sunrise, and began to speak aloud in his own tongue the call to the gods for their favour and guidance, the sacrificial prayer of his tribe, of the people of the enduring crow.

This, he knew now, was why his steps had been directed here. Never in all the years of his people had any of them made this sacrifice in the first morning light at the great stone henge, the temple made by the gods for man . . . *Aie!* never; for if any had then it would have been honoured in the tribal memory never to be forgotten no matter how many seasons and years should pass. He had been sent here because the gods had marked him as surely as he had marked the young ram that lay with wide-staring eyes and heaving flanks on the stone slab at his feet. Over the levelled sword raised before his eyes, he called the prayer and then began to name the great gods so that none should be missed and work against him and his dreams . . . Father Dis; Taranis the thunderer; Teutates; Esus; Coventina of the sacred grove of Nemeton; Cernunnos the horned one; Epona the hooved one; Nonus the wise and forgiving one who, when his wife deceived him with another, because he loved her, claimed the child for his own; Dagda; Nodons of the silver hand; Badb the goddess of battle who had flown high above the chariots of the great queen, and Lug the fair-haired who stirred the corn seed to life and set the blossoms of all flowering trees to swell into fruit . . .

He chanted the litany of names as the great rim of the sun began to wheel above the horizon. When he was done he reached down, took one of the ram's horns in his left hand, drew the animal's head back, and with one fierce slash of the sword cut its throat. The ram kicked in its death agony and its blood ran dark over its tawny fleece and moved darker still across the rough face of the stone slab. Baradoc watched the ram die. Then he stepped back and looked through the great stone archway at the linked twin circles of raised stones over and through which the swifts were screaming and hunting the insects raised to flight by the new sun; and he looked for some sign that the gods had heard him and were pleased with his offering. Always the gods gave some sign but it lay in the eyes of man to discover and read it. And the gods gave him their sign.

There was a flutter of wings from the top of a small thorn which grew close to one of the far stones. Baradoc, catching the flash of red wings and the blue-black head, saw that it was a shrike. The bird settled on a side branch of the shrub. In its mouth it held a limp, dead wren it had killed. As Baradoc watched he saw the butcher bird with a quick stabbing twist of its head impale the wren on one of the long thorns to rest there among the dead beetles and bees of its larder until hunger should bring it back to feed. For a moment or two he was sure that this was his sign, but his mind had scarcely turned to the reading of its message for him when from the top of one of the far stones a bird, at first a slatey-blue shadow against the darkness of the stone, winged down fast. It streaked low over the sheep-bitten grasses towards the thorn, the sun metalling its dark wings with a high gloss and lighting the pale, rufous patch of its gorge with a golden glow. The shrike seeing it coming rose with a cry of alarm from the thorn and flew away, hugging the ground and swerving in and out of the thorn patches. After it in fast pursuit, swinging and turning, and fast closing on the shrike, went the other bird, and Baradoc watched, knowing now that this was the true sign for the other bird was a merlin, the smallest of his country's falcons. On the lip of the down beyond the great henge where the land began to fall away to the river valley Baradoc saw the merlin strike and kill in mid-air, saw a great puff of feathers spread in the air and then, as the merlin disappeared below the crest, heard its distant exultant killing call. The gods had spoken plainly to him, filling him with a deep and exulting pleasure and pride. Was not the bloody butcher bird the Saxon threat from the east and the swift, sudden killing of the merlin the vengeance and victory which would one day come from the west?

He turned away from the stones towards the shelter. He saw that Tia was standing outside watching him, and he knew that if she began to question him, maybe to mock or tease him, then he would be hard put to hold his feelings back. These things had nothing to do with women. He was no child now, no youth, but growing in stature and strength to fit the manhood that was closing about him.

Tia said nothing. She had seen him make the sacrifice, but the killing of the shrike had been to her no more than part of the morning stir of nature. As he came towards her she saw his face set brown and hard and the dark intensity of his eyes and she guessed that he moved with his dream of the future glowing and blood-stirring within him. For the first time then it came to her that of all the people she had known in her life none had had this fire in the heart and brain. Her brother and his neighbours and friends, the well-to-do, and the country people, the farm and estate workers, the shopkeepers and traders, British or mixed-blooded, had carried no real anger and resolve, no dedication to any cause except the small concerns of their day-to-day existence. Her brother had longed and had still half-believed that the legions would return from Gaul even in the face of the truth which was there for all to read. The great Empire, already split and split again was, like many a stranded jellyfish she had seen on the sands below the villa, fast shrinking to an ignoble death. That she could now have such thoughts surprised her, but she knew that it was being with Baradoc which had begun to open her eyes and her mind to such things. She had seen her brother and their neighbours make offerings and small sacrifices to the gods, had herself revered the lares and penates, and she knew now that the gods were not to be deceived because there had never been in her face or the faces of the others that which made Baradoc as he came towards her now a figure who for face wore a bronze mask in which only the eyes lived.

She gave him the morning greeting and then, while Baradoc began to strike their shelter and pack their belongings, went to their fire. Overnight they had banked the pile of red embers with new wood and dry grasses and covered it with turves. She pulled the turves aside and blew the slow embers into fire and fed brittle, dead thorn kindling on it. She put bear grease in the skillet and began to cook the last of the fish which they had caught the previous day. While they were cooking she mixed some of their ground corn with water and beat it into flat cakes with her hands to fry when the fish were done. The dogs sat and watched her and she threw them the last of their dried meat which had gone rank and high. They ate it with relish.

The pattern of their days was set now. They ate well in the morning and then travelled until the late afternoon or evening when they would eat again. Water for drinking they carried in their leather skin. Water for washing they took as they travelled using the first spring or river. A wind eddy blew smoke into her eyes and mouth. Weeks ago it would have made her cough and her eyes water. Now she was hardly aware of it. All could be borne because Aquae Sulis came nearer each day. Irreverently as she cooked she thought that it was a waste to sacrifice a young ram. She held in her mind the thought of a shoulder or leg being spitted over the fire. Not for a while yet could she even dare to make a joke of it because there was still a silence in Baradoc which she guessed would not go until they had eaten and begun their march. At this moment Baradoc came to the fire, carrying their two wooden platters, and squatted down on his hunkers. He smiled almost shyly at her, as though there were only a few hours gone since they were strangers and said, 'We should travel well today. The country is open and we can keep to the ridgeways.' He nodded to the westerly sky. 'I think too these parts are more peaceful. No scavenging birds, crows, ravens or kites wheel in the sky and the wind is free of rolling smoke clouds.'

Wiping her sticky, floured hands on a cloth Tia, her words surprising herself, quietly said, 'Since I've been with you it seems to me that my body and my brain have been wakened from a kind of sleep. Not so long ago I took my pleasant life and ways for granted. Other people were shadows that moved around me. I had no curiosity about them and little about myself. Now my mind is full of questions.'

'That is the way it should be. Without questions there are no answers. And without answers no truth, no progress, no future.'

'Then I am free to ask questions?'

'Why not?'

'About you?'

'If you choose.'

'You have a living dream to free your country. Once your forefathers had that dream and turned it against my people. Time has settled that struggle. Now your enemy is a new one . . . the Saxons.'

'And your enemy too.'

'True. But tell me, why do you hate the Saxons with a hatred that is fiercer than a smith's furnace? Why do you have an anger in you that is harder than iron against them, so unbending that it must come from more than a love of your country and your dream for its future?' She leant forward and turned the frying fish in the skillet to brown their sides, hiding her face. 'What did they do to you?' She looked up slowly after a while and saw his face unmoving, the mask set over it again.

Baradoc, each word a chip struck from an icy mass, said, 'I had a father and was taken from him into slavery. I had a master and was his slave. But even while a slave he became my father. He taught me the arts he knew. He even taught me things about my own and other tribes I did not know. Everything I am and will be is forever marked by his wisdom and kindness. He gave me my freedom and understood, since I did not leave him at once, that there was more I wanted from him. And then the Saxons came. He hid me in the roof loft and, sword in hand, met them in the courtyard of the villa. I saw it all through a gap in the tiles. They ringed him and taunted him and baited him. Age made his movements clumsy. Slowly and savagely they speared and axed him. They made his dying long and a drunken sport. And when he was dead they hacked with their blades at his body, danced on it and kicked it, defiled and degraded it. That night I swore to the gods that I would take the sword against them so long as any rested in this land, and I made a vow that the first Saxon I ever killed I would dedicate to him.' He paused for a moment, the mask slowly faded from his face and the thin edge of a smile wreathed his lips as he went on, 'So that is the answer to your question — and Lady Tia it is not one which I expected ever to come from you. From today the people around you will no longer be shadows.'

And Tia, serving his food, wondered at this love in him for his dead master and for his country, and there was pity in her for the woman he would some day take to wife for she would have to live in the shadow of those loves.

The Villa Etruria

For the next two days, the country being open and untroubled, they travelled easily and finally reached one of the small branches of the headwaters of the Abona river. The valleys of the downland with their clear chalk streams held small settlements and farms. The southern slopes were worked with terraced strip fields, the greens of sturdy growths of wheat and barley and oats patchworking the land. Now, too, they came across flocks of cattle and sheep herded and guarded by family groups who lived and slept under rough shelters on the downs. Sometimes they talked to these people and bartered the game which Baradoc killed for cheese and milk. Money none of these people would accept as payment. True value lay in barter, goods for goods.

With the days an easier relationship sprang up between Baradoc and Tia. Something had awakened in her which gave her understanding and a growing admiration for his character and strength of purpose. In him, too, grew an acceptance of her which discounted all her race and breeding. She was a travelling companion, the two of them bonded in a growing friendship. Since the going was easier now, she marched mostly at his side instead of trailing behind. As they journeyed they talked more because she seldom had any urge to tease or mock him. Instead she was full of questions about his people and his life and about his days with his master. One evening as they sat beside the slow moving Abona where they were camped for the night she asked him about his cousin who had been made a slave with him and why he had betrayed him and left him hanging from the tree in the Anderida forest to die.

Baradoc said, 'When he was given his freedom he left my master but he stayed in Durobrivae and worked there for a smith and armourer. He has a cunning in his hands as great as the cunning in his mind. And he heard from meeting travellers who came to the smithy that my father had died. At the moment his father is head of the tribe — but only until I return. What he did to me in the forest he did first for his father, and then for himself. With me dead then one day he would lead the tribe.'

'What's he called?'

'Inbar, and our tribal name is Ruachan. After the Saxon raid in which my master was killed he came to me with a friend and we all travelled together. Not until they strung me to the tree did he tell me that my father was dead.'

'And you mean to kill him?'

'We shall fight and when he lies on the ground with my sword at his throat his life will belong to me. Then I shall give it to his father, who is a good man, and he will choose whether the sword strikes or is sheathed.'

'And what do you think he will say?'

Baradoc gave a dry laugh. 'Lady Tia, the questioner. How should I know? But if the word is to kill, then I shall kill him and he will be laid in the burial grounds on the cliff hill. But if the word is to spare him, then Inbar must rise and go from our lands forever. Whichever way the loss is great — for Inbar has many skills and his dreams are mine and his hatred of the Saxons is mine. With so much craft and cunning and courage it is a great grief that the gods at his birth flawed him.'

Tia lay back on the grass and stared at the evening sky. High above she could see the black shape of Bran wheeling slowly on a rising air current and then, suddenly in a moment of play, falling quickly, twisting and turning, the searing sound of the wind against his wings coming clearly to her. Cuna came and sniffed at her face and she raised a hand

and fondled his muzzle. Tomorrow or the next day they would reach her uncle's villa and this episode in her life would be closed. But, although her meeting with Baradoc had sprung from tragedy, she knew that for her too — even as the gods had flawed Inbar to bring her to rescue Baradoc from the oak — they had fashioned time and movement to give her this period with him so that her eyes should be truly opened and her mind truly awakened. For a moment or two the thought of Aquae Sulis had no pleasure. All that she could look forward to there as the years passed would be of little importance. Menfolk, she thought were the lucky ones . . . they had a freedom to dream and then to act and create . . . Women were only shadows against them. In her reverie she heard the low, soft growling of Cuna as he played with a broken stick. Then she heard him yelp loud and Baradoc suddenly laughed.

She sat up to see that Cuna in play had attacked the loose roll of their fishing net which lay near the shelter and was now tangled in its meshes. As he rolled and twisted she laughed too. Leaping and jerking inside the web of net Cuna lost his balance and began to roll down the slope of the bank. Before she could move he had gone over the edge and landed in the river.

Laughing still Baradoc jumped up, took the long fish spear and lifted the netted Cuna out of the river. He held him up and Cuna yapped indignantly until Tia reached for him and sitting down began to disentangle him from the net. Free, Cuna shook himself, spraying her with water and then, as they both still laughed, began to race around in wild circles leaping from one to the other in mock attacks, delighted with the attention he had brought on himself. While Lerg and Aesc looked on impassively, Tia caught Cuna and held him to her breast and calmed him down.

Baradoc, watching her and the dog, said after a moment or two, 'Of the dogs he's the one you like best, isn't he?'

'Yes, yes I do. He's so small, but so brave, and he makes me laugh.'

'Then when I leave Aquae Sulis he stays with you. He is yours.'

'Oh, no I couldn't — '

'He is yours.' Baradoc stood up, his eyes turning away from her. 'The gift is made. Now I will cover the fire against the morning.'

He moved away to gather turves and grasses to damp down the fire. Watching him, holding the wet Cuna in her arms, Tia, flushed with the pleasure of the gift, knew how great a gift it was, for of all the dogs she had long guessed that Cuna, the droll and the bear-baiter, was first in his affections. She knew, too, that as long as Cuna was hers so long would the memory of Baradoc be strong and green with her.

★ ★ ★

The Villa Etruria was two miles to the west of Aquae Sulis. It stood on a gentle river-bank slope, well above the winter flood line. From the main arched entrance to the courtyard, stone steps ran down to a small landing place on the Abona. They had come to it by the road which ran west to the small port of Abonae near the mouth of the river, reaching it in the late afternoon, the lowering sun striping its red tiles with black ridge shadows while the breeze rippled the branches of a row of mixed limes and poplars that flanked the slopes on either side of the building. Part of the bank had been cut away and the villa had been built into it. A covered way ran round the large courtyard, backed on one side by the kitchen, servants' quarters and store rooms. On the other side was a small bath house with the hypocaust that served it. Between these wings the main rooms of the villa faced square across the court to the river. In the centre of the courtyard was a spring-fed well, encircled with a carved stone parapet and roofed with an ornamental canopy from which hung a large bronze bucket. A little beyond it giving shade to the yard grew a tall sweet chestnut tree, a tree, Baradoc knew, which the Romans had brought to his country in their early days. When corn was short the old legionaries had milled the chestnut fruits to add to their scanty cornflour issue. Flowers were everywhere, growing up the pillars of the covered ways, spilling over the tops of tall red urns and rioting from the beds which lined the pathway around the yard.

Lying on his couch that first night it was a long time before Baradoc could find sleep. Lerg and Aesc slept outside his door, and outside Tia's bedroom not far away he knew Cuna would be lying. Thinking of Tia he smiled to himself. When he had asked her where the villa was she had said nothing about the river. She had lived until now without her eyes being truly opened. When they had come down the river into the bowl of hills that held Aquae Sulis he had been surprised to see how small the town was. He had imagined it to be much larger. There had been no sign of trouble or past disturbance and although they had drawn some curious looks from people, mostly because of the dogs and Bran on his shoulder, they had been met kindly and given directions to the villa. But although the town was small he saw, on their way to the villa, that there were many more like it scattered along the Abona and on the hill slopes.

The villa itself had not surprised him. As a slave he was used to such places. But for the first time in his life, because of Tia, he was a guest. When they had arrived he had insisted that Tia go by herself into the villa to her uncle. He had sat on the river steps with the dogs, watching the swallows making water rings as they dipped to the river surface and the flight of the bronze, green and blue dragon-flies hovering and darting above the yellow flag blooms.

Finally, with his steward at his side, Tia's uncle had come to greet him. Ex-Chief Centurion and Camp Prefect Truvius Corbulo was well over eighty. He walked now with slow, awkward steps because of his rheumatism, helping himself with a long vine staff, old and polished with use, probably a relic from his army days. His hair was white and he was a tall man, a little bowed at the shoulders but carrying himself with a natural and professional dignity. His eyes were blue, a deeper blue than Tia's, and although they looked warmly on Baradoc he could guess that in the past many an erring legionary had quailed before them. It was easy to imagine Chief Centurion Truvius of the Second Legion in the days of his prime . . . plumed helmet, armoured in mail cuirass and strapped shoulder plates, a pleated leather kilt, a senior officer's highly decorated boots, sword hanging on his left side, his staff of rank in his right hand and, sweeping from his shoulders, the folds of a red paludament, the cloak of authority.

He had greeted Baradoc and in a short, but friendly speech, thanked him for all he had done for Tia and had then put him in the care of his steward. For a moment as they had moved into the courtyard the steward, his eyes on the dogs and Bran, had begun to say a few words . . . a mumble about should the animals go to the stables and the young Briton . . . Truvius had jerked his old head round, eyed the man without words and had moved on. From that moment Baradoc had been looked after as a highly privileged guest. He was taken to the baths where he stripped and — as he had often done in his old master's house and in the public baths at Durobrivae — passed through the cold and tepid rooms to the hot room where, once the sweat had begun to break through his skin, he lay and was shaved and then his body scraped and curry-combed by the bath servant, relishing the man's skilful strokes with the curved bronze blade of the strigil.

When he had come to dress it was to find a fresh-laundered tunic and under-shirt awaiting him with highly polished sandals of soft green leather, the leg thongs worked with a running design in fine silver thread.

Lying now with the silence of the house about him, a soft down-stuffed mattress giving him the feeling of floating on air, he realized the shock it must have been for Tia savagely to have been thrust out of the luxury of her old life into the wilderness with him. And this house *was* luxurious, though small. It had been built of the local limestone. Even the pillars supporting the roof of the open corridors that ran around the courtyard were of stone. The wall openings of the reception room and the dining room were glazed with green and yellow squares of glass. The dining room floor was covered with a large mosaic, six hanging bronze oil lamps gave light and on plinths along the walls stood family busts. One angle of the courtyard corridor where Truvius had his collection of birds had been faced, too, with glass, a rough, green whorled glass through which the light came broken and uneven as through water. But of all the things in the villa none had surprised him more than Tia when she came into the

214

ante-room before dinner where he and Truvius waited for her, drinking a fine white wine the like of which he had never tasted before and which he guessed must have been imported from Gaul — the grim thought passing quickly through his mind that he hoped the old gentleman had a cellar well enough stocked to last him his days because there would be little more fine wine from Gaul until the country grew settled again, and only the gods knew when that would be. It was with this thought in his mind that he had turned to see Tia enter.

In the darkness now the picture of Tia glowed bright and vivid in his mind. Her short hair, combed and arranged in tight curls, shone like a gold flame and was trapped by a red velvet band that ran across her clear brow and behind her ears. From one shoulder hung a blue silk robe, leaving the other shoulder bare. A transparent, diaphanous short mantle fell in light, moving folds to her waist, while on her feet were soft blue-dyed slippers worked with a close pattern of small seed pearls. The sight of her had made Baradoc catch his breath. Gone was the forest-and-downland, dirty-faced youth who had travelled with him. Here was a beautiful young woman, perfumed and elegant, a young goddess coming into the room like a vision.

The contrast shook him. For all his life with his old master, all his experience, he had felt suddenly that here was a new world. A memory of his tribe's settlement had gone darkly through his mind . . . the men in their rough skins, the women, young girls and children, sun-and-weather bitten, who worked over the cooking pots, hands greasy and calloused, and tilled the hill plots and on the feast days could only find for finery a mantle or cloak of cheap wool, for ornament some solitary armlet or neckpiece, some brooch set with coloured stones . . . *Aie!* it was another world for the people of the enduring crow, but not another world which could never change. It must change . . . Rome had gone . . . another realm must rise and no invader from the east was going to create it. He had come back to the present as Tia, teasing mockery in her eyes, had said, 'Well, Son of a Chief, Baradoc — do I get no greeting? Did you lose your tongue as well as the dirt and sweat of travel in the bath house?'

Baradoc had smiled and said, 'What could my tongue say, Lady Tia, that could match what my eyes see? Can the beauty of a bird be told by counting the colours that paint each feather, or the silver glory of a salmon be known by the tally of its scales?'

Tia laughed and turning to Truvius, had

said, 'I should have told you, uncle, that Baradoc is a poet as well as a warrior who one day dreams of sweeping the Saxons from this land.'

Truvius, handing Tia a glass of wine, had answered, 'When a man sees beauty and cannot find poetry in himself then he is a man, too, who finds no courage in himself when he faces danger. And now — stop your teasing. You have kept us over long waiting to eat.'

For the first time in his life — for not even in his old master's house had this happened to him — Baradoc ate in Roman fashion, reclining on one of the three sloping couches set around the low table and waited on by the steward. Although Truvius showed little hunger, shifting often, too, in discomfort from his rheumatism on his couch, he and Tia did full justice to the stuffed olives and preserved plovers' eggs, the cold lobster — which had been brought upriver from Abonae — and the young broad beans and carrots, followed by slices of grilled venison, their appetite lasting right through to the dessert of dried figs and walnuts. Throughout the meal the steward had hovered round, refilling their wine glasses, bringing fresh napkins and water bowls for them to clean their hands, and watching always over the comfort of Truvius, ready to help him turn, prompt with a fresh cushion to ease his stiff body.

At the end of the meal Truvius, giving them a wry, humorous look had said, 'Twenty years ago I could have matched your appetite. Forty years ago, when I was still in service, after a day's march I could have eaten and drunk you all under the table.' Then looking at Baradoc, he said, 'So — you go to the west to rouse your people? And why should you not for my own have forsaken you? But remember this when you come of age to lead and fight . . . ' He coughed a little, shifted stiffly on his couch and sipped at his wine. 'When Claudius sent General Aulus Plautius with the Second, Ninth, Fourteenth and Twentieth Legions against your people, the Cantiaci, the Regnenses and the Atrebates, then man for man, courage for courage there was no difference between defenders and attackers. There seldom is. But there was this difference in Plautius's men — discipline, one leader and one plan of battle. He wins battles who makes the enemy fight on his terms, on his chosen ground. Remember, boy, for so with kindness I can call you from the mountain of age on which I now sit, that your tribes must find a leader, just and severe, whom men will love and he must find for himself new battle skills and tactics that these barbarian Saxons have never known and . . . ' He had broken off in a fit of coughing and the wine spilled from the glass in his shaking hand, but when the steward came to him, he waved him away testily and, after a while went on: ' . . . I would ransom my soul if such a thing were possible to be your age again, and to fight for this country, for it has been good to me and I have grown to love it more even than my native Etruria . . . Aye, I would gladly fight without rank as a simple bowman or spearman if the gods would will it. But the gods give but one portion of life to each man. When his eyes close for the last time they wait on the other side of darkness to greet him with his reckoning and his reward or punishment.' He was silent for a long while, his old head nodding, his mind wandering, then he looked at them and a smile lit his lean face and he said, 'Would that I had died in battle. I find old age a bore to myself and a burden to others . . . '

In bed now, hearing an owl cry by the river and catching the stir of Bran who roosted on the ledge of the window, Baradoc could remember every word the man had said, and he knew that the memory would never leave him. One leader and each man disciplined, and new battle skills and tactics that the

Saxons had never known. Then, driving those thoughts away, there came into his mind the picture of Tia, a daughter of the house of Corbulo, a young woman who stirred his heart but who, now that their journeying was done, was as far above him as the stars. Somewhere he knew there was a woman he would marry and make his own . . . but already she had been betrayed . . . *Aie!* the heart was a house of many chambers and the doors of some once shut could never be reopened.

★ ★ ★

The next morning as he stood outside the kitchen quarters and saw to the feeding of the dogs and Bran, Tia came to him and when the dogs had eaten they walked down to the river.

With a brusqueness which he did not intend Baradoc said, 'You are safe with your uncle, and this part of the country, too, seems settled. I must go on my way. Today.'

For a moment or two Tia was silent. Then she said sharply, 'You cannot leave today.'

'Why not?'

'Because it would offend my uncle — and it would offend me. Would you treat him as though he were an innkeeper? And myself as a . . . a sack of corn you deliver for the kitchen?'

'I meant nothing like that.'

'He is old. The steward tells me that he has suffered two heart attacks in the last few months. There are times, too, when his mind wanders and he is like a child. His days are numbered, son of a chief Baradoc. You will not shadow even one of them with the discourtesy of leaving so soon. You are a guest. We both owe you a debt of honour. That cannot be paid quickly as you toss a coin on to a tavern slab in return for a beaker of beer. This country will not fall apart, nor your dreams vanish for the delay of a few days. And stop scowling. It puts ugly lines across your brow.'

Baradoc laughed and shrugged his shoulders. 'I meant no rudeness. But you're right to scold me.'

So Baradoc stayed on at the villa for the next three days. On one of these days Tia and her uncle travelled to Aquae Sulis and made their prayers at the temple for the spirits of her brother and his wife, and Truvius gave orders to a stone mason for a slab to be carved commemorating them. When it was made he intended to place it in the wall of the villa overlooking the river. Baradoc travelled with them but did not go to the temple.

Instead he wandered around the town. Many of the wealthier people had already left it and from the shopkeepers and working people that he spoke to it was clear that there was a deep feeling of unrest in them, a shadow of the fear which already clouded the east. But their chief anxiety centred on the Cymric tribes beyond the Sabrina river, and the tales which each new traveller brought that the hill tribes were moving. The Silures, Demetae and Dobunni who had never been truly under the old rule, saw the prospects of easy and profitable pillage, the pleasure of wielding firebrand and sword, and the prospect of slaves to sell or to work their mountain farms and herds. Rumours flew like bats at night. So, Baradoc guessed at Isca in the west, on the moorland borders of his own country, there would be the same rumours. Bands of his own people, the Dumnonii, would be moving or gathering to move, small chiefs eager for the quick pickings, and in their greed never dreaming that, creeping mile by mile over the years, their own destruction or bondage was seeping west-wards. In those few days he realized, too, that many of the outlying villas around the town and along the Abona had been closed or left in the care of servants.

Sitting with Truvius that evening in the

courtyard, the dogs lying before them, the sun firing the plumage of the birds in their aviary, the steady movement of worker bees about the flower urns and beds, the old man said to him, 'Sulis is a town of shadows, and many of the villas around here hold nothing but ghosts. Some of my friends have gone to Londinium and some to Gaul. But wherever they go they will find no real ease. There is no making terms with an enemy full of land hunger. Some will pay a tribute for their own safety, but each year the demand will be greater. In the end everything will be taken from them. The gods have called a term to the bright days of glory and now we begin to enter the darkness of a changing age. A man can do no more than to cherish his own honour, to fight for it and to die for it. The rest is in the hands of the gods. I have lived by war, and I would that I had died by war . . . '

His words trailed away, his eyes closed and his head dropped to his chest. He had drifted away into sleep, maybe into a dream of the bright, hard days of his manhood. Then one of the birds from the aviary screeched loudly. Truvius's head jerked up, his eyes blinking. Then he cocked a grey eyebrow at Baradoc and smiled. Nodding at Lerg he said, 'In my young days with the legions I would have given you a handful of gold for a dog like that. Aye, and I would rather travel with such a dog for companion than many a man I have known. My Tia was lucky to find you.'

Baradoc shook his head. 'I was lucky that she found me.'

'You were both fortunate. She says that you must be well rewarded.'

'I want nothing.'

'This I know. But I make a gift from an old soldier to one who still has to face his first battle.' He raised his right arm letting the folds of his toga fall away from it. On his wrist he wore a thin, much worn gold armlet. He slipped it off and handed it to Baradoc. 'This is the first battle decoration I won . . . when I was little more than your age . . . others and greater came later, the torques and discs and silver spearhead. But this was the first for no great act of bravery, more a moment of youthful rashness. Wear it.'

Baradoc took the thin, worn armlet and slipped it on. For him it would always hold the memory not only of the old Chief Centurion but also of Tia and would always rest on his right arm.

Each evening they sat in the courtyard talking before the time for bathing and dinner came; the three of them and the three dogs and the steward bringing them cool drinks and small dishes of salted nuts and sugared fruits to eat. It was an oasis of well-being and peace — which was shattered on the evening of the day before Baradoc was to leave.

They were sitting in the courtyard in the shade of the tall sweet chestnut when Cuna sat up and whined. At the same moment Lerg and Aesc rolled to their feet from where they were lying and both of them turned their heads towards their master. From a branch on the chestnut tree Bran launched himself, his shadow racing across the flower beds, and he rose into the air and began to circle over the villa.

Tia said, 'Why are the dogs uneasy?'

Baradoc stood up. None of them were armed. He signalled the dogs to keep their station. As he did so there was the sound of footsteps from behind him. He turned and saw the steward and his wife and the house servants come through from the reception room to stand in a close group at the top of the steps leading down into the courtyard. From the room behind them six men appeared and ranged themselves along the face of the covered walk, six men with long hair and bearded or moustached, six men wearing belted tunics of skin or wool, the cloth crudely striped in greens, reds and yellows. All of them were armed with spear and sword and all of them were weather-browned and hard-muscled, short wiry mountain men. Before the three in the yard could make any move or sound, the man beside the steward, taller than the rest, a bronze torque about his neck, raised a hand as though commanding silence and then pointed beyond them to the archway that framed the top of the steps leading down to the river.

Baradoc swung round quickly. The dogs held their station, waiting some sign or command from him. But he gave none. A tall man stood inside the archway carrying sword and spear, a throwing axe thrust in his belt, a short cloak hanging from his shoulders over a finely dressed deer hide tunic, his legs bare of sandals or gartering. From behind him, rippling in like shadows, without sound, like some flawless movement of a dream, came six other men in hillmen dress and they split on either side of him in even ranks, and each man carried a heavy hunting bow, raised and arrowed, the bows partly drawn and each arrow head pointing at the group in mid-court. For a moment or two it seemed that the invasion was part of a dream, and the dream a spell which held the whole company frozen in a coloured frieze that a word or movement could erupt into violent life.

Cuna broke the spell. With a sudden, short bark he raced forward to the man in the doorway. Before Baradoc could stop him, he

226

leaped up and seized the edge of the man's tunic and hung on to it, swinging from its folds and growling. The man looked down at Cuna, then laughed, and putting his spear behind him against the archway wall, reached down and lifted Cuna by the scruff of his neck, pulling him free of the tunic skirt. Laughing still, he held Cuna aloft, yapping and growling.

Baradoc moved forward quickly, seeing the arrow points swing to follow him. He went up to the man who stood smiling still with amusement at the suspended Cuna.

Baradoc said, 'Put the dog down. He is young and bold and not yet fully broken to command.' Without thinking he spoke in his own tongue. The man, no smile on his face now, tossed Cuna to him. Baradoc fondled the dog's ears for a moment and then dropped him to the ground ordering him to go to Tia.

The man watched Cuna trot to Tia, eyed her briefly, and then turned to Baradoc and said quietly, 'You speak my language, but not with a Cymric sound. You dress like a Roman landowner's son, but your hands are marked with hard work and you have the gift of silent talk with your dogs. Tell the big hound to come to me in peace, but say it in words, words that only I know in my tribe, words that in all the tribes are only given to the few.'

From behind Baradoc the voice of Truvius came testily, angrily but bravely, 'What does he say? What does the ruffian want? By the gods — that I should be so old and feeble . . . ' He broke off suddenly in a fit of coughing.

Without turning Baradoc said in Truvius's tongue, 'These are hillmen from beyond the Sabrina. Their leader could be a man who prefers reason to force.' Then, turning briefly, seeing Tia holding Cuna, the old man bowed forward, head doddering, in his apple-wood seat, he spoke briefly to Lerg.

The great hound moved forward slowly, the sunlight sliding over his rough pelt. He went up to the man in the archway and sat back on his haunches. The man put down his hand and with the back of it gently touched the black wet nose of Lerg. Lerg sat unmoving. The man withdrew his hand and said to Baradoc, 'What did you say to the old man?'

'That you could be a man who prefers reason to force, a man who does not use the sword or spear without true cause.'

'You speak their language well?'

'Yes. I served a Roman master as a slave for years.'

'And still keep their company?'

'I did them a service. I go home to my own

people beyond the river Tamarus.'

'Aie . . . now I know the strange notes in your words although they are mine. There is more sea than mountain, more fish than fowl, more fog than snow. That you speak their tongue is good. You can speak for me and save the legs of old Machen who nurses a mead-skin downriver with the rest of my men.'

As the man was speaking Baradoc studied him. He was taller than most hillmen and he had a full handful of years more than himself. When he smiled there was no guile behind the eyes, but when he frowned there was force and authority in him. That he would not leave the villa empty-handed was inevitable, but if he, Baradoc, could hold him to fair speaking then Tia and Truvius might be spared any personal violence.

Baradoc said, 'I will speak for you.'

'Good. But first I would know who you are.'

'My name is Baradoc. I am the only son of my father, the son of great Ruachan, chief of the tribe of the enduring crow.' He pulled aside the shoulder of the light tunic he wore and exposed the tattoo of his tribe's bird. He went on, 'I return to my people to raise them and all our kind against the Saxons and . . . '

'Enough!' The man cut him short. 'Such

229

talk is everywhere among the tribes but it is no more than the empty chatter of house-safe sparrows as the hawk flies over. My business is of today — and here in this villa.'

Anger was so strong in Baradoc that he had to hold down the words he would have spoken. Prudence alone moved him, as he said, 'I have named myself. Who are you?'

'I am Cadrus of the Ocelos.' The man touched his right shoulder. 'I bear their mark here. We are from the hills beyond Gobannium, and Eurium. But this day we are from Abonae which my people hold after crossing the Sabrina.'

'You go to Aquae Sulis?'

'No. We are not enough.' He looked around the courtyard, smiled and said, 'We are content to take the straying goslings. The fat goose can wait until another time.'

Baradoc knew the joke had been made for him alone. The mark he carried on his shoulder was of the goose with the golden feet and bill, the Ocelos tattoo.

'And from here? What do you take?'

'All weapons, save yours. All treasure and money. And some of the household for slaves. All this without force unless force is offered. Go to the old man and tell him this, and then stay with him and the girl while my men do their work. Who is the girl, his daughter?'

'No, his dead brother's daughter. She came with me from beyond the Anderida forest. She lived with her brother and his wife. Their villa and homestead farm were burnt and pillaged by their own people . . . the ones who fearing the Saxon coming turn in madness on their own kind. The brother and his wife were killed. She escaped into the forest and I brought her here.'

Cadrus nodded, and said, 'Go tell the old man and then the three of you hold your place while my men do their work.'

Baradoc went back to Tia and Truvius. Cadrus began to give orders to his men. Four were left spaced around the courtyard, their bows held ready, while the others began to go through the house. Cadrus stood in the archway and as the house was sacked, the weapons and looted treasures were piled alongside him, gold and silver plate spilling on to the stones, small leather pouches of coins from Truvius's room, a casket of jewels . . . nothing of good value was overlooked down to the smallest bronze brooch, the tiny hand lamps of beaten copper — and amongst it all the silver chalice given by Asimus which had stood in Tia's bedroom.

Baradoc told Tia and Truvius what Cadrus intended. The old man heard him in silence until the end and then he raised his grey head and said, 'So it must be, for the man who holds the sword and the spear is master. What they take from us is nothing. The years have made me helpless, and the times have made victims of the innocent. All my servants are free people. Now they go to slavery in some wild hill fortress.'

Tia said firmly to Baradoc, 'The man is of your kind. He holds you in good faith. Go to him and ask him to spare the servants.'

Looking down at Tia as she sat on a stool at the old man's feet, Cuna resting against her leg, Baradoc said nothing. But the shadow of unease which had been with him from the moment that Cadrus had glanced towards Tia was now grown blacker in his mind. Truvius lived now in a dream of old age. The world about him had long lost meaning. His life lay in the past, his days now were a crawling serpent of slow hours that wreathed about him and found him impatient for the final sting. But Tia was at the beginning of her days. Cadrus's face had been unmoving as he had glanced at her, but his eyes had mirrored the quick stir of his emotions. The silver and gold and spilled treasures on the archway floor were bright with colour under the sun, but the westering evening sun also quickened the sheen of Tia's golden hair, the jay-blue depths of her eyes, the plum red curves of her lips and the smooth soft nut-brown warmth of her bare arms and legs, bold against the creamy fall of the wide-skirted tunic which she wore.

Baradoc said, 'This is no moment to ask for a favour which will not be granted. The hillmen have no bellies for field or farm work. Fighting and hunting is their work. A slave is a high prize, to be put to the plough or the cattle folds, or to be sold to the coast traders from Erin.' But the more he could have said he kept to himself for a woman slave who was fair in all men's eyes was a treasure not to be passed by. *Aie* . . . even in his own tribe it happened. Tia stirred angrily and began to speak. He broke in sharply and said, 'Stay here and say nothing. One wrong word could put Cadrus out of humour.' And then, as Tia looked up at him tight-lipped, he saw her face slowly change and he knew that she had read his thoughts.

From behind him Cadrus called sharply to the man who guarded the servants outside the reception room. Prodding them with the butt of his spear the man moved them down into the courtyard and across to Cadrus. They halted before him, the old steward and his plump wife who worked the kitchen, the strong middle-aged man who kept the bath house and stoked the hypocaust for water and

233

house heating, and a younger man who did general work about the villa and kept the small stable of two horses which drew the old man's four-wheeled carriage when he drove to Aquae Sulis or went to visit friends.

Cadrus raised a hand and beckoned Baradoc to him. He nodded at the group and said, 'I take the two younger men. They are full of years and work. The old man and the woman would not be worth the food they would eat. They can stay.'

Baradoc turned to the servants and told them Cadrus's decision. At once the steward and his wife moved quickly to join Truvius and Tia. Of the two men the elder stood passive, but for an instant the head of the other turned, sweeping round the courtyard, and he half moved as though to escape. The movement was halted by the sharp hiss of a flighted arrow loosed by one of the men near Cadrus. The arrow bit deeply into the ground at the man's feet, the long shaft vibrating savagely. From the men on guard around the courtyard and from the others who had now come from the building rose a roar of laughter. Only Cadrus was silent. He watched as his men, needing no signal from him, roped the hands of the servants behind their backs and then fastened heavy leather collars about their necks, each one joined to the other by a long length of strong, plaited hide rope. Cadrus watched all this done and not until they were led away through the archway towards the river did he turn to Baradoc.

He said, 'What is the girl's name?'

'Gratia.'

'You speak grudgingly. Tell her to go gather a warm cloak and strong sandals and any woman's things she needs. Tell her that in obedience she can walk free and unshackled but if she kicks like a young heifer and would escape from the path then she will be roped to the others for she now belongs to Cadrus.'

There was no surprise in Baradoc. No tribesman would have left her free. He had now long known in his heart that this moment was coming, had faced the dilemma and had known only one answer to make to it, an answer with the strength of tribal custom behind it, an answer with which all of his own race would keep faith, but an answer which Cadrus, his eyes trapped now by Tia's grace, might sweep aside with a single sharp word to bring a flight of arrows to destroy him. No matter to Cadrus that the breaking of tribal faith might some day turn the gods against him. Tia's beauty shining in his eyes had blinded him. As he paused now and faced Cadrus with a stony face, Baradoc knew that with a single lie he, too, could be forsaken by the gods and they might let Cadrus have his way without marking his future.

Baradoc said coldly, 'She cannot go with you. She is betrothed to me. Not even Cadrus of the Golden Goose can take the future wife of a man of the tribe of the enduring crow as a slave. The gods would mark your tribe forever with shame for the crime. Your women would be barren, your hunting grounds empty and your hilltops a waste land where not even the eagle or the fox would harbour She is promised to me, she stays with me.'

Without hurry, no movement of muscle in his face to betray emotion, his eyes steady, Cadrus raised his sword and held it out point forward so that the sharply honed tip just touched Baradoc's breast. He said evenly, 'Your tongue is swift in the battle of words and cunning. You are distantly of my blood and we share the same gods. If the feud fire had been lit between our tribes I would kill your father, slaughter your house and burn your huts and there would be no shame for you would do the same to mine. There is no feud, and you speak fair that I cannot take for slave a woman who has promised herself to you.' His hard face creased with a quick smile, and there was a touch of mockery in his voice as he went on, 'But it is in my mind that you speak falsely for her sake. I would know from her without any word from you whether you speak the truth. From this moment you stay dumb as the slow-worm. And, if she denies you, then I kill you as I would slaughter a young bull for the sacrifice!'

Without taking his eyes off Baradoc, the sword point always against the loose fall of his tunic, he called to one of his men, 'Fetch me Machen here for I need one who speaks the bastard tongue.'

From the outer side of the archway he was answered at once by a slow, lilting voice, touched with the edge of lazy laughter. 'Who sends for Machen when Machen is here fresh from mead sleep?'

A tall, thin middle-aged man, his face grizzled with long copper-coloured stubble, dressed in a rough habit of brown, its ragged skirts swinging as he walked, the loose cowl hanging down his back, came through the arch and stood alongside Cadrus.

With hardly a glance at Machen, Cadrus, sword never moving, pointed with his free hand to Tia and said, 'Tell the girl to come here. I would take her as slave, but this young bull of the tribe of the enduring crow denies me the right, saying that she is betrothed to him. She understands not our tongue but you will ask her the questions I give you in her own bastard language. If she denies the young bull, then he dies.'

'She knows you want her as slave?'

'No. They sit there knowing nothing — the ancient eagle of the legions and the sleek young falcon — and their world spins dying under them as yours spins when the mead takes you. You know their language and the gods have given you an ear for the music of song and the music of truth. If you tell me she says that he speaks the truth she can be no slave. If you hear the false note of a lie then she becomes my slave and this one dies.'

Baradoc felt the point of the sword prick him briefly as he finished speaking, and from the corner of his eyes he saw Machen move across the yard to Tia and Truvius.

Tia watched the man as he came to her. He moved slowly but easily and there was the ghost of a smile about his lips. Beside her sat Truvius, his hand in hers, mumbling to himself, staring straight ahead, his eyes blinking slowly with the fixed rhythm which marked his periods of withdrawal. Disaster had taken the villa. He had faced it for a while and now was lost to it, sheltered by the blind comfort of mindless senility.

In her own tongue Machen said gently,

'Leave the old man and come with me. Speak no word to your young tribesman friend.'

Tia rose. Of all that had gone on between Baradoc and Cadrus she had caught only a few of the words she had come to know of their language. They gave her no grasp of the trouble between them, except that her own instinct and her knowledge of the ways of tribal raiders told her that there was some argument about slaves and herself. She went with Machen across the yard and up to Cadrus. He looked at her boldly, his gaze moving over her from head to foot, and she saw his mouth tighten, his shoulders tauten as he drew sharp breath, and a sudden glitter fired his eyes. From her deep woman's instinct she knew at once that in some way she was a prize that Baradoc had disputed with him.

She stood at the foot of the semi-circular steps rising to the archway and Machen stood with her, translating for her the questions which Cadrus made in their own language, and all the time Cadrus spoke and then Machen translated, Cadrus kept his eyes on her.

Machen asked her, 'Cadrus would know how you met this young man?'

'In the forest of Anderida after my brother and sister were killed and I was making my way to Aquae Sulis ... ' There was a nervousness in her which she held down but not entirely could she keep its note from her voice as she described how she had cut Baradoc down and they had then journeyed together.

'For how long have you travelled?'

'A month or more.'

'Cadrus and our people have made this raid for weapons, treasure and slaves. He takes two of your good men and also he would take you.' Machen paused, expecting some quick response or outburst from her. Women spoke or cried out before thought or common-sense could govern emotion. This young woman said nothing. Her forehead slowly creased and her mouth tightened into a thin line. He waited and when she said nothing, he went on, 'This man of the tribe of the enduring crow disputes his right by tribal law. He says that you are betrothed to him. If this is so then you cannot be made slave. Speak truly — are you promised one to the other and one by the other?'

With the question, Tia, although she could not see him fully from where she stood and there was no sound or movement from him, knew the full reading of Baradoc's mind. It came to her now as it came from him to Lerg and the others, not words, not direct sense,

240

but wholly in a magic that by its force turned the body and the brain to paths of understanding. Yet she knew that, without this, she would have known, for to save her there had been nothing else Baradoc could do.

She said firmly, 'It has been a secret between us which I was to tell my uncle this night. Yes, we are betrothed.'

Machen turned to Cadrus and said, 'She says he speaks the truth. They are promised to one another.'

Without emotion Cadrus asked, 'Does she speak the truth, my Machen? Tell me and swear it by your faith, by the gods of the sacred oak groves, by the white purity of the tree-suckling mistletoe, and may your soul shrivel and there be no after-life for you if you swear me false.'

Machen without hesitation said, 'I swear that she speaks the truth which is in her.' But to himself, because the mead was still warm in him and there was a respect in him for the girl's bold and quick-witted response, he had no fear of imperilling his soul and his life hereafter. There were truths that grew between people which they could not know themselves until some sharp moment of destiny brought them to light. Even now the girl did not know the full truth in her, but one day she would.

Cadrus, his face suddenly softening to a smile, shrugged his shoulders and said, 'Oh, Machen of the mead-breathing mouth, may the gods rack you if you lie because of her gorse-bloom hair and pretty forget-me-not eyes.'

'I speak not falsely. There is no truth that lies so deep that my ferret-mind cannot unwarren it.'

Cadrus said, 'Ask her if she knows what it is to marry a tribesman. She comes of high Roman blood. She knows only one way of life. This — ' he waved his hand around the yard. 'It is in me that she has deceived you, good Machen.'

Machen turned to Tia and said, 'Cadrus doubts you. Aye, he even doubts the truth in me. Answer now his question.' He put to her the demand which Cadrus had made.

Tia, confidence growing in her, speaking as though some outside power and intelligence answered for her, replied, 'I would marry him because I love him and he loves me. I would go to his people and their hard life because this country which my uncle and my father and all their kin before them helped to create now falls apart in misery. My uncle will not live long. I am ready to follow my love to find a new people and a new life.'

She stood watching Machen and Cadrus as

they spoke together, no more than an odd word of their talk having any meaning for her, and she kept her eyes from Baradoc who stood wooden-faced with Cadrus's sword still at his breast. Then as Machen turned to her to speak again, she saw Cadrus lower the sword and slide it into the leather and wood scabbard that hung from his belt.

Machen, now smiling openly at her, said, 'Cadrus whose heart can be softened by a woman's ready wit as mine by good mead, salutes you. He accepts my word that you speak with a frank and true tongue. Now do as I say and he wishes. Go to the treasure which we take with us — ' he nodded towards the piled weapons and household loot which lay heaped on the top of the broad archway steps, ' — and choose any one thing you value and bring it back here to me. Go now.'

Tia walked across to the piled loot and looked down at it. What of all she possessed was of great value to her? What of all the life she had had until now was dear to her? Her family were all gone except Truvius and his days were few. These hillmen would go and the house would echo like a shell as she moved about it and the day would come when she would be alone in it. Baradoc would have gone to the west, and the lie she was living at the moment would have gained her only an empty freedom. Tears misted her eyes and almost without knowing it she bent and picked up the silver chalice and walked back to Machen. She gave it to him and he passed it to Cadrus.

Cadrus stepped up to her. He raised the chalice, touched his brow with it and then handed it to Tia. 'Tell her,' he said to Machen.

Machen, the dying sun threading his beard with copper glints, looked Tia deep in the eyes and said, 'There is a long skein of kinship between the Ocelos people of the mountains and the people of the enduring crow. Before the wedding kinsmen bring gifts. This is Cadrus's gift to you. If times were different we should stay and make feast after the marriage. Now we stay only to make the gift and to join the ceremony. I am a priest whose power and authority no tribe, not even in the far north or the west, not even over the sea with the Scotti or beyond the first of all the great walls with the Picts, can question. Take now the hand of this man of the enduring crow and go both of you to your uncle, and stand before him for his blessing so that I may join the hand of husband to wife.' Then with a quick flicker of laughter in his eyes, he added, 'This must be so because the good but still doubting Cadrus to know truth to be true would see it sanctified in deed.'

Cadrus turned to Baradoc and, his eyes now friendly, said, 'There is one in the mountains with such a fire in his belly as you have against the Saxons. In a few more years come to me and I will take you to him, but first you must grow to full manhood and have sons to follow you should you fall in battle. Go now — take your Roman filly, but think not that she will be easily schooled.'

Without a word Baradoc moved to Tia. And Tia, with a nervous shiver as though her body moved in the spell of a vivid dream, turned and took his hand. They went across the courtyard towards Truvius and the tribesmen with lowered bows and rested weapons watched them. Long evening shadows striped the paving and flower beds. The aviary birds took the last of the paling light on their enamelled wings, and the sound of the worker bees about the shrubs by the running spring water of the well made a heady droning. They walked, neither looking at the other, and behind them came the three dogs and from the end of the red-tiled roof Bran, his sable plumage lacquered with the sun's last glow, sat still and graven like a carved corbel. They stood before Truvius who sat, his head sunk on his chest in sleep, his old vine staff resting across his knees. Tia reached out a hand and touched him. Slowly he raised his head and blinked the weight of sleep from them, then smiled and said. 'What has happened? What is it my Tia?'

Tia, her hand in Baradoc's, said, 'We come to you, my dear uncle Truvius, for your blessing.'

The Flood Riders

Tia woke just before first light. As she lay in the darkness she heard Cuna whine gently from the foot of her bed. She spoke quietly to him and he was silent. About her the ravaged house was still and the memories of the previous day flooded through her mind, bright and dark pictures each stirring emotion. She saw the eyes of Cadrus on her as she had faced him. There was good and bad in the man. Her body shook with a spasm of remembered fear as she thought of the life which would have been hers had she had to follow him as a slave. Baradoc had saved her from that, but she could not guess at what cost to himself, to his pride and his deep sense of tribal customs. True, Machen — who for some hidden reasons of his own had taken her part — had guided and shielded her as she stood before Cadrus, and then had carried out the simple pledging ceremony in the courtyard, joining her hand with Baradoc's after Truvius had given them his blessing. Dear uncle Truvius . . . Sometimes she wondered whether there were not, as well as his true lapses into senility, also times when he pretended them either to cloak his own helplessness or from a deep wisdom which compensated for the vigour and mastery of his old days now long denied him. And Baradoc? By his quick thinking he had saved her, had stood by her while Machen joined them, his face giving no sign of any emotion he felt. Strange Baradoc . . . with his burning dream of the future. As he took her hand, he would have been already rejecting the picture of himself leading a Roman woman into the homecoming gathering of his people . . . their wild and noisy greetings turning to silence as they eyed her? Well, he need have no worry. He had saved her from slavery. She would not nor could not make any claim on him. When he got back to his people he could say that she had refused to follow him, refused to be a wife and one of his own holy men could with a few words break the tie that bound them.

Cuna whined again, louder. In the silence that followed Tia heard two sounds, the brief protesting *cark* of Bran from somewhere in the courtyard and the sharp note of metal momentarily striking against stone. Cuna whined again, a low muted note and swiftly there was an understanding clear and vividly all-embracing in Tia. Baradoc was going. Sword or fish spear had swung against the stone parapet of the courtyard well as Bran, from the ironwork canopy over it, his favourite nighttime roost; had hopped to his shoulder; and Cuna had whined because . . . poor Cuna, who had been pledged to her, sensed that the others moved away and longed to go with them.

Tia got out of bed, wrapped a cloak about her shoulders, and went barefooted from her room into the open corridor. Part of the yard lay washed in moonlight as pale as the underside of a willow leaf and the chestnut's shadow was dark as a thunder-cloud over the archway that led to the river. Baradoc, Bran on his shoulder, the two dogs at his side, dressed now in his rough clothes, the old sword at his side, his travelling bundle slung over his shoulder from the head of the fish spear, stood in the tree shadow at the foot of the archway steps. For a moment Tia was tempted to stay where she was, to stand and watch and let him go. The thought was in her that, if at any time since their marriage he had asked her whether she would have travelled with him, she could not have known what true answer to give. There was much between them, but nothing of lovers or man and woman. At her side Cuna whined and she knew that for Cuna's sake she could not let Baradoc go without a move from her.

She walked down the corridor, past the aviary where the bright birds were now, as they roosted, dark, strange-shaped fruit on the shrubs and twisting creepers, and out on to the uncovered terrace by the archway. Baradoc heard her, and was still as she came up to him. They stood in the tree shadow and their faces were stiff masks as though they wore them like the theatre players of some high drama.

Tia said quietly, 'So you go?'

'Yes.' Baradoc's voice was thick as if some inner anger half strangled it.

'At night and without farewell?'

'Because of what has been and the way it has been, yes. I come from a different world. There is no place in it for you even if we truly loved one another.'

'You would be ashamed to bring a Roman before your people as a wife?'

Baradoc was long in answering. Then he said, 'Be content, Lady Tia. What was done was to save you from Cadrus. Not to gain you for myself. When I reach my people the priest will set all aside.'

'You do not answer my question.'

'No, I would have no shame before them. Now, tease me with no more questions for you know that our paths no longer lie together. I take the ford across the river and

250

the mining road west to the hills.'

'Then you shall take Cuna with you. I give him back.'

Baradoc hesitated briefly and then, with a small shrug, he said, 'If you so wish.'

With an abruptness that surprised Tia, he turned sharply and moved through the archway, his bundle swaying on the spear, the dogs at his heels. She stood in the shadows, watching him, now in full moonlight, move down to the reed-fringed river and turn along the bank.

When he was gone from her sight she went back into her room and lay in the darkness, seeing him moving through the night, the dogs around him, and Bran on his shoulder. Although she was restless with the stir of many mixed emotions she told herself firmly that Baradoc was right. What had been done had been done to save her from Cadrus. There was nothing more between them. He had his world and she had hers . . . though the gods knew that hers was changing shape and meaning rapidly and she could see little of promise in it. With Truvius she belonged to the past.

When morning came, as she had done every day since she had arrived, she gathered flowers from the courtyard and went to Baradoc's room after the servant had cleaned it to refill the small earthenware jar on the table by the window. She knew that, until some new guest used the room, she would do so every day because this until then was Baradoc's room and much of him lingered there for her still.

As she arranged the flowers and stepped back to look at them she saw on the end of the table one of her uncle's flat ivory writing tablets, and she knew that Baradoc must have taken it from the reception room where her uncle kept it at hand to make notes of household affairs as they occurred to him, no longer able to trust his errant memory. She picked it up and held it under the light from the window. The smooth wax bed was stylus-scored with writing in her own language. She read the words and at first there was a confusion in her mind through which they slipped, almost avoiding capture. Then she read again. This time, although her eyes were slowly touched by tears, nothing of the message was lost to her.

I would have built for you a house with a
roof of green rushes and a flower-pied floor.
A thousand sea-birds would have greeted the
golden girl with a brow like a lily, the
young queen who rode the perilous paths
without harm or hurt.

252

And as she stood there Truvius, leaning on his staff, came into the room. She turned and ran to him and he put an arm around her and held her as she wept.

★　★　★

A spear's throw from the rough road Baradoc sat with his back against a rock, facing the west, eating a handful of dried grapes and a piece of hard cheese. The sun was shrouded in a low, rolling mantle of grey rain-promising clouds. There had been little morning movement on the mining road, a few carts making for Aquae Sulis with country produce, a handful of miners on their way back to the lead mines in the low limestone hills over which the clouds now were close-wreathed. The men had given him news of Abonae. The hillmen had taken it some days before and most of the people from the settlement had fled into the country to hide. Cadrus and his men would go back across the river in their hide-sheathed boats taking their spoils with them. There would be no putting the place to flames. Cadrus would leave it like a lean cow to fatten and calve again until it was time for another raid. Cadrus was not like his ancient forefathers senselessly sacking and plundering with no thought of the future.

There would come a day when Cadrus would cross the river and take Abonae to stay, and then move on to take Aquae Sulis and stay . . . all the Cymric tribes would do the same, moving eastwards until the day came when they would have to face the real enemy. One day someone would have to arise with the strength and power to command Cadrus and his kind, to shape and wield their courage and skills and make of them an army with a mission and a true faith. He broke the cheese into small portions and tossed a piece to each dog and Bran and he smiled to himself as he realized that to Cuna he had tossed the largest piece. The gifted dog. The twice gifted dog. Against his right hand he could capture still the bodily memory of Tia's hand in his as they had stood before Machen and had listened to his ritual words . . . Aie, one day if the gods sent the chance his way he would meet Cadrus again and he would —

The thought of Cadrus was driven from his mind as Cuna suddenly leapt to his feet, barked and began to run towards the road. Baradoc called sternly to him, but the dog took no notice. At the same time, although Lerg and Aesc held their place. Bran from the top of the rock against which Baradoc leaned, took off, dropped low, his great wings almost sweeping the seeding heads of the long grasses, and then rose, beating his way above the road. In those few moments a wild hope swept through Baradoc which shook his body as though a swift fever had gripped him, firing his blood. He jumped up and ran towards the road. Far down it he saw a low cloud of dust racing away like wind-flattened smoke. Clear to him came the sound of horse-hooves beating against the hard ground.

Standing by the road, watching her ride towards him, he knew that this was what he had wished for but had cherished only as an idle dream that defied all sense and reason. No matter the manner of their joining he had no claim on her. Only she was free to turn the ceremony of duress into the truth or denial of love. Now she came riding the single horse, which being free at grazing, Cadrus's men had overlooked, and he knew that even had he left the road earlier and moved without benefit of track or path to the hills she would have found him because, no longer to be denied, the heart had its own knowledge of human courses as the swallow went unerringly south in autumn to return to the same hut eave each spring.

With Cuna barking around the horse's legs she halted before him, her growing hair free and shining in the wind, her eyes smiling but uncertain with a soft shyness. Behind her a travelling bundle was packed across the horse's back and she was dressed as he was in her old travelling clothes. Going to her and looking up, he took her hand, feeling it now in truth as a little while before he had felt it in memory. With a touch as brief and light as the wing of a passing moth he kissed her palm, and the shyness went from Tia. Her lips, up-turned with a faint touch of mockery, she said, 'O, son of a chief Baradoc, who was too cowardly to speak the truth, but wrote it on wax in the night — is that how your love will be? Easily scribed and as easily wiped away?'

Baradoc raised her hand, touched his brow with it, and then kissing it again, said; 'No, Lady Tia. What I wrote on the tablet was the shadow of a dream which I thought would die at daybreak. Come down now from your mount.' He held her arm as she slipped off the horse and stood by him, and he went on, smiling, 'Now we both have our feet on the ground and live no dream.' He raised her hand and kissed it. 'This is the kiss of my true love and the true pledge that joins us. From this day, as there is only one royal sun, so there is only one queen in my life. Your honour is my honour and any who misnames it shall have only the swift charity of my sword.'

For a moment Tia said nothing. Then, the teasing in her eyes masking her joy, she said, 'O son of a chief Baradoc, your old master gave you a skill with words that snares my heart . . . Aye, and did so, I know now, from our first day together. But this day, I have ridden hard and far and without food. If you would not hear the belly of your love grumble then feed me.' She leant quickly forward and kissed him on the lips. Before he could hold her, she bent and picked Cuna from the ground and began to fondle him.

Baradoc led the horse to the rock and made Tia sit on the ground on the goats' hair cloak and he fed her from the small store he had brought from the villa with him. He fetched water in a skin from a nearby spring for her to drink and, when she had finished, he poured water over her hands that she could clean them. There were few words between them and when their eyes met it was as though a light passed between them too strong and too strange yet for them to endure its flame but briefly. Man and woman they would be but until that time came there lay ahead of them the groves of courtship to be threaded hand in hand, and a sweet and slow discovery of one another which would bring their love to full term.

They slept that night in a dry cave on the

lower slopes of the hills, lying so that in the darkness they could reach out and touch one another. Until sleep took them, it was mostly Baradoc who talked, both to ease his own shyness and joy and also to have her begin to know about the journey ahead and the life that waited for them with his people. He told, too, about these hills which they must cross, where now most of the mines were worked out or abandoned, and the great stretch of marsh-and-lake land that lay beyond which must be crossed before they would reach the coast where the barren moors ran down to the sea in steep headlands, and then of the long following of the shore line westwards which would at last bring them to the country of his own people, until finally he heard Tia's breath-note slow and her body stir briefly to find comfort as she fell into sleep. Then as he lay awake he thought of old Truvius who, Tia had told him, had sent her after him with his blessing, of Truvius who had once said to him as they talked in the courtyard together, 'All countries are greater than the people who take them by the sword. They shape conquerors to their ways and work in them a new love which is a mystery above any human love. I came with the legions from Etruria. I shall die here content to be of this land . . . ' And as with Truvius so it would be with Tia.

One day she would know herself to be not only his wife, but one of his people, and their children would be of his country.

★ ★ ★

The high summer rain fell steadily the whole of the next day. Because there was no hunting with success through the slow driving swathes of rain as they climbed the long scarp to the crest of the range, they turned aside to the road and found a small mining encampment of meagre huts and a rough tavern where they bought cheese and oat cake and dried fish, and six eggs for their evening meal. The tavern keeper told them that in the last weeks there had been few travellers coming or going through from the west because the marsh people would boat none across the lakes and swamps. He advised Baradoc to take the long route round to the south but Baradoc's mind was set on crossing the marshes for it would save them two or three days' travel and there was a growing eagerness in him now to reach his own people.

They crossed the top ridge of the hills in a grey shroud of rain-cloud and picked their way slowly down the steep westward face through rocky ravines and sides of loose stones where the horse, laden with their goods, had to be led and sometimes forced to keep the track. That night on the lower slopes they found a herder's hut, its wattle sides and bough-thatched roof half burnt away in some old accident or act of pillage. Baradoc cut fresh branches from a nearby thicket of alders and repaired enough of the roof to give them shelter. Even so, the rain drifted in upon them and they passed the night with more discomfort than sleep, but because they were together and their shyness was easing they made light of the hardship. Baradoc said, half in joke and half in earnest, 'You could be lying warm and comfortable and clean in your bed at the villa, Tia. Even now I would take you — '

With a suddenness that startled him, Tia suddenly reached out and put her hand across his mouth, stopping his words, and she said without anger but with a sharp note of command, 'Never talk like that again. I belong with you.'

As she withdrew her hand Baradoc took it and said, 'Then I never will. When you command I obey.' He chuckled. '*Aie* from that first moment after you had cut me down and I opened my eyes to see you I became your slave.'

Tia smiling, shook her head. 'You talk, and your tongue runs away with you, my brave heart. You will never be anyone's slave.'

When they awoke the next morning the rain was still falling, driving before a strong southerly wind in dark, swaying curtains. They ate a scanty cold breakfast of dried fish and were wet through to their skins before they had travelled half a mile. The western slopes of the limestone range eased and finally levelled out at the fringe of the great river-and-lagoon scored stretch of marshes that lay across their path. Skirting the first stretch of towering rushes and reed-mace growths they came across a well-used path. In places the path had been firmed and strengthened with faggots of cut withy branches and bound bundles of reeds. Frogs called from the dense growth on either side of the path, bearded tits and sedge warblers flew up in alarm before them and once a marsh harrier came drifting over on great, silent wings and cried harshly as it turned away from them. After a time the path brought them to an opening in the marsh growths and they stood on the edge of a small piece of cultivated ground, the tilled dark marsh soil green with lines of growing vegetables and lank rows of still unripe barley. Beyond the cultivated ground was a narrow lagoon inlet. Built on wooden piles a little way out in the water was a reed hut which was joined to the land by a rough wooden causeway. From raised poles along the causeway and at one side of the hut fish nets were strung. From the eaves of the roof hung plaited osier cages and coops in which fowls and pigeons were penned. Tame ducks and geese swam free about the hut piles, around which rising flood water from the rains swirled fiercely.

Baradoc halted at the edge of the cultivated ground and gave a loud shout. He shouted three times before any movement came from the hut. Then a short thickset man appeared and came to the head of the causeway.

Baradoc, giving the horse's halter to Tia to hold, walked forward slowly a few paces holding his hands above his head. The man on the causeway made no movement.

Baradoc drew the sword from his belt and thrust it upright into the ground and then walked forward further. At this the man came slowly down the causeway.

Baradoc watched him as he approached. In one hand he carried a light spear and his other hand rested on the haft of a long knife which was thrust into the belt at his waist. He was bearded and long-haired and dressed in a sleeveless tunic made of otter skins roughly thonged together, the garment worn and greasy and ripped in places. The man stepped off the causeway and walked to within a few paces of Baradoc. He stood in silence for a while eyeing him suspiciously The skin around his right eye was red and swollen. The rain ran off his bare arms and legs and the sour smell of his body came strongly to Baradoc. The man's gaze went from Baradoc to Tia with the horse and dogs standing at the fringe of the reeds.

He said gruffly. 'What do you want?'

The words were in Baradoc's tongue, but heavy with the marshmen's accent and surly with suspicion.

'We go to my tribe in the west. The people of the enduring crow. We have money and will pay for a passage across the marsh lands.'

'Who is the woman?'

'My wife.'

'The word has been given that none can cross the marshes.' He gestured to the south. 'You must go round. Besides I have nothing that would take your horse.'

Baradoc said, 'We want to cross quickly. To go round will take many days. The word was not given against your own kind. Marshmen have eaten in my father's hut many times. We have the same tongue, the same country.'

'Maybe. Show me your mark.'

Baradoc pulled his cloak and tunic aside and showed his tribal mark of the crow. 'We want to cross now. If this rain lasts another day not even you could take us against the floods.'

The man pursed his lips. 'What do you know of the marshes and the rains? Nothing. This is the rain of Latis who weeps for the return of her lover.' A smile briefly touched his dirty, weather-marked face. 'She could weep for a day or a week. No man can tell.'

Baradoc, who knew of the goddess of bogs and marshes, Latis, who was worshipped only by the marsh people, said, 'Then let us leave Latis to weep long if she must. You could have us on the other side by nightfall. Also — ' he paused, for he had seen the man's eyes stray more than once back to the horse which Tia held, ' — as well as paying you we would leave the horse. Two people with one horse travel no faster than a man alone.'

The man was silent for a moment and then, grinning, nodded his head, and said, 'Leave me the horse. I need no other payment.'

From that moment there was no trouble. The horse was handed over to the man, who told them his name was Odon. From his hut appeared his wife and son who was a sturdy boy, his face still smooth and untouched by any beard growth. At a word from Odon the boy dived off the edge of the causeway and swam across the lagoon inlet to the fringing reeds. He disappeared into them. In a short while, he reappeared poling a strong, light draughted boat made of overlapping hides stretched over a framework of willow poles. The inside had been roughly daubed with a mixture of marsh mud and chopped straw and sedges, all set hard by baking in the sun, and then given a coating of fish-glue whose rank smell still persisted.

Between them they loaded up the possessions which Baradoc and Tia carried and the dogs. Tia sat forward in the blunt bows, while Baradoc was in the middle of the boat and Odon stood in the stern to pole the craft. At his feet lay a broad-bladed wooden paddle which he would use in deeper and more open water.

At first the boy wanted to go with his father and he refused to leave the boat. After a few angry words between them Odon swung his pole menacingly and the boy jumped over the side and waded ashore, shouting defiantly at his father.

As Odon poled off he laughed and said to them, 'He's as wild as a wolf — but he's a good son. I had two others but they died of marsh fever.' He shook his head to free his hair and eyes of the rain which still fell, and went on to Baradoc, 'There's a baling pot near you. The boat is sound. But with this rain it gathers water. You'll need to use it.' He dipped the pole and they began to move down the narrow inlet.

For the next two hours Tia sat in the bows, the thick woollen cloak draped around her growing heavier and heavier with the rain which soaked into it. Now and again as Baradoc and Odon talked in their own language she could pick up a scrap or two of what Baradoc said, but Odon's words because of his accent escaped her altogether.

Sitting there she was, although wet and uncomfortable, surprised by the calmness and happiness of her feelings. She had no true idea of what lay ahead. This was no journey on which she could combat hardship by the thought of some haven like Aquae Sulis ahead. Now the future was almost unknown to her, but she had no dread or concern about it because her spirit was content with the calm knowledge that whatever happened now she and Baradoc were together, not as strangers held by chance, but as man and wife tied by love. The discoveries they had yet to make about each other held no fears either because in the end they had come together freely, neither disaster nor expediency forcing them.

She sat with the dogs at her feet as the boat slid down the inlet and, after a while, Bran who had been circling overhead dropped down and perched on the low prow of the boat. Odon, seeing the raven, said something to Baradoc who answered, but Tia could not understand what they said. Odon, now that the bargain had been made, seemed pleasant enough but there was something about the man which she did not like, something that had nothing to do with his dirty, unkempt appearance or the strange cast given to his face by the constantly twitching, diseased eye. Baradoc had told her that the marshmen had long grown apart from all the other tribes. Travellers who were ferried across the marshes by them, even though well-armed, always did so at their own risk. They were men more at home on the water than on the land, and were almost as much at ease in the marsh channels as the fish and wildfowl on which they lived. It was odd, she thought, that in this country — now her own country — which had long been civilized by her ancestors there should still be wildernesses like this which had rested unchanged and untouched by the legions. Nearly five hundred years of Roman rule had left places like this and the wild mountains from which Cadrus came much as they always had been. Beyond Isca and the mining hills which they had crossed no great military roads ran. Westward was an almost unknown land and it was westwards that she was now going. Just for a moment the thought of all the strangeness that lay before her touched her with a sudden stab of wonder at her own impulsiveness in accepting the challenge of the unknown which her love for Baradoc had provoked. Then, looking up, she found Baradoc's eyes on her. He smiled quickly, wrinkling his nose at her and a quick flush of warmth spread through her, making her oblivious of the pouring rain and her own discomfort.

Hour after hour they moved through the marshes, sometimes crossing wide stretches of lagoon, sometimes snaking through narrow channels that were overhung with high reeds and rushes, sometimes sliding out into stretches of river where the brown waters rolled and swirled so strongly with the rain flood that Odon had to fight his way with strong strokes of the paddle to ease the boat out of the main stream and into a side channel to keep his course. There were times too when Odon had to force the boat across lagoons thick and matted with weeds: water parsnip and tangles of water-lilies, and yellow spiked flags and white-starred clinging crow-foot, so thick that Odon sweated and grunted as he poled them along.

Tia grew used to the sudden up-flinging of

a fishing heron disturbed by their coming, to the quick fire-flash of kingfishers arrowing away from them, to the noisy alarm calls of mallard, teal and widgeon rising from their feeding grounds, churning the water to a creamy spume with their thrusting feet and beating wings, to the sudden shocks which she had had at first when the weird booming calls of bitterns rang through the rainy air. Now and again Baradoc pointed out to her an otter sliding through the water, or the white marked head of a water snake as it curved sinuously away from them, and, so often after a while that she became used to it, the fierce turmoil of the water's surface as shoals of small fish flung themselves into the air to escape the rush of some great hunting pike or perch. The rain came down steadily. Odon sweated at pole and paddle. Baradoc baled now almost without let. Bran sat huddled on the bow of the boat. Cuna shivered and whined, and Lerg and Aesc crouched without sound or movement watching Baradoc, withdrawn into some immemorial dream of their own which banished time and discomfort.

In the early afternoon they came to a wide weed-free lagoon. Near the shore stood a small group of huts built on poles over the water. From the causeways and platforms around the huts a group of marsh people watched them pass and Odon gave them a wild, ringing cry of greeting as they swept by. Sometime after this they entered a tract of swamp land where alders and willows crested the reeds of little islands and the shallow stream they followed closed until the rushes at times overhung the boat. The air was fetid with the bubbling marsh gases that broke from the water as Odon's pole disturbed the thick mud of the channel's bed.

After a while the stream began to broaden and eventually the boat slid out to a small lake into which a river ran from the south and emptied from the north end. Nearly half-way across this lake, short of the main river flow which coursed through it, a solitary hut stood on poles. It had no causeway because it was too far from the shore, but there was a wooden platform around it. Odon, taking the paddle, swung the boat towards the hut.

He said to Baradoc, 'The hut is empty. We rest for an hour and eat.' He looked up at the sky. 'Soon I think the rain will stop. By nightfall I can put you on a safe path to take you through the far side of the marshes.'

Odon edged the boat into the side of the hut platform, dropped his paddle and held on to the timber frame of the platform. He held the boat steady as Tia climbed out and the dogs jumped up with her. To Baradoc he said,

'You go up. There's a rope in the bows you can make fast. I do the same here.' Holding on with one hand he took a hide rope from under the seat on which he was sitting.

Baradoc climbed on to the platform, walked to the bows, and knelt to take the bow rope. As he did so, and before he could reach the rope, Odon dropped his rope and giving a strong push on the platform's edge sent the boat gliding away from the hut. As it drifted away he picked up the paddle and turned the boat back in the direction from which they had come. Over his shoulder he shouted, 'The word was given that none should cross. I would have taken you for you are a tribesman. But I take no woman who is not of the blood and who speaks only the foreign tongue.'

Turning his back on them he began to paddle strongly away. Baradoc and Tia, taken by surprise, stood and watched him. He was going and taking with him all they possessed, leaving them stranded in the middle of the lagoon. Then, angrily, Baradoc swore loudly, and the anger was at himself for his stupidity. The rain and the monotony of the journey had dulled his wits. For a moment his instinct was to dive in and swim after the boat, but he knew at once that Odon could easily outpace him. All their weapons and belongings were in the boat, except for the sword which he wore. Even if he got to the boat Odon had a spear . . .

Then, the dullness clearing from his mind, he turned to Tia, unbuckling his belt and beginning to strip, and said, 'Give me your dagger.'

'But Baradoc, you can't — '

'Give me your dagger!' he cried harshly as he stripped himself naked.

Tia handed him the dagger which she always carried. Baradoc took it and then turned towards Bran who had flown up on to the rush roof of the hut. He called loudly, 'Saheer! Aie! Saheer!'

Without another glance at Bran or Tia, the dagger between his teeth he dived into the water and began to swim as fast as he could after the boat.

From the platform Tia, her heart thumping, watched him and she saw that he would never catch Odon. The man, seeing him coming, was paddling hard for a reed channel at the northern end of the lake. No man swimming could ever overtake the boat. Then, harsh and seering through the rain, she heard the strong wing-beats of Bran. Bran came down through the wind-driven rain and flew low over the water after Baradoc. Tia heard Baradoc whistle to Bran as the bird hung at his side. The raven wheeled away from him and began to beat quickly towards the boat.

Standing on the hut platform, the dogs about her, alert and quivering as they watched, Tia saw Baradoc swimming as fast as he could through the dark waters, saw Odon paddling towards the reed channel, and Bran moving after the boat on strong wing-beats. The raven rose in the air behind the boat and then came down in a slow, heavy stoop at Odon, passing over the man's head, raking it with his talons and then swung back to hover and beat with talons and great beak at Odon's head and face.

Odon raised his paddle and swung at Bran. The bird slid away from him only to come back at the man, first from one angle and then from another, forcing him to twist and turn on his seat as he struck upwards with his paddle. Again and again Bran dived at Odon, baulking and side-slipping to avoid the paddle blows. Once as Odon slipped on his seat, Bran landed on his shoulders and drove rapid thrusts of his great black beak at the man's neck and face.

Odon screamed with sudden pain and Bran, hovering away from him called loudly *cark, cark*. As Bran came in again Odon dropped the paddle and picked up his light spear. He stood up in the boat, blood running from his face, and slewed and turned as Bran attacked him, but Bran now kept well clear of the quick spear thrusts, circling and diving and calling loudly all the while.

As Odon could no longer paddle, the boat lost way and drifted, and Baradoc rapidly began to overhaul it. He saw Odon glance round to mark his progress. When he neared the boat he circled away to the bows, well clear of any spear thrust that Odon might make, safe in the knowledge that Odon would not risk throwing it for a frenzy now had taken Bran who whirled and swooped at Odon. One unguarded opening given to Bran and the raven would strike for Odon's eyes. Baradoc caught the side of the boat and with a great thrust of his arm and shoulder muscles lifted himself over the side. The boat tipped as he rolled aboard and water swirled over the gunwale. He heard the hoarse bark of Bran and a sudden fierce cry of pain from Odon. As he scrambled to his knees Odon, with blood running down his neck where Bran had struck him, raised the spear and hurled it wildly at him. Baradoc threw up an arm to protect himself and the blade of the spear scored the length of his right forearm and flew past him into the water. Then Odon, to escape Bran as the bird came swooping at him, dived overboard and disappeared. Oblivious of his wound, Baradoc stood, dagger now in hand, and watched the brown waters while Bran circled slowly overhead. Odon he knew would swim like an otter. And Odon now without a weapon, he knew, would not return to attack. Suddenly Bran called and went downwind through the rain wreaths towards the distant fringe of reeds about the channel opening through which they had come into the lake. Odon's head and shoulders appeared above water, but as Bran dived at him he sank quickly below the surface and Baradoc knew that when he surfaced again it would be in the safety of the reeds. He called to Bran and the raven, after a slow circle over the waters of the mouth of the channel, beat back to him upwind and dropped to the bows of the boat. Baradoc went to the stern, picked up the paddle and began to work the boat back to the hut.

★　★　★

The wound in Baradoc's arm, though long, was not deep. Tia, tight-lipped, tore strips of cloth from an undershift which she had brought with her and bound it. They had unloaded their possessions from the boat which was now securely tied alongside the hut platform. Above them the rain beat steadily on the weathered and decrepit rush roof. The hut was empty except for an old pile of reeds laid out as a bed in one corner. Seeing Tia's anxious, drawn face Baradoc raised his free hand and touched her on the cheek. He said, 'Don't worry about Odon. He won't come back.'

Tia, knowing now more than she had done at the time how fearful she had been for Baradoc's safety when he had climbed into the boat, said, 'You could have been killed.'

'Left here without a boat we would both have died.' He smiled. 'We've got his boat, and that's no bad bargain for the horse — and we can find our way out in time.'

'Why didn't he keep his bargain? You are of the same blood.'

Baradoc hesitated. To tell her the truth, that it was because of her and her race, was impossible. The same prejudice would arise again in the future but this was no moment to bring it to light. He said lightly, 'The same blood, maybe — but his has become diluted with the fever water of the marshes. He was over greedy for a good bargain.' He looked up at the leaking roof, the sound of the rain beating on it mingling with the noise of the flood water rushing against the piles below them. He went on, 'Odon was wrong or lying

276

about Latis. She still weeps for her lover. I think we should stay here the night. In this rain and with darkness coming on we should be helpless. We can make an early start at daybreak. I'll see what food we've got.'

Tia shook her head. 'You do no woman's work. Sit and rest your arm. And while I do it you can tell me about Latis . . . ' Her voice trailed away. Impulsively she moved to Baradoc and pressed her face against his breast, holding him. She felt his arms move around her and slowly the comfort of his embrace eased the shaking in her own body and killed the fear she had known for him when she had seen him climb into the boat and Odon had flung the spear She raised her head to him and Baradoc touched her cheeks gently and then bent and kissed her on the lips.

They slept on the old bed of rushes that night, moving it below a sound piece of roof to escape the rain drips. While she lay in the darkness before sleeping Tia thought of the story of Latis which Baradoc had told her as they had sat eating and sharing their cold and short commons with the dogs and Bran. Beside her, his arms ready at hand, Baradoc slept. She drew close to him to find the warmth and comfort of his body to join with her own. Latis still wept . . . Latis who, sitting by the side of a river had seen a great silver-armoured salmon swimming in the waters below her and had fallen in love with it. To please her the gods had changed the salmon into a young warrior who had stepped from the waters into her arms. But each year in the winter the warrior lover moved back into the waters, became a salmon, and swam away to sea not to return until the next year's floods brought him again up-river to step silver-armoured into her arms. Latis who sits beside the drought-starved waters and weeps, flooding the rivers with her tears to bring her lover back from the sea, hastening to her up the spate-filled stream . . . thinking of this Tia smiled to herself as she lay warm and relaxed against Baradoc, remembering his words, 'Latis's memory is a pebble, smooth and round, taking no mark. She weeps in and out of season without knowing why until the great fish leaps the last fall and into the pool at her feet.'

Latis wept all that night and was weeping the next morning. When they looked out the flood waters had risen so much that the boat floated level with the hut platform and would soon be in the hut itself. A brown torrent, carrying drift and flood debris, swept through the lake and the fringing rushes stood now with only their flowering tips above water.

One look made two things obvious to Baradoc; they could not stay in the hut and in this flood there was no hope of finding a way across the miles of marsh they still had to cross. There was only one course open to them They must follow the river down to the sea and then make their way westwards inshore until they were clear of the marshlands.

They loaded the boat with their belongings. Baradoc pulled one of the framework timbers from the hut wall and with his sword and knife fashioned a rough second paddle so that they both could sit in the stern and handle the craft between them. With the animals sitting up forward and their belongings stowed amidships they went downstream on the summer spate-filled river, a rolling flood of creamy brown water running so high now that they could see far over the marsh stretches on either side. Great skeins of wildfowl wheeled in the sky above them, disturbed and made restless by the flood. Above them hung the birds of prey, the hawks, the sea eagles and the peregrines while like dark ghosts the harriers flew over the green tops of the almost submerged rushes. They had no need to use their paddles except to keep the boat on course. When Tia had got used to handling her paddle, Baradoc now and then left her to hold their course while he baled the rain water out of the boat. By mid-morning, the simple-minded Latis gave up weeping. The wind shifted round into the east and slowly the sky began to clear of the low, heavy clouds which had dominated it for so long.

The farther north they moved down the river, the larger it grew. At noon they came to a wide lagoon. To one side of it they saw a hut with the water well over its platform. They paddled out of the main stream and across to it. When there was no answer to Baradoc's shouts, they eased alongside the platform, tied up and Baradoc splashed along the flooded boards and into the hut. The marsh family who inhabited it had clearly left from fear of the rising waters. Such stores as they could not take with them were lodged high up under the roof or on the rough shelving either side of the door.

Baradoc found dried fish, a basket of wild duck eggs, a hard circular slab of bread, three smoked eels, a water skin half-full of thin, barley beer and a small wicker cage in which sat three miserable looking hens. He loaded them all into the boat and left payment for his takings with some of the money which Tia had brought with her. As he got back into the boat and they pushed off, Tia said, 'Look.

280

the flood must be going down.' She pointed to the wattled side of the hut where a dark, wet band showed a hand's breadth above the water.

Baradoc scooped some of the lagoon water into his hands, tasted it, and spat it out. 'No — the flood's still running high. The tide is going out. We must be nearing the mouth of the river. The water's salty here.'

By mid-afternoon they were running down the looping estuary of the river. Mud-flats were showing above the dropping tide and echelons of gulls and waders were beginning to work them. On either side of the estuary the marsh ground spread dense and high with reeds. To the westward, over this sea of moving greenery, they could just make out, like a brown mist in the distance, the hazy rise of the first low hills beyond the flatlands. A little while later they were free of the mudbanks and the bordering marshes, moving into the sea on the breast of the river waters that curved like a dark ribbon across the turquoise and jade waters of the sea, a ribbon that thinned and faded and frayed as the sea slowly took it and made it part of itself. When they were well clear of the land the tide, running hard, took them and swept them westwards.

Tia, stiff and tired with the labour of their

river ride, dropped her paddle and rubbed her sore hands. A handful of black-headed terns wheeled and dived around them. A seal surfaced briefly and watched them with lustrous eyes. The sun slipped free of the clouds, the slow roll of the waves ran musically under their keel and, now and then, threw silvery fans of spray back from their bow. Latis's mind had wandered from thoughts of her lover and she wept no more. Baradoc cut portions of the hard bread and smoked eel and handed them to Tia. As he did so he held one of her hands, raised it to his mouth and kissed the rough palm. Neither of them said anything. The sea birds wheeled and called above them and the sea was a run of coiling bright green and blue, its slow parading waves feathered and foam-laced as the steady wind caressed them.

The Fortress of Birds

That night they paddled ashore to a sandy beach walled by high dunes. Climbing the near dunes Baradoc saw that they were backed by a wilderness of marshes which stretched inland and away to the west. They pulled the light boat ashore, well above the high water mark, and tipping it on its side, propped it up with their two paddles to make themselves a shelter in whose lee they could sleep After some difficulty Baradoc made a fire, starting it with dried grasses from a mouse's nest which Cuna dug out of the dune side. They killed a hen and boiled it in a mixture of their thin, musty beer and some rainwater which Tia had baled from the bottom of the boat to fill their own water skin as they came down the river. The duck eggs from the hut they found were already hard-boiled so they cut them up into the cauldron to thicken the broth and added some mussels which Baradoc foraged from the low-water rocks. As soon as their meal was cooked Baradoc smothered the fire with sand for while they were in the marshlands he knew it was wise not to attract attention to themselves.

Even so, as they ran the boat into the water at first light the next morning and began to paddle away, four marshmen came over the dune tops and ran into the water after them, shouting and waving their spears. Seeing that they could not stop them, they went back to the beach and began to throw stones at them from their slings. For a while, until they moved out of range, the water around them was pocked with the splashes of the stones which came flying towards them humming viciously like hornets. They paddled well out and then turned along the coast pushed by the tide which had just ebbed and was running out strongly westwards. All that morning as they worked at their paddles they now and then saw small parties of men, women and children come over the dunes and down to the water's edge to watch them, all the men armed and from their manner hostile. Odon clearly had passed the word about them.

'But how could he do it so quickly?' Tia asked.

'They have signal fires and other ways. Some say they have trained birds like the pigeons they keep to carry messages, and some say they shout to one another across the marsh stretches, like the booming of bitterns and the word travels. I don't know. The marshmen have always lived apart and they have a magic which they never betray to outsiders. No matter that Odon betrayed us — we have taken his boat and that means more to him than his wife.'

With a smile Tia asked, 'And what in your tribe do you value higher than a wife?'

Baradoc smiled too. 'You know the answer for it is the same with Romans. Your honour and then my honour.'

They paddled all that morning while the tide ran. When the water finally slacked and began to turn they were clear of the low stretches of dunes and marshes and moving along a coast where now the cliffs began, rising higher with each mile they passed. The cliffs were topped with trees and green hanging valleys, some of which held a few huts and they could see the patchwork of small fields.

They turned in at low tide to a small beach, cliff-buttressed and with no sign of habitation, and they ate and filled their water skins from a small cascading stream that came down the rocks. It was here that they decided that as long as the weather, which had now set fair, lasted they would stay with the boat and work their way along the coast by water. Ashore the travelling would be hard because they were reaching that part of the coast where beyond the ever-steepening cliffs the land ran back in a high moorland plateau, full of bogs and running streams, and without roads, a place of desolation which travellers avoided by travelling far to the south. On the sand with a stick Baradoc drew a map for Tia showing the river which rose on the moor and ran south to the old legion fortress of Isca and then on to find the sea which separated Britain from Gaul. Then he outlined the other great moor which lay west of Isca where two other great rivers ran northwards rising not far from Nemetostatio, an abandoned legionary outpost, to join each other before meeting the sea in the great bay guarded on the west by the high promontory of Hercule beyond which the coast ran away sharply to the south-west towards his own homeland.

Watching him as he talked, the sunlight glinting on his new growing beard, marking the line of the fast healing cut on his bare arm, Tia was aware that it was almost as though she had never really looked at him before, that the Baradoc she had cut down from the tree and with whom she had travelled to Aquae Sulis had been more boy than man. But this Baradoc before her now suddenly seemed to have sprung across the threshold into manhood. This Baradoc was her husband. He was leading her into a strange land beyond the Tamarus river, to a life which would close around her and claim her for the rest of her years — and she was not only totally unprepared for it, but had hardly given it any serious thought in the happiness which had flooded her as she had galloped away from the Villa Etruria to join him. Searching to make some amends for this, to put her immaturity and unpreparedness to a proper test she said quickly, 'From this moment we speak only my tongue in the morning. The rest of the day we use yours. I should be a wife without honour if I go to your people and cannot talk to them freely. And each night before we sleep you will tell me about their history, their legends, and their beliefs and their gods. I would not shame you with my ignorance or my dumbness.'

Baradoc said nothing. No matter all they had gone through together, no matter that out of the forced nature of their betrothal had come the truth of their love for one another, there had been a curtain between them through which they could speak and see, but through which no warmth greater than the even glow of comradeship had passed. As though the curtain were tangible, he reached out now and pulled it aside. He put his arms around her and drew her to him, both of them half upright, kneeling on the soft ground. He kissed her and felt her lips move with his, felt her arms fold about him as his held her tight to him. And they held together so moulded to one another until Cuna suddenly barked and jumped up at them, and then they collapsed sideways on to the sand map. To Cuna's barking, as Baradoc looked down into the even depths of her blue eyes, Bran added his harsh hunting call and above him the gulls, disturbed by his black, wheeling shape, began to scream and wicker in a fierce chorus that came echoing back from the tall cliffs. From that moment there was no longer any Lady Tia and no longer any son of a chief Baradoc, nor any curtain between them.

The following days moved to a pattern which was brightened by settled fine weather, and the quiet swell and fall of the summer sea imposed on them something of its own easy rhythm. They moved with the tide when it began to ebb westwards whether it was day or night. They slept sometimes in daylight, sometimes under moonlight, sometimes on the warm sands, sometimes in the boat as it rocked under the stars. Tia began to learn Baradoc's language fast, and she lay often with her head against his shoulder as he told her about his people and their history, spoke their poems to her and taught her their songs.

One night they slept in the summer hut of a friendly old fisherman at the head of a small beach at the foot of a gorge through which tumbled and roared a swift moorland river. Behind the hut were wooden racks on which the old man hung his gutted and broached catches to dry. When autumn came he would take the dried fish loaded in the panniers of his pony over the moors, along the heather tracks to sell or barter to the people in the settlements in the valleys south of the moor. He was an old man who knew nothing of the world outside his fishing station and the small settlements he served. From him they bought hooks, gorges, lines and a small net so that they could do their own fishing, and when they left he gave them a great slab of heather honeycomb which they wrapped in dock leaves and kept cool in their cauldron.

Before they left the old man, nodding at their boat, said, 'The gods have been good to you with the weather. Not for many years have I known it so settled. But when you come to the mouth of the Two Rivers, even though the gods still smile, take to the land.' They left him and idled along the coast for many days, working the tides, or sometimes passing whole days sheltered on secure cliff-guarded beaches, wrapped in the laziness and bliss of the sun and their own happiness.

Then came a day when the high cliffs, their tops flaming now with purple heather bloom, dropped away and before them was the wide bay of the Two Rivers curving southwards in a great arc to the estuary mouth where the river waters moved over the bar in a welter of foam to fight the sea. Beyond the river mouth the land was shrouded in a heat haze, but Baradoc knew that somewhere close in the haze was hidden the great promontory of Hercule and suddenly there was in him a sharp urge to idle no more. He decided that they would cross the bay, abandon the boat, take to the shore, and follow the coast west-wards to his homeland. But as they crossed the bay, although they had the tide with them, they met the spew of the strong waters of the Two Rivers. Paddle as they might they were pushed farther and farther out to sea and the pearl-grey heat haze, thickening over the dis-tant shore, slowly began to roll in a cloaking mist over the water towards them.

Within an hour they were wrapped and lost in veils of heavy mist and the sea which had been kind for so long stirred and strength-ened and began to run in a long swinging swell, deep and powerful, carrying them up its dark slopes and then drawing them down into wide valleys of foam marbled water. Through the mist came now and then the cry of some solitary seabird and sometimes a glimpse of the black-winged, surface-hugging passage of shearwaters and shags.

The three dogs, hating this new movement of the sea, huddled together miserably in the bows. Bran, plumage bedewed with mist drops, sat bedraggled on their piled belongings amidships, Baradoc and Tia now having no sense of direction sat in the stern, the boat drifting and rising and falling. Within an hour Tia was violently seasick and Baradoc made her lie down on a couch of their spare clothes in the bottom of the boat. Although he spoke cheerfully to her, he was worried by this sudden turn in the weather. In the past days he had always been careful to hug the shore as closely as possible and only to journey when the tide was with them on its westerly course. Now, because of the mighty outpouring of the river waters, they were farther out to sea than they had ever been and in the mist he had no idea of the direction of the boat's drift. Worse still, he knew that in a couple of hours the tide would turn, and in a few more hours it would be dark. By morning they could have drifted far out to sea, maybe out of sight of land. The prospect was not a happy one, but he kept his anxieties to himself. So far they had seen no other ships but he knew at this time of the year that the foreign trading vessels from Erin and Cymru would be on their way west and south — about to clear the great toe of Britain around the promontory of Belerium to avoid the autumn storms, heading for Gaul, Iberia, and the Mediterranean. If they met one of them there was every chance that they could be taken up as slaves. Silently he put up a prayer to the gods that the mist would clear soon . . . but the gods gave no answer, except for Latis. As the mist darkened with the coming of night she began to weep again and her tears were almost as fine as the mist, thickening it and wrapping it about them in a damp, clinging cloak.

By the time full darkness was with them Tia had recovered, but she had no desire for food and Baradoc would not eat by himself. They fed the dogs and Bran and put down water for them in the frying skillet. Then the two of them sat in the stern, their cloaks drawn over them, pressed close together for warmth, the darkness now so thick that although they could hear the occasional stir of the dogs forward they could not see them.

★ ★ ★

Tia slept, leaning against Baradoc, his right arm about her. She dreamt that she was back in her brother's home and riding with him as he made his morning rounds, seeing the oxen drawing their ploughs across the long strips of lynchet fields, hearing the laughter from a shearing party as men clipped the early summer coats from the sheep, riding through the beech woods on the down tops where the swineherd watched his beasts rooting through the dead leaves for the last of the past year's mast, and looking forward to the moment when they would turn down the long home combe to the beach where they would strip and take their swim. Coming back through the fishing village they would buy fresh lobsters and crabs, carrying them across their saddle fronts, alive and moving in their straw-plaited skeps. And as they turned from the beach they would rein in and watch the fishing boats, riding high on the combers, come in from their early morning netting with crowds of gulls and terns wheeling and calling noisily above them . . . In her dream the screams of the gulls rose until she was slowly drawn from sleep to find that the noise had followed her. For a moment or two she had no idea what had happened or where she was. Then slowly memory and the present came back to her.

She stirred stiffly and sat upright. The darkness of night had gone, but the mist was still with them. She could see the dogs sitting in the bows, their coats dewed with the fine rain which still fell. But the sea no longer rose and fell in the swinging motion which had made her sick. It lay around the boat flat and calm. Not far from them came the screaming and calling of unseen seabirds.

Baradoc, seeing her awake, said, 'Take your paddle. The gulls are crying from cliffs, I think. A little while ago the sea calmed as though we had come into the shelter of land.'

They dipped their paddles and began to move the boat towards the sound of the crying gulls. After a few moments a rock, fringed with waving seaweed, appeared close on their right. They paddled on and suddenly Aesc rose from the bows, shook her coat and began to bark.

Tia said, 'Aesc smells land.'

Almost before she had finished speaking the bows of the boat grated gently on shingle and the mist ahead of them darkened, then swirled apart and briefly they had a glimpse of grey rocks footed with a small stretch of pebble beach. Baradoc went to the bow, slid overboard up to his waist and then began to drag the boat forward. Lerg and Aesc jumped over and swam to the beach and disappeared into the mist. Baradoc let them go. If there was any danger close at hand they would soon give warning.

Tia, as the boat slewed sideways to the beach, jumped over. Between them they drew the boat up on to the beach clear of the water.

As they walked across the narrow scallop of beach Lerg and Aesc came to them out of the mist. The morning light was strengthening quickly and the air, which had been still and heavy, was slowly touched with the breath of an awakening breeze which began to shred away the veils of mist. They saw that the small beach was flanked closely by rocks on either side and backed by the steep broken rise of a cliff.

Baradoc said, 'The mist is lifting fast. We'll make the boat safe and then find out where we are.'

They took all their possessions out of the boat to lighten it, carried them above the high water mark of sea-wrack and drift wood, and put them safely on a wide shelf of cliff rock. Then they pulled the boat well above the tide mark and to make it safe Baradoc tied the long bow rope to a heavy boulder. As the mist about them slowly thinned they ate and drank some water. Then, wearing his sword and carrying his spear, Baradoc sent the dogs ahead and they followed them up a narrow, over-grown track which zig-zagged and curled up the cliff through screes of loose shale and shillet and patches of scrub and low wind-shaped thorns. Sea thrift padded the rocks and patches of brown seed-headed foxgloves, willow herb and gorse filled the small gulleys and gentler slopes. Before long they were above the last, dying trails of mist and out into the strong sunlight. The cliff line ran far to the north-east and the rocks were covered with colonies of seabirds, the air full of their cries. Here and there on the higher slopes they could make out the movement of grazing goats and sheep. To the south-west the cliff line, much shorter, ran sheer for a while and then dropped sharply to the sea, ending in a small island joined to it by a line of rocks which the dropping tide was now uncovering.

Without a word to Tia, Baradoc turned and began to climb higher and after a while they came through a narrow, twisting valley to the top of the cliffs. Before them stretched a wide run of grass and heatherland rising gently to the north. Just below the skyline stood a group of round, stone-walled huts roofed with weather-browned turves. Baradoc dropped to the ground and pulled Tia down with him, his eyes never leaving the huts.

Tia said, 'What is it? Do you know where we are?'

'Yes, I think so. We're on the island of Caer Sibli — the fortress of birds. Only a handful of people live here and they don't welcome strangers. Look — ' he turned and pointed southwards where the haze over the sea had cleared ' — that's the main coastline over there.'

Tia saw, away across the growing sun sparkle on the sea, a faint hazy line of shadow against the lower sky. Then looking back at the huts she said, 'I don't see any smoke from cooking fires or any sign of life. We're short of food and we come in peace. Why should they harm us?'

'Because they are the Lundi people.'

'Lundi?'

'That is their name for their tribal bird. The birds you saw on the cliffs as we climbed, the ones with solemn faces and painted beaks that others call puffins.'

'But why should we fear them?'

'Because nobody ever knows what is in their minds. The sea-raiders and the trading captains know this island. They land and rob them and take those who do not hide in the cliff caves for slaves. Sometimes, too, when there is famine on the mainland the tribesmen come out in their boats and steal their sheep and goats and take their maidens. Once there were many of them. But over the years they have become only a handful. Maybe their huts are empty now because they are at the far pastures with their cattle. Wherever they are we would risk too much by meeting them.'

Baradoc rose, took her hand, and began to lead the way down to the beach where they had left their boat. Tia went with him without question, her legs aching from the long climb to the island top. The sea and the cliffs below them were alive with the movement of birds, puffins and guillemots, cormorants and gannets moving in restless colonies on the rocks or fishing the waters. Above them, soaring and preying, hung sea eagles, ospreys, great black-backed gulls, kites and peregrines and ravens. She had never seen so many birds at one time. Half-way down when they stopped to rest Baradoc said, 'The tide is running out and the wind is in our favour. We can cross to the mainland by nightfall. The little food we have will serve us.'

He was happy, as he moved on, for if the gods were good to them, a handful of days would see them back with his people. The thought of return, as it always did now, made him picture the scene. He would come down the valley to the great rocks, to the place of his people, to the stone and timber-framed houses, past the hillside plots, to the noise of shouting children and barking dogs whose strangers' greeting would be muted as he and Tia walked into the stone-paved, walled meeting place overlooking the sea, with the wind blowing the drying nets and the boats drawn safely up from the long strand, and he would stand with his hand in Tia's and the other holding his sword and he would call aloud for Inbar . . . *Aie,* even before he called for his own mother if she still lived, he would call for his cousin and before he entered his dead father's house or took meat again with his own people he would settle the score which had to be settled.

Walking behind Baradoc, her clothes dry on her now from the strong sun, Tia watched Cuna snap at a butterfly that crossed the track before him and thought of the Lundi people who lived on this island whose hard life had taught them that there was danger in greeting any stranger. She smiled fondly to herself as the memory came back jewel-bright to her of Baradoc talking his day-dreams to her one evening as they lay close together on warm sand, his dream . . . maybe his only dream . . . of a Britain proud and free of all Saxons, where one day any man might walk its length and breadth unarmed and unafraid . . . Baradoc the dreamer of peace — but also the warrior husband, the man she loved, whose sharp spear tines shone from the whetstone and whose sword never lacked its bright edge.

So they came down together, jumping the sea-smoothed beach boulders, on to the tiny crescent of sandy shingle, growing now as the tide ran out — and both of them were suddenly robbed of all movement.

Their boat was no longer on the beach. The large stone to which the bow rope had been tied lay in its place, and from it the shingle and sand were scored with the broad mark where the craft had been dragged down to the sea, pulled by the stern for there were no footprints showing. Tia looked out over the waters. There was no sign of the boat, only the winging and diving movement of the myriad sea birds and the long, lazy rhythm of waves breaking over the rocks and washing up on to the shore, seething and hissing softly.

Without word or cry they ran together to the mooring stone and then walked, as though in a dream, down the scored mark to the water and stared out at the diamond glitter of the sea. Then, with an anguished cry, Tia turned and ran back up the beach to the rock ledge where they had left all their possessions. None of them had been taken. They rested, piled on the ledge, just as they had put them there.

'Why take the boat and leave these,' cried Tia angrily.

Baradoc said nothing, but he stepped closer to the rock face below the ledge. On its flat face writing had been freshly scratched with the sharp edge of a piece of shillet.

Baradoc said, 'Read the writing. The answer is there if you can understand it.' Then the passion of frustration in him burst and he struck the rock with his fist and cried out bitterly, 'What have I done that the gods make sport of me like this?'

On the rock face was written in Tia's own language:

Cronus in the dream spoke thus
Name him for all men and all time
His glory an everlasting flower
He throws no seed

Tia turned slowly to Baradoc, a frown marking her suntanned brow. 'What does it mean?'

'Ask the gods!' he said angrily.

'Who is Cronus?'

'He, too, is a god, but not one of ours. From my old master I know about him. He was the god of all Time, the god of the Golden Age and the father of Zeus.'

'Why should someone steal our boat and then write that?'

Stifling his rage, Baradoc said, 'How can I tell you? But it is said that many of the people who live here, because of their close breeding, are strange in the head.'

'To take our boat and leave our belongings they must be mad. What are we going to do?'

Baradoc, catching the trembling note of anxiety in her voice, put his arm around her and said calmly, 'Accept what the gods have sent and face it. The boat must be hidden somewhere around the island shores. But we can't go looking for it without being seen by the islanders. So there is no choice left us but to go to them.'

'But they're dangerous, you said.'

'So they are. But if they had meant us harm they would have waited in ambush for us here and killed us and taken our boat and our possessions.' He pointed to the rock ledge. 'Look, the boat is stolen but the bow and the arrows in their quiver are left. That is either a sign of madness or a sign of peace.' He tightened the buckle of his sword belt, handed Tia his spear and picked up the bow and the arrow quiver, and said, 'I leave you with Lerg and if anyone — '

'Baradoc!' Tia interrupted him, her face taut, 'You leave me nowhere! Where you go I go. Until we read the truth of this mystery my place is by your side.'

Baradoc hesitated. Then seeing the firm set of her mouth, the stubborn tilt of her chin and the light of defiance in her eyes, he shrugged his shoulders and said smiling, 'What kind of wife have I taken that she overrules my words? The women of the enduring crow are meek and lower their eyes when their men speak.'

Tia said, 'So they should when the time is right. But that time is not now, though — ' she grinned ' — the gods know I will take no pleasure in climbing that cliff track again.'

She turned from him and began to make into a bundle such food as they had left. As she picked up the almost empty water skin Baradoc said, 'There will be no need for that. There will be water on the high heath land.' He turned and looked at the writing on the rock again. The words had been scribed by someone who knew the Roman tongue well. No wild Lundi islander could have written them. Maybe marooned on the island was some priest or learned hermit, his brains addled with the fancies that solitude had brought him.

★　★　★

That day, their first on the island, was a strange one. The mist long gone now, the sky bright and clear with a warm breeze blowing from the south, the sea a maze of serpentine currents below them, the air pierced with the cries of the seabirds, they climbed the cliff track. Near the island top where a small stream ran down a narrow valley they stopped and drank at a pool overhung with ferns, the rocks padded with vivid green moss.

When they reached the plateau they hid for a while and watched the nearest group of huts. They saw no sign of life. Before moving Baradoc sent Lerg on ahead to the huts. He looped away across the rough grasses, lost now and then in the tall patches of bracken, and they saw him move around the huts and disappear into one of them. After a while Lerg came out and sat on his haunches in the doorway.

Baradoc and Tia went forward with the two other dogs, while Bran circled in low flight above. There were four huts and they were all deserted. Their walls were made of piled stones, the roofs of driftwood poles — for there were few trees on the island — were thatched over with layers of heath bundles and turves. For protection against the strong sea winds the thatch was held by a network of twisted heath ropes from which hung large stones. All the low doorways faced south-east to cheat the fierce westerly winds that swept the island top in the autumn and winter gales. Outside each hut was a pile of old limpet and mussel shells, fish and animal bones and other cooking debris. Each hut had a stone hearth in the centre, long cold now and the ashes blown about the floor. Above the hearths was an opening in the roof to take away the smoke. Each hut, too, had a raised platform away from the door which served for bed, and three of these still held piles of sewn seal skins and rough woollen coverings. And each hut looked as though the owners had suddenly, in the midst of their normal life, just walked out and left everything. Earthenware pots still held stale, dust-filmed water; skillets and cauldrons stood by the cold hearths, some with dried and rotten fish and porridge in them; a string of coloured clay beads lay on the floor by one of the beds and from the walls hung fishing lines and nets. In niches were set scallop shell holders full of congealed seal oil with rush tapers for lighting. The floors were covered with soft, dark peat earth which still held the footprints of the people who had lived there.

Beyond the huts was a large granite-walled enclosure for cattle penning, the gateway of driftwood and latticed rushes broken and lying on the ground. In a sheltered corner of the outside wall stood two wind-crabbed and twisted damson trees on which the fruit was slowly turning colour.

All that day while the light lasted Baradoc and Tia explored the island, moving always with the three dogs well out ahead of them and Bran — disturbed by the myriad bird life — was soon lost to his own devices, but came winging back to them from time to time calling hoarsely. The island was almost four miles long and in its widest part towards the southern end a mile broad. It ran narrowing to the north like a roughly shaped flint dagger, the cliffs on the westerly side so steep and sheer that Tia drew back with fear as she looked down at the breaking waters and the white stippling of seabirds on the rocks and coasting above the sea. On the easterly side the land was gentler, sloping through bracken combes and small hanging valleys to much lower cliffs.

It was in one of these combes towards the tip of the island that they came upon another group of huts, lying below the crest of the plateau, the doorways looking out to sea and to a great rock outcrop far below where a colony of gannets roosted. All the huts were deserted, but here the insides showed signs of violence. Some of the roofs had been burned, the cooking vessels about the hearths were smashed, bed platforms broken and the nets and fishing gear strewn on the floor. Grain storage pots lay broken and cracked and corn and flour lay yellow and mouldy over the trodden peat. Behind the huts a walled field held crop strips, long neglected, the pods on the rows of beans now black and split, the barley in full ear smothered with poppies and weeds and thrusting bracken growths.

On the seaward side of the field, in a small marshy hollow from which a stream ran thinly, a great rock outcrop thrust up from the short turf before the fall of the true cliffs, and here Baradoc and Tia found some of the islanders.

They were all men, and there were eight of them, and they lay as they had fallen in battle with their backs to the craggy face of the rock pinnacle. Sun and weather had worked on their raggedly clothed bodies, and rats and foxes and seabirds had picked their bones clean. All their weapons had gone except for a broken spear, a sword snapped short almost to the hilt, and two round padded bucklers, skin-faced over wooden frames, their centres crowned with wide bronze bosses. One of them had been split almost to its centre by some weapon stroke, and in the bleached skull of the skeleton alongside it was wedged the iron head of an axe with the wooden handle broken off short below the socket. Bracken and yellow rag-wort had grown up around the men, mildew had spread over their rough tunics and the rain and sun had stiffened board-hard their cloak skins. They lay there in the sunshine, the bees working the new bells of the heath blossom, butterflies zig-zagging across the gorse and brooms at the rock foot, and the meadow pipits and larks calling from the streamside and sky above them.

Without a word Tia and Baradoc turned away from the scene of violence. They knew what must have happened . . . Tia seeing it all in her imagination, though she would have wished to close her inner eyes on the sight: the long keels of sea-raiders or traders who would barter and sell human or any other goods ghosting into the island by night, the sudden assault maybe at first light when all the men, women and children would be in or close to their huts . . . and here, this handful of men who had found time to snatch their weapons and make their stand, choosing death to the slavery which would await them in far places.

Suddenly Baradoc said vehemently, 'What kind of thing is man that he does this to other men? What kind of gods watch over this land that they delight in such savagery and the slavery and slaughter of the innocent? To kill in a true cause is a just thing. To kill and enslave for a handful of gold is an evil, a poison which must be stamped out as a man brings the sharp of his heel down on the head of the adder in the path before him.'

Listening to him Tia felt her body strung with a cold tremor of pity for the women and children of the island huts. In her memory was suddenly the vision of Cadrus's face as she had stood before him and his eyes had gone over her, the look searing her as though it had been a fierce flame. She felt Baradoc's arm move around her shoulders and he began to lead her away.

★   ★   ★

They passed that night in one of the huts at the southern end of the island. The three dogs kept watch outside and Baradoc lay on the sleeping platform with Tia, awake and with his weapons close to him. Tia slept and sometimes talked in her sleep and Baradoc guessed that she was haunted by dreams of the men who lay, bleach-boned and fleshless under the tall rock. Every little while he went out and joined the dogs. The night was clear and the great stars of Orion's belt blazed in the heavens. To the north a curlew called and occasionally an owl came drifting like a lost spirit over the land. Southwards, hidden in the darkness, lay the mainland. Anger stirred in him as he thought that in a handful of days they would have been back with his people . . . and now, until they found their boat, they were trapped on the island. Tomorrow, although he would make a closer search around the whole shore line, his common-sense told him that there were a hundred places among the tall cliffs and rugged bays and inlets where the boat could be hidden without much hope of discovery. Maybe, too, whoever had taken it had set it adrift and it was now miles away. But — and his anger and frustration flared in him at the thought — *somebody* had taken it and, unless that person had left the island in the boat, he was here to be found. That thought, because all anger seeks a firm hold, filled his mind with a desire to find the person and, mad or sane, to face him with the bitterness that ran so strongly in him. He wanted to be back with his people, to present his wife to them, to take his place with them, to deal with Inbar, his cousin, and to be free to take up the true cause which stayed ever with him, like an always open wound when he thought of the

Saxons and of the night they had circled his master and hewn him down, shouting and jeering and laughing in their drunken sport.

But the gods, as he slowly came to acknowledge as the days that followed slipped from the coil of time, were against him. By himself he searched the island, climbed down the sheer cliffs, risking life and limbs, swam across inlets and gullies that boiled with surging, foaming waters to explore caves and clefts, and lay sometimes motionless for hours on a commanding rock point watching for some betraying sign of human life, until with the passing days the fire of his impatience died.

They settled in the largest of the huts and furnished it with their own possessions and pickings from the other huts. They lacked neither for shelter, food nor water. There were fish to be netted or hooked from the rocks, and wild on the island roamed the animals of the islanders, sheep, goats and pig. After a few days a handful of the islanders' fowls made their way back to them to scavenge their scraps and stayed to lay eggs for them. Now and again Baradoc, stalking with his bow, shot a seal basking on the rocks and they had its flesh to eat, its pelt to repair clothing and its blubber to render down to oil for the lamp sconces in the hut's wall niches. There was peat to be cut and driftwood to collect for their hearth fire and as the year waned they took the islanders' abandoned short-handled sickles and cut the weed-choked grain crops, and they collected the hard beans from the rows of blackened pods and Tia ground them on a stone quern to add to their flour when they made bread or to thicken their fish and seal broth. As autumn came in they found a small valley where blackberry bushes grew and feasted on the fruit and pulped some with the meagre crop of damsons and stored it in earthenware jars to sweeten their bread in the days to come. Salt they scraped from the dried hollows of the sea rocks where storm pools had long evaporated.

While the good weather lasted they both kept their eyes alert for any sign of ship or passing craft and often looked longingly at the distant mainland, and wherever they were along the island coast they searched always for some sign of their boat or of the stranger who had taken it. They wore little clothing, swam together from the rocks and hid from each other the core of longing they held to escape from the island, and only Baradoc ever went into the combe above the gannets' rock where the dead island men lay.

Against the coming of winter they laid up in one of the other huts a store of cut peat turves, dried strips of goat and sheep flesh, smoked fish and the small harvest of grain they had garnered. Baradoc repaired their hut thatch and twisted new ropes to hold more stones so that when the first gale did sweep over the island the hut stood firm and secure.

It was after this gale that Baradoc, hunting with his bow at the northern end of the island, had his first glimpse of the stranger. Lying in the bracken watching a herd of goats, waiting for them to crop closer so that he could take one, he saw them suddenly scatter and move quickly away. Distantly over the skyline close to a sheer cliff drop a brown clad figure appeared and stood looking out to the western sea approaches.

Aesc raised her muzzle as the scent of the stranger came downwind and from the throat of Lerg at Baradoc's side came a low rumble. He gave the dogs the word and they went upwind fast and steadily. Baradoc held his place, knowing that once they reached the stranger they would hold him until he arrived.

The two dogs raced across the plateau to take the stranger from either flank. Whether the man — for he was clearly such — was aware of their coming or not Baradoc could not tell. As the dogs closed silently on the man Baradoc rose and began to run after them. But before he was within two bow shots of the man, he saw him drop quickly below the skyline.

When he reached the dogs there was no sign of the stranger. The land dipped away into a small bowl that stood at the head of a great landslide of rocks that ended in a cliff face that dropped sheer and unbroken by path or by any ledge or shelf wider than would give scant roosting or breeding place for sea-birds.

Far, far below, the long westerly swells of the dying storm rolled and thundered against the cliff foot, sending great spouts and fountains of grey water creaming into the air. Yet more surprising than the sudden vanishing of the stranger who could have had no escape route it seemed than over the cliff was the behaviour of the dogs. They stood a few paces apart where they had come to a halt to hold the man and when Baradoc commanded them to the search they ignored him. Aesc, the wind ruffling her long coat, gave a tired yawn, then sat and began to scratch her flank with a rear foot, and Lerg, under Baradoc's angry gaze, lowered his head and avoided his master's eyes. For the first time since he had trained them they were refusing to obey his command . . . a high wave of anger swept through him and he would have shouted at them, berating them, but he checked himself. Some power greater than his own held sway over them. There was no fault in them which merited his anger.

He left them and searched about the bowl and the cliffside, but could trace no way by which the stranger might have escaped him. In the end he gave up the search. As he walked away the two dogs turned and followed him. When he found the flock of goats he sent the dogs in to cut one out and they obeyed him. Back with Tia, not wishing to worry her, he said nothing of having seen the stranger.

Two mornings later Tia, rising early while Baradoc slept, went out to collect eggs from the hens. On the threshold of the hut she found an earthenware crock, a looped thong handle about its neck, full of goat's milk and by its side wrapped in broad dock leaves a large piece of goat's cheese.

The Island Parting

When Tia told Baradoc about the milk and cheese, he said, 'It must be a gift from the stranger. Some days ago I saw him, but he slipped from me by casting a spell over the dogs.'

After Tia had got the full story from him, she said, 'Although he may have taken our boat and destroyed or hidden it, I can't think he means us any harm. Why leave such a gift otherwise?'

Baradoc shrugged his shoulders impatiently. 'What you say is true. But he has stopped us from reaching my people. Even if we had the boat it would be dangerous now to put to sea. At this time of the year a single cloud in the sky which would be the pride of a summer's morning grows to a storm before hot broth can cool. With a good wind and a good tide and a fair sea it is all of a day's hard paddling to reach the mainland. By myself I would take the risk, but in winter I would never put you in such peril.'

For a moment or two Tia was silent, looking down at him where he sat on the edge of the bed platform pulling on a pair of rough goatskin sandals he had made and binding the broad thongs about his sun-browned calves. For her he had made soft sealskin sandals on which with his own hands — for when he needed he could work as fine and surely as any woman — he had sewn a beaded outline of the enduring crow, the bird of his tribe, now the bird of her tribe, and a bird which haunted the island's cliffs in pairs, their jet wings flashing in sun and rain, the scarlet of their legs brighter than rowan berries. The sun glinted on his tawny beard which she had close cropped for him with her finely honed single-edged dagger. As he looked up at her, his dark eyes warm and as lustrous as bloom-free damson fruits, she knew that she loved him and could love no other. And knew, too, that he loved her as he could love no other woman, but that a greater love which she made no claim to rival lived with him — his love of his country, his passion to see it free and to bring all men to the peace of a just and honourable life. She moved to him, put down a hand and lightly touched him on the cheek and then softly ran her finger across his rough, weather-cracked lips, and said, 'You would not only put me in peril, my brave heart.'

Baradoc tugging at a thong, raised his head to her, kissed her finger, and asked, 'Who else?'

'You do not know?'

'All I know is that this spell-weaving stranger acts out some madness which, with so much waiting to be done elsewhere, holds us here till spring comes. *Aie* . . . we are well set enough with food and drink and shelter, but time passes without true action and golden hours are lost forever.' He struck his hand irritably against his head and went on, 'In here I have already schemed the way and the means. We begin small, smaller than a mustard seed, but the growth will come. First, with my own people, and then gathering a good company of men of reason and courage from other tribes, we must train and learn to love discipline as did your people's armies. We shall need men with the grain of your old uncle Truvius as he was in his prime and — '

Amused, well used to this kind of outpouring, Tia suddenly pressed her hand across his mouth. Holding it there, she said, 'Crow man — cease your clifftop croaking and listen. Maybe this stranger acts out some madness. But in my mind it is more a wise magic, far beyond that which you hold over Lerg and Aesc. Milk we have not had for many weeks. And for long now there has been in me a craving for milk, aye, and cheese. Does that mean nothing to you, that a

318

woman should have such cravings?' She took her hand away, and laughing said, 'Now you look moon-faced at me, empty-eyed and empty-headed like some simple wit sitting on the Forum steps understanding nothing but that the sun shines and he is warm. Did your great master teach you nothing about women and their terms? Did you think that lying on warm beaches at night after the marsh crossings, happy in one another's arms to escape the cold before dawn there would not follow one day the slow flight of the white stork?'

Baradoc frowned at her. 'Now you talk in riddles.'

Tia shook her head and reaching down held his tawny hair, gently tugging at it. 'You, whose eyes are like a hawk's and can mark the stir of the far grasses as a vole makes passage foraging, it seems are blind when you look at me. Do I have to grow as round-bellied as a full moon before — '

'By the gods!' Baradoc leapt suddenly to his feet and grasped her shoulders. 'You're with child!'

Smiling teasingly at him, but trembling with her own happiness which she had had to contain until there was only certainty in her, Tia said mockingly, 'My lord Baradoc, my brave heart, I have never met anyone so quick at understanding. Yes, I am carrying your child and have done for these last few months.'

Baradoc drew her to him and, holding her, smothering her face against his shoulder, hugged her. Then he kissed her and stood back, looking at her, his face creased with joy, and said, 'It will be a boy, won't it? It must be a man child, to grow to arms and courage and honour and — ' He broke off abruptly, shame-faced, and took her hands gently in his. Then, his voice low and shaking, he went on, 'Tia, my Tia . . . boy or girl, it matters not for there can be no shadow of difference in my love for either, and no shadow ever over the love which binds you to me and me to you.'

'That I know. But I know, too, and you need have no shame in it, that you would if it were possible bribe the gods with ambrosia, nectar and high sacrifices to grant that our first-born be a son.'

Shaking his head, Baradoc put his hand about her cheeks, and said, 'You tease me and for my slowness you are right to do so. But you are wrong. I go now to make a sacrifice to the gods, but I shall ask them for one thing only — that when the day comes they keep you safe for you are the bright bird of my life.'

From that moment there was a fire and an

impatience in Baradoc which made even the shortening days of winter seem long. To ease the itch in him for action as the old year rolled slowly towards the new, he set about building a boat which would carry them to the mainland when the spring came. He took drift wood and poles from some of the huts and slowly thonged them together with hide strips to make the framework of the hull. All this he did on a slope above the beach where they had originally landed, well out of reach of the highest tide or winter gale. He worked sometimes from first to last light, and the hours he had to lose to hunting for their pot he grudged. Most of the seals had moved away from the island now that the breeding and rearing seasons were gone, but he killed them whenever he could and scraped and cleaned the skins until, with other skins which he foraged from the bed platforms of the abandoned huts, he had enough to fashion an outer and an inner skin about the framework of the boat.

There were times at night as he sat in their hut lashing the skins together with thin strips of hide and sinew when Tia would rise and deliberately blow out the sconce lights and scold him to bed. There were nights, too, when he woke in the darkness and thought about the child which Tia carried and saw them returning to his people. Yet more often he lay working out some problem in his boat building. He had no pine pitch or clay to caulk it. Between the inner and outer skin, he decided, he would pad the space with a mash of chopped up reeds and rushes to be gathered from the bog patches in the middle of the island, working into the cut rushes pig fat and seal blubber rendered down in a cauldron over a fire. The mess would harden after being laid on and should make the boat water-tight enough to take them to the distant coast. Not a day passed, except in the fiercest gales when to step outside the hut into the shrieking wind and rains was to be buffeted to the ground or on those days when the island was wrapped in a windless sheet of thick mist that made the climb down to the boat too dangerous a task, that he did not labour at the boat with knife or axe or a small broken saw which he had found in one of the huts.

While he worked his mind flighted to the future. The child would be a son, the gods must grant him that. The task that lay ahead when he finally returned to his tribe would be more than the years of one man could achieve. He would gather and train the tribes of the west, they would in the end come to his way of thinking and acknowledge him, call him Pendragon, swear faith and follow him, the dragon head leader. In full time the years or death in battle would finally take him, but not without the comfort of knowing that a son stood at his side ready to step into the leadership and go forward with the fight.

As Tia grew bigger with her child, he made her keep close to their hut and he took from her all the work he could. He grew even harder and leaner of body, but his spirit flamed bright and steady, and Tia, knowing and understanding the passion in him, made no complaint. She loved him, knew his love for her, and knew the truth of him that under the warrior he would be lay also the poet and dreamer. There were few mornings when she woke to find him gone in the dark to catch the first light by the time he reached the boat that she did not find scratched with a stick on the smoothed out peat and earth floor some message from him. On a rainy morning he wrote, *The day weeps its sorrow for the summer suns that are gone, but in my heart like a wren in its moss bower my love for mother and child is warmth of a hundred suns.* And on a morning of rare frost which white-laced the grasses and dead bracken, she read, *Three things that are wondrous fair — winter silver on the spider's web, the moon's broken gold on the moving waters, and the smile which is a rose on the lips of my sleeping love.*

There were times after the turn of the year when Baradoc sensed often that he was being watched as he worked on the boat. Whenever the feeling struck him he would see, too, that the dogs had marked the scent of another, but they would stand near him and make no move of their own or at his command. Although he searched the cliff sides and the rocks he could see no one, but he knew that the one who watched must be the stranger who still occasionally left small gifts outside the hut, a stranger who clearly meant them no harm and who — although he must have taken their original boat — showed no concern that he should be making another for one morning he had left outside the hut a sharp-pointed stout thonging needle for which Baradoc was grateful because he had been sewing his skins together by making a hole in them with the point of Tia's dagger and threading the thongs through by hand. But no sight of the man did Baradoc ever see, though sometimes on moonlit nights, unable to sleep, he would wander the cliff tops and northern plateau land, bow in hand, to shoot wild pig or goat or to pick off from a grazing flock one of the grey geese which had come to the island to winter. Knowing, too, that the man must eat and would have fire for warmth and cooking, his eyes were always alert for the signs of smoke along the cliff tops and rock pinnacles but he never saw any.

Sometimes, lying warm under their skins, holding Tia in his arms before they slept, he talked about the man and once Tia, who needed no words from him now to read his mind, said, 'Since he means no harm and by his gifts shows kindness why do you worry about him?'

'Because I don't like mysteries. I have seen a man walk to the edge of a cliff five hundred feet high and disappear over it where none but a seabird could know safety. He takes our boat ... *Aie*, and I'm sure cast it adrift to keep us here. Yet now he does nothing to stop me building my boat. Even helps me with the gift of the needle. Is he mad or is there purpose in this?'

'I don't know.' Tia stirred in the darkness to ease her burdened body. 'Maybe he's someone like Brother Asimus. A priest or dreamer, someone perhaps who has been shown the future. Asimus had a dream and waited for us to come. Maybe this man had a dream too. From his writing on the rock it would seem so. The gods use such men.' She gave a little chuckle. 'It is no good you saying you don't like mysteries. The gods won't change their ways for you. If Asimus had said that his god had sent him a dream to say that one day all that you dream and long for would come true — well, you wouldn't question it. You'd have no bile against mysteries then, would you?'

Baradoc was silent for a moment and then said, 'Why would I? I would understand it. But the riddle written on the rock, and a man who walks out into space over a cliff . . . well, such things tease me even in my sleep. Like someone tickling my nose with a straw, not waking me but breaking the peace of my rest. If I were not so busy with the boat and the hunting I would find him and speak boldly with him because the child you carry would have been born amongst my people, and there would have been women to serve you when the time came.'

'I would have liked that, yes. But I am not frightened. You are here. That is all the comfort I need. Birth is a natural thing, a tide which takes a woman so that she needs do no more than drift with it. Now sleep.'

She lay in the darkness when he was asleep, listening to the sough of the wind over the thatch and the singing notes it made through the ropes from which the great stones hung. She felt Cuna jump slyly in the darkness to the foot of the platform and curl against her leg and there was suddenly a bright picture in her mind of the child — boy or girl, no matter which, though she prayed always for a son out of duty to Baradoc — a child tumbling and playing with the dogs, their child. Would it have her eyes and Baradoc's hair? Then, feeling the child move within her, she put her hand to it and drifted into sleep.

★ ★ ★

In the end it was the stranger who revealed himself to Baradoc. The year had long turned and spring was moving and awakening. The migrating birds were flocking back from the south and Tia made Baradoc take down the old bird-catching nets left by the islanders for there was sorrow in her with each small bird that got caught in the narrow meshes. Some days now the wind blew gently from the south and the air was so clear that the mainland shone as in a crystal, and the smoke of distant settlement fires rose like dark threads against the dunnock egg blue of the pale sky. The seabirds were nesting, and the boat-work was finished except for the making of two paddles, and there was a fire of impatience in Baradoc to haul the boat to the water so that he could lay the flat stone ballast in it to settle its trim.

One morning as he sat in the sun outside the hut shaping the last of the paddles from a length of rough plank, the flotsam from some ship's wreck, Tia came to the doorway, her long hair caught back with a piece of braided wool, a loose robe, leaving her arms bare, sweeping almost to her feet, and said the wish was in her to eat fresh eggs. During the winter of their few hens three had died, two had been killed by a fox, and the last had been taken by a golden eagle which had coursed it across the cattle fold, made kill and was away before the dogs could reach it.

Baradoc absorbed said, 'I'll get some gulls' eggs when I go down to the boat.'

Tia, her chin set stubbornly, reached down and took the paddle board from him. 'I want eggs now, my brave heart. A dish of beaten eggs and herbs. The desire is with me and with the babe.' She smiled, putting her hand to her front, 'He kicks from the need and greed for eggs. And we want not gulls' eggs but the eggs of the lapwings on the north land heath.'

'But I have work to — '

Throwing the board from her, Tia cut him short, 'You have no work that will not wait. We need eggs. If we do not get them the babe will kick me to death.' She eyed him teasingly for a few moments, and then went on slyly,

'He kicks as only a man child could kick. Would you have me tell him some day that the first time he asked his father a favour it was denied him?'

Baradoc sighed, stood up, put his hands on her shoulders and kissed the tip of her nose. 'Lady Tia, I am your servant. Should you ask the eggs of a phoenix I would find them for you.' Then looking across the bright waters to the mainland and the distant shoulder of Hercule's promontory, he went on, 'If the weather holds, then we shall soon be across. You have enough time to run yet to see us with my people and the babe born where he should be born.'

'The child will be born where he is born — and that is in the hands of the gods. Now fetch the eggs.'

Baradoc went north with the dogs to the downland where the lapwings flew, their cries sharp and wailing as they circled and tumbled close above his head, their broad wings cutting the air with a hissing and searing sound like water steaming and spitting from red hot stones. But before he could find any of the nesting hollows Lerg growled and Aesc gave a sharp warning bark.

A bowshot away Baradoc saw the stranger, and saw him more clearly than he had ever done before. The man stood on a hummock beyond a shallow, marshy depression which held a broad pool whose waters flowed in a stream to cascade thinly over the nearby western cliffs. He wore a long brown coarsely woven habit, its hood lying back over his shoulders, while about his waist was wound a thick rope girdle.

Forgetting his quest for eggs, without giving any command to the dogs, Baradoc began to hurry forward. The dogs went with him. The man turned and walked from him and, without a glance backward, his pace kept measure with Baradoc's so that the distance between them remained the same. Something told Baradoc that this was no pursuit, that the man had decided that he no longer wished to avoid him.

The man moved across the downland towards the edge of the western cliffs and passed out of sight over a rocky rise in the ground. Baradoc following, crested the rise in the ground and hurried down its far slope along a goat path he had often used. Old bracken growths with the first green of the new crosier heads breaking the earth covered the slope and amongst them lay a scattering of large weather-and-lichen marked boulders. There was no sign of the man, but to the left of the path Baradoc saw at once a large flat rock which was tilted at one end towards the sky. Since his memory held now a familiarity with this place and many others on the island, he knew that the rock had never so pointed skyward before.

He ran to it and saw that the rock, working on a natural pivot against other rocks buried in the ground, had been swung upwards at one end and downwards at the other to make a pent over an opening in the ground, a cavity with a stony floor away from which, through a boulder-framed archway, ran a tunnel almost the height of a man.

Baradoc lowered himself into the hole and looked through the stone archway. Light seeped through it. Leaving the dogs at the top of the hole Baradoc began to move down the tunnel which after a few paces grew in height so that he could stand with ease. He moved forward, hand on the hilt of his sword, through a light which grew stronger and stronger. From ahead there came to him the growing sound of the call of seabirds and the low thunder of waves breaking at the foot of the cliffs. The tunnel ended with a down-flight of wide steps.

Baradoc stood at the top of them looking down in amazement. Below him was a wide rock-vaulted chamber, lit by sunlight that came through a great fissure in the rocks on the far side. On one side of the fissure hung a long heavy curtain of skins, thong-looped to a pole along which it could be pulled to close the entrance. The floor of the cavern was strewn with dried bracken and rushes and a wall embrasure held a bed close to which stood a rough table flanked by a long wooden form. Around the walls rock ledges and ships' timbers formed shelves and cupboards. To one side a turfed-damped fire smoked feebly on its hearth. Near the curtained opening a goat, her udder milk full, was stalled in a pen made of rough drift-wood timber. Standing by the pen, one hand scratching the head of the goat, was the stranger.

Before Baradoc could take in more, the stranger moved across to the foot of the flight of steps and looked up at him. He was of no great height, but stoutly and strongly built and, Baradoc guessed, had seen twice the years he had. Jet black hair hung to his neck and he wore a close-cropped beard. His eyes were friendly and had the wet brown shine of closed sea-anemones.

Baradoc, his anger against this man stirring anew, said, 'Who are you who stole my boat? And why at last have you brought me here when at other times you disappear like a wild goat over the cliffs, or watch hidden and cast spells over my dogs so that they take no heed of my commands?'

The man smiled and the whole of his face

was briefly wrinkled and lined like the skin of a hoarded russet apple.

'I give no name in answer to a question. But the questions not asked are answered. Between these two lies the virtue of patience. One sees the fire and the smoke at a distance but the warmth is not felt until the hearth is reached. But since questions stir always in your mind like angry wasps and there is an impatience of desire in you like the unending breaking of sea waves against a rock, I give you some ease of the mysteries.'

'You talk in riddles.'

The man nodded affably and began to unloop from his waist the thickly plaited girdle until he held in his hands a long length of stout rope. He walked to the rock cleft overlooking the sea, saying, 'Come and see a mystery answered.'

Baradoc crossed the cavern and standing at his side looked out. For a moment he half-drew back to kill a sudden stab of vertigo. The cliff face fell sheer to the sea hundreds of feet below where the long swell thundered and crashed at its foot, the waters, foam and current marked, heaving and moiling were alive with the swimming and diving seabirds and over-traced with the flying lines of others as they passed between their feeding grounds and the roosts and new season's nesting places.

The man said, 'A rope is no mystery. You double it, put the loose loop over a cliff-top rock and then move down it to swing like a spider at the end of its thread and enter. Then you pull on one end of the rope. The whole comes to you — and the mystery is dead.' Smiling, his eyes mischievous, he turned and put out his hand towards the hearth. 'I breathe the fire to full life at darkness. Only the eye of the night owl could see the shadow of smoke against the sky and the stars. Learn, then, that a question is answered not by speaking it for another to answer, but by seeking the truth of it in yourself.'

Momentarily Baradoc, though the man was being friendly enough, felt higher anger spark in him at the manner of the man's approach to him, as though he were some pestering child intruding on the time and talk of his betters with idle questions.

He said brusquely, 'I am no child to be teased with idle riddles, nor plagued first with the theft of my boat and then puzzled by your gifts and spells. You chide me without cause.'

To his surprise the man said, 'Why should I not chide you gently as a father to an over-eager son? I speak for your own good because I have read the runes and dreamt the dreams.'

'Forget the runes and dreams. You took our boat. Why?'

'Because it was written so. Listen — for many years I lived here with the islanders. When they were killed or taken by the sea-raiders I alone escaped for the gods in my flight led me to this cave, and here at night they speak to me. But I am no islander. My feet have trod many countries from Asia to Gaul and Erin. But this is my country and there is no part a mystery to me from Vectis to the far north to the lands of the Cornovii and the Carnonacae, to the far Orcades and Ultima Thule. I have read the papyrus rolls of Londinium, Lutetia and the Great Empire City. I have talked with devils and demons and magicians and sorcerers and taken no harm but much wisdom. And in sleep and in full eye-wake the gods have shown me the past and the future, and I have learnt that while the past is a jewel fixed forever in its setting the future is a river which the gods have set in its course but which time and man's works can loose from its bed to new courses. The gods have dreamt it, but man with his waking dream of power, conquest and greed mars all.' He paused and the red gleam of his lips showed through his beard as he smiled ruefully. 'Keep faith with the true dream. Mis-shape it not by impatience and greed for false glory. One day men will call you Pendragon as many before have been called. But the true king comes to meet glory and betrayal and then to sleep until all lands groan with the labour and distress of chaos and he comes again and the true march of the centuries begins anew . . . ' He broke off and moved slowly to one of the cupboards on the cavern wall.

Listening to him Baradoc knew that for all his quiet speech, his sober, even manner, that the man was mad; not mad with any violence of talk or manner, but mad with the innocence of one touched with the disease of the gods, one for whom the air was full of voices and for whom the shape of solid things, a bush, a rock, a tall pine, a running stag, wavered always as though seen through water and became the fabric and fancies of a phantom world.

He said stubbornly, 'You set our boat adrift.'

'I did. But now you have built another.' The man spoke without turning as he opened the cupboard door. 'But if you would leave this island safely with your woman and child, put it not to the water until the first red-gorged swallow comes winging north, and until that time comes say nothing to your wife of our meeting.' As he finished speaking the man turned and came back towards Baradoc. In his hands he held a shallow basket made from woven heath stalks and lined with a soft bed of moss. Resting in it were eight mottled lapwing's eggs and a slab of soft, creamy goat's cheese set about with a thin garland of snowdrop blossoms, the white petals flushed with faint green like new grass breaking through melting snow. He gave the basket to Baradoc and said, 'Take these to your wife. And remember, the war steed, which is the heart of man, smells the coming battle and stamps for the charge, but the warrior, which is the wisdom of man, must check the reins and draw the curb until the horn is sounded high and clear. Now return to your woman and wait for the first swallow to come hawking and winging over the cliffs of Hercule.'

★ ★ ★

Baradoc said nothing to Tia of his meeting with the stranger. This, not so much because of the man's injunction, but because as the child grew in Tia she had moods that flighted from periods of high gaiety and laughter over small things to times when she sat silent, touched with some hidden anxiety which she would deny if he questioned her. He guessed that at such moments her thoughts were on the day of labour and birth to come, when from wife she would become mother. Often that anxiety was turned towards him, making her reluctant to have him leave her to hunt or to put the finishing touches to the boat. To tell her of the stranger and of the nonsense he had talked would only give her food for brooding. When he gave her the gift basket, he said that he had found it nearby on the wall of the cattle fold.

'But how could he have known I wanted plovers' eggs?'

'He didn't. There was only the cheese in it. The eggs were the ones I collected.' It was the first time he had ever lied to her, but though he did it for her sake there was an unease in him for the rest of that day.

On the day he finished the shaping of the last paddle, the fine weather withdrew. For three days a gale blew from the northeast with a wind so strong that the spindrift from the waves breaking over the rocks sheeted across the high island top in swirling veils of salt mist and spume. Unable to make a trial of his boat and settle the ballast stones, unable to hunt, Baradoc sat around the hut full of impatience. He wanted the child, which they both had decided had a full month yet to reach its time, to be born amongst his people. The warning of the stranger that he should not try yet to make the crossing he had quickly put from his mind. Although some birds were already in passage, it would be weeks before the first swallows came skimming across the sea. Once let the weather settle and they would make the crossing. Since he would then be in country he knew and with people who were friendly and near to his own tribe in faith and kinship he would take loan of a quiet mare and Tia could ride in comfort.

After a few days the gale wore itself out as the sun went down. When Tia woke in the morning and sat up on the bed platform sunlight was streaming through the open door and Baradoc was away. She smiled to herself, knowing exactly where he would have gone. His impatience to try the boat had been like an itch covering his whole body while the gale had blown. She rubbed the sleep from her eyes and stretched her arms. As she did so the child kicked hard within her and a swift pain shot through her stomach of a kind she had not known before. She put her hands on her swollen flesh and spoke aloud to the babe so that Cuna, who never left her now, turned his head and looked at her. She slipped off the platform, threw off her bed gown, and went to the wooden tripod holding their shallow washing bowl. Baradoc had long ago made the tripod for her and before he had left he had roused the fire and put the cauldron on it full of water for her washing. As she bent to fondle Cuna's ears she saw that Baradoc had scratched a message for her on the peaty floor. It read:

The gods raise the door-latch of night
To let the silver morning in
Sleep veils the brook-lime blue of your eyes
The gay bird of love in my heart begins
    to sing
Returning, I will lay a chaplet of purple
    vetch about your hair
And, kneeling, call you queen.

She smiled to herself, but even as her love for him stirred her she relished the wifely pleasure of knowing that in the reading of his lines she could read also through his love the small guilt behind the offering. She liked him near her these days but the pull of his boat was strong. Stripping to bathe herself, the sunlight through the door gilding her brown body, the fine down of her arms and legs trapping its brilliance in a soft golden mist, she said to Cuna, 'Our master Baradoc weaves a net of fine words to hold us content while the gay bird of love in his heart sings of

340

his dreams.' The child kicked hard in her again and she leant forward to ease the quick pain that flared in her loins.

On the beach Baradoc placed lengths of trimmed tree trunks he had beach-combed along the shores to make rollers over which he could run the heavy boat down from the sloping bluff on which it had been built and across the shingle to the water. Stripped to a loin cloth he hauled the boat down, watched by Lerg and Aesc, while the seabirds wheeled and called about the little cove and a colony of painted-faced puffins watched him, shuffling and nodding. The sea was gentle with the last of the dying swell from the storm, and for the first time that year the sun was almost summer-fierce on his body.

He slid the boat into the water and holding it by the bow rope let it float free. It swung gently on the swell, riding high but listing to one side. He pulled it half out of the water and packed stones in it to trim it even. Three times he pushed it out, and then pulled it back to make the balance just. Finally it floated on a level trim and with enough freeboard to take himself and Tia safely out to sea. But before he could risk that he knew that he must prove its caulking sound. They could not safely leave the island in a leaking boat. He climbed into the craft and taking up a paddle began to work along the shore. A bowshot to the south was the small island promontory that sheltered the cove from the westerly winds. As he moved the dogs followed him along the rocks. The boat answered true to the paddle and a surge of pleasure filled him as he thought of the long days of work he had spent on it, and, now, here was the reward of his labour and determination. If the weather turned fine and steady, then in a few days they would be moving to the mainland, to the place of his people, to the birth of his child and then to the days and weeks . . . *Aie!* . . . months and years if need be which it might take to rally all men against the coming enemy.

As the little island drew nearer he swung the boat away from the shore on a tight turn to take it back to the beach, but the bow came only partly round and then fell away against the push of a current that curved along the shore and swept seawards along the projecting island. Fighting the thrust of the current with his paddle Baradoc turned the bow of the boat into it at last, only to find that the thrust was so strong that the current still took him, sweeping the boat stern first along the island shore and dragging it out to sea. For one wild moment he was on the point of abandoning the boat and swimming ashore. The thought of losing all his past labours held him. He decided to round the island point, find calmer water in its lee and beach the boat in the first cove or inlet he found.

★ ★ ★

At the moment when Baradoc cleared the point of the island, Tia was sitting in the sun outside the hut plucking a mallard duck which Baradoc had taken with a sling stone in the marshy hollow around the mid-island pond. The light breeze set the soft breast down floating into her face. She sneezed suddenly against its touch in her nostrils and, as her stomach muscles contracted, pain hit her so hard that she dropped the bird and clamped her arms about herself tightly. The child kicked and the pain came again and then again quickly. Tia groaned from the force of it and Cuna came and touched her cheek with his wet muzzle as she bent forward.

As the pain went she heard the sound of footsteps over the hard ground between the huts. She looked up quickly thinking it was Baradoc. A man came up to her, walking slowly. He was dressed in a priest's brown habit and as he came to her he smiled. There was no fright in her. She guessed he must be the stranger for he carried in his hand a thong-looped jar down the sides of which ran goat's milk that had slopped free as he walked.

Straightening up as the pains left her Tia said, 'My husband, Baradoc, is down at the beach with his boat. It would be another and great kindness from you if you would fetch him.' She smiled. 'I think my child has his father's nature and is impatient of the long wait.'

The stranger looked westwards to the sea which ran like beaten silver to the hazy line of the horizon, and for a moment his eyes closed as though the glare or some remembered grief overpowered him. Then he turned back to Tia and, smiling, said, 'All will be well with you. Your husband will come in full time. But now it is written that it is your term and there is no waiting for him. Go to your bed and I will stay by you. Yours will not be the first child I have brought into this world. You need have no fear of me, nor have any shame that a strange man helps you. I give my name, which is Merlin, freely to you and so all strangeness dies.'

He took her by the arm, led her into the hut to the bed platform and put the milk pot down at its side. Then he turned to the hearth fire and began to fill the cauldron with water from the hanging skin.

Tia said, 'You could go to the cliff top and call my husband. It is better that he comes.'

Merlin shook his head. 'There is not time enough. Be brave and be patient. Baradoc will return and when he does it will be to be greeted by his son. Now undress and lie beneath the covers. Your son as you say is impatient like his father. He will not wait for him, for there are many who already wait for the child's coming.'

As Tia began to strip Merlin went out of the hut and although she could not see him, she could see the shadow of his body cast across the doorway and, without knowing why, the sight of it was a great comfort to her.

As she pulled the bed covers over herself the sharp pains came again; and then began for her a time when all thought and feeling and the march of all her senses lost shape and sequence, a time when she lived in a dream through which loomed always the calm and comforting face of Merlin and the touch of his hands on her were those of a woman, and the sound of his voice as peaceful and lulling as the rustle of aspen leaves under the breath of an idle breeze until finally, as though from a great distance, came Merlin's voice with a high note of happiness in it, saying, 'Take

345

your son in your arms. He was hard on you in birth, for the birth of great ones makes the gods jealous of losing them to this world, but in life your son will never be less than gentle with you.'

★　★　★

At the moment that Merlin placed the child in Tia's arms, Baradoc saw the vessel bearing down on him. It came riding towards him on a freshening north-easterly wind. The great main sail was set and curved like an arching yellow shield as the craft ran free before the wind. At the bows the white foot waves creamed high and flared in a great spate along its sides, below the long row of lodged war-shields that lined the gunwales. At first Baradoc had thought it a trader coming down from some Sabrina port, but as it drew nearer, the island from which he had long drifted, low on the horizon behind it, he saw from the sail and the shields that it was no peaceful ship. Racing down on him, already fetching a little from its course to reach him, he knew that it brought no hope. Black anger was added to the misery already in him as he sat, naked except for his loin cloth, watching the ship overhaul him, seeing the long line of multicoloured shields hung over the freeboard, and clear now the two men at the great stern oar and other men in the bows, their heads all turned his way, the sun and sea glitter reflected on spears and swords, and above them, swollen and straining in the wind, the wide curve of the saffron-coloured mainsail blazoned with the wingspread of a great black raven across its full breadth. From the bitterness of despair in him rose the memory of the stranger's words . . . *If you would leave this island safely with your woman and child put the boat not to water until the first red-gorged swallow comes winging north.* What kind of black sorcery, what fine cunning with words from the gods or the stranger's madness was this? He had put the boat to water, but not to leave the island, only to ready it for leaving . . . *Aie,* but face the truth, there would have been no waiting for the swallow.

There was no virtue in trying to escape. If he had taken to the water they would have filled him with arrows or harpooned him like a seal or porpoise. He waited for them and the anger was so thick in him that it cloaked all other thought and he let it rest, a curtain between himself and the guilt and shame which would come in time.

The great ship passed him, an order was shouted loud, ringing across the waves to him, and then it came about sharply. The high sail boom was lowered quickly and the fine leather sail gathered safely by the crew. The ship ghosted up to him and three long-handled boat hooks grappled him to its side. Looking at the men, leather and wool jacketed and tightly long-hosed against the weather, he knew that they were none of the kind he hated, the land-hungry Saxon men, but Viking sea-raiders who had probably over-wintered in Erin or Cymru.

They took him aboard, cast his boat adrift, and marched him, held securely between two crewmen, to the high carved bows where stood a man he had met before, a tall powerfully built man wearing a silver-winged bronze helmet, a saffron-coloured tunic with the raven device, and a broad sword swinging from his whaleskin belt. His face was black as sea coal.

The man looked at him unmoving for a long while as the wind whistled softly through the rigging and the waves slapped idly at the ship's sides. The man smiled and bit his under-lip with fine white teeth in pleasure, and then he said gently, 'By Thor, what day of omens is this that out of the sea is thrown up an old friend, my young horse-thief with the great wolf hound?' He laughed and cried mockingly for all to hear, 'Have you turned then penitent and paddle now to Erin to join a Christian monastery?'

For a moment Baradoc was silent, mouth and chin set stubbornly and the blackness stayed sourly in him, but through it came now the dim touch of hope. He said, 'I go to my people beyond the point of Hercule, a few hours' sail for you. Put me ashore, Master Corvo, and you can name your ransom money. I am the son of a chief.'

Corvo was silent, while the crew watched and the ship rolled gently. None moved except the two men at the stern oar who kept the bows dead up into the wind with their strokes. Then the man spoke and he said savagely, 'The son of a chief? And what am I? The son of a black slave woman begotten by a drunken sea-raider — and gold means nothing to me until we reach the warm south lands to spend what we have. But this trip death has trimmed our crew and I need men — not money.' His voice rising fiercely, he called, 'Put a collar on him and chain him to the rowing benches!'

Baradoc was led aft. As he went he saw far, far to the northeast the sun gilding the green tops of the island and to still himself against useless violence and the black passion of regrets and lost happiness he clenched his hands and bit his lip until blood flowed to hold back the anguish that engulfed his heart.

Envoi

Grief had paced out its first fierce measures, encircling her heart and shadowing her mind with the heavy folds of its sable mantle. Baradoc's boat at the whim of the tides and the caprice of the veering winds had drifted back to the island. Merlin had swum out and brought it in to the little cove where its keel had first touched water. When Tia saw it and wept Merlin told her that Baradoc still lived and would return to her for he had seen the future in the dreams the gods gave him.

Now with the passing days warming the rocks and all the island balmy under the touch of growing spring, the young bracken a foot high, the sea samphires and the thrift pads moving towards bloom, and the sureness of Merlin's faith that one day Baradoc would return becoming her courage and strength, Tia found a peace and a fortitude that served her strongly.

She lived now, for safety against sudden raiders and for human comfort and companionship, in Merlin's cave where Lerg and Aesc slept each night under the boulder entrance and Cuna at the foot of the child's small wicker crib, while Bran roosted on a rock spur outside the curtained fissure opening. At night the brazier glowed like a red eye and the fat tallow candles, their light flickering in the draughts that idled through the high curtain, cast moving shadows over the rough vault of the cavern's roof. Sometimes before she slept and Merlin moved to finger snuff the lights she would look down at the child in the crib at her side and find him awake, his dark eyes, dark as his father's, watching the shadows play on the vaulted roof. She would put out a hand and gently touch the warm cheek and smooth the down of his pale, mouse-coloured hair already flecked with the copper glints he drew from his father, and the down-soft touch under her fingers always brought back the morning of Baradoc's going and she saw the rough writing on the peat floor . . . *Returning, I will lay a chaplet of purple vetch about your hair and, kneeling, call you queen.* And she remembered again the moment when bearded Merlin leaned over her and put her son into her arms, the early born, the longed-for son, and standing back from her said after a while, 'How shall he be named?'

Without hesitation, for this had long been settled between herself and Baradoc, she said, 'He is named after the father of his father, and is called Arturo.'

Merlin nodded, smiling, and said, 'It is a good name. A name for all men and all time.'

And so she lived now, cared for and protected by Merlin, waiting for the time when Arturo should be grown enough to make the crossing to the mainland. She would go to the people of the enduring crow and claim her place among them and rest with them until Baradoc returned. So, while she waited for Merlin to name the day of the crossing, she lived with him as she had once lived with her brother, in openness and companionship. He knew her mind and learnt of her past and the story of her meeting with Baradoc. But the one thing she kept locked in her mind, hidden even from Merlin, was their meeting with Asimus and his gift to them, because the true ending of that story belonged only to her and to Baradoc.

She used for the first bathing of Arturo the silver chalice to hold the warm water with which she sponged his body and cleaned his apple-bloom cheeks. When the child was a month old, sitting cradled by her arm on her knee, his naked body shining in the sunlight through the sea entrance, the cry of the seabirds and the slow booming of the swell against the rocks echoing around the cavern, it happened that Arturo, crowing in baby delight, reached out his small fat-wristed hands and put them on the sides of the chalice. Through the water, seen only by her, the ice-bright silver of the bowl was misted and clouded with a crimson flush as pure and unflawed as the rosy gorge of the swallow which had made its nest above the cavern's sea opening.

Postscript

In this book — the first of the trilogy — I have made no attempt to follow strictly the lines of the accepted Arthurian legend — largely because I do not think it bears much relation to truth. What the truth was nobody knows. That there was a truth is indisputable. King Arthur and the Quest of the Holy Grail are unshakably part of our national heritage.

Although there are no incontrovertible facts about King Arthur, the renown of his life and deeds in the Dark Ages was lodged for over six hundred years in folk memory. And folk, being what they are, invariably alter and embroider a good story. William of Malmesbury, Geoffrey of Monmouth and then Sir Thomas Malory were landed with the result. Lesser as well as better writers have followed them. Acknowledging that I come in the first of these two categories, I feel no shame in entering the lists poorly armed but securely mounted on a horse I have ridden for years called Imagination.

We do hope that you have enjoyed reading this large print book.

Did you know that all of our titles are available for purchase?

We publish a wide range of high quality large print books including:
Romances, Mysteries, Classics
General Fiction
Non Fiction and Westerns

Special interest titles available in large print are:
The Little Oxford Dictionary
Music Book
Song Book
Hymn Book
Service Book

Also available from us courtesy of Oxford University Press:
Young Readers' Dictionary
(large print edition)
Young Readers' Thesaurus
(large print edition)

For further information or a free brochure, please contact us at:
Ulverscroft Large Print Books Ltd.,
The Green, Bradgate Road, Anstey,
Leicester, LE7 7FU, England.
Tel: (00 44) 0116 236 4325
Fax: (00 44) 0116 234 0205

Other titles published by
The House of Ulverscroft:

BIRDS OF A FEATHER

Victor Canning

A fortunate man, Sir Anthony Swale is married to a loyal wife; he lives in a grand house in Somerset and leads a very privileged life. He devotes most of his time to collecting rare art treasures, particularly from behind the Iron Curtain. And he will pay any price for the right piece — including treason. But then his treachery is discovered — and agents working for the Government decide it is time to take discreet action . . .

THE BOY ON PLATFORM ONE

Victor Canning

Cheerful Peter Courtney, a fourteen-year-old, is an unusual boy. Exceptionally gifted, he's able to repeat, fully, any text which is read to him once — even in French. When his widowed father's business fails, he takes Peter around London's social clubs to perform professionally. Because of his skills he finds himself involved with the Secret Service. He is required to use his gift to receive important information regarding traitors to the British and French Governments — but this places Peter and his father in danger. Now they must escape and leave everything behind . . . in hiding from an assassin who is thorough and systematic.

TALES OF MYSTERY AND HORROR: VOL. III

Edgar Allan Poe

These *Tales of Mystery and Horror* include the story of Bedloe, a wealthy young invalid, who has a strange tale to tell his physician, after he experiences a form of time travel, in *A Tale of the Ragged Mountains* . . . And *The Conversation of Eiros and Charmion* is a very strange tale of a comet approaching earth, causing it to contain pure oxygen. The result of this has a devastating effect on people . . .